THIRTY-FOUR

Going On...

BRIDE

BECKY MONSON

This is a work of fiction. Names, characters, places, and incidents either are the product of the author's imagination or are used fictitiously, and any resemblance to actual persons, living or dead, business establishments, events, or locales is entirely coincidental.

To the man I call hubby. Thanks for making me your wife. And for taking out the trash. I love you.

PRELUDE

Look, I get it. Weddings don't always go as planned. I had no visions of grandeur that my wedding would go without a hitch. But this? This is ridiculous.

To start, our witnesses are a couple of hippies. Both with long hair (one has dreadlocks) and tattoos up their arms. Then there's the officiant. I'm not sure, since I have little (or no) experience with this, but I think he's high. Like, as a kite. And the icing on the cake? Lia—yes, the same Lia that claims to be a witch—is next to me. She's designated herself as my maid of honor.

The only person standing here that should actually be standing here is Jared. I'm pretty certain his deer-caught-in-headlights look mirrors my own facial expression. How did we get here?

I know how we got here. And it's all my fault.

BECKY MONSON

CHAPTER 1

"Pick it up, Julia! You can do this!"

I'm in the seventh circle of hell.

"Come on! Let's move faster!" My sister Anna yells over the construction that we're currently passing. As expected, we get a few whoops and whistles tossed at us from the workers. Pity flattery, I'm sure. Well, maybe not for Anna, but certainly for me. There's absolutely nothing attractive about me right now.

To start, I don't know if I've ever sweated this hard in my life. I look like I've taken a shower fully clothed. I'm sticky and perspiring, and it's not even that hot outside. It's a typical day near the end of May in Denver, Colorado. How did I let Anna convince me to do this? Oh that's right, there was no convincing. She forced me. "It'll be good for you," she had said, lying through her devil teeth.

At this point I don't know if my lungs will ever be the same. They actually ache with pain. And then there's the ache in my calves, and really every other part of my body. Whoever thought of running as an extracurricular activity should be shot. A form of torture, yes. Exercise? I'd rather get a tooth pulled without Novocain.

To call it running is a bit of an exaggeration on my part. I'd call it jogging, but even that seems wrong. What I'm doing is barely lifting a foot off the ground with a slight bounce. You couldn't even call it speed walking. I know, because a speed walker zipped right by me earlier. I'm pretty confident a toddler could walk faster than I run. Or jog. Or whatever.

I knew my lucky genes would catch up with me someday. Up until last year I could eat whatever I wanted; I never thought twice about it, and apparently neither did my butt. But then I went to work at a bakery and subsequently decided to purchase said bakery. I suppose since I'm constantly surrounded by food — the good kind, no kale on the premises — I've been eating more than I thought I had. There's a lot of taste testing going on, of course. And I'm quite sure a lot of emotional eating as well, since owning your own business can be rather stressful at times.

So my sister Anna, who also happens to be the devil as well as my wedding planner, convinced me to lose ten pounds before the wedding.

Only twelve more to go.

Clearly dieting is not my forte. In fact, I'm pretty certain since the word "die" is part of it, it's probably not healthy for anyone. I have learned one thing, though: if you want to slow down time, if life is passing you by too rapidly, go on a diet. Time will slow down to a snail's pace, or even slower. Every day is a lifetime of suffering.

"Julia, I think the ants on the sidewalk are going faster than you," Anna says as she literally runs a circle around me. Her curly dark brown hair is pulled up into a perfect ponytail, her full-face of makeup completely intact ... not one drop of perspiration. *Not one.*

"Yes, those little buggers are fast," I say through breathing that can only be compared to someone with emphysema.

"Do you need a break?"

"Yes," I declare, dropping onto a bench we just happen to be passing. Kismet! Thank you, gods of laziness.

"Julia," Anna says, jogging in place in front of me as she checks her pulse, "we've only been out for twenty minutes. You can't possibly be that out of shape."

"You give me too much credit," I say, leaning my head back on the bench, trying to find some air. It's the Mile High City, after all. The air is thin — it should be against the law to suck in too much of it.

"This is torture. Do you make Jonathon do this?" I ask.

"No," she says. "Jonathon isn't getting married in three months." She tilts her head to the side and eyes me suspiciously. "You said you've been exercising in the evenings."

"I have!" I object loudly to her allegations. How dare she.

"What exactly have you been doing then?"

"Walking," I say flatly.

"And was there any heart elevation during this walk?"

I shrug. "I'm sure there was."

"Julia, leisurely walking home from work is not exercise," she rolls her eyes.

"Not according to the latest issue of *Health* magazine," I retort.

"You read *Health* magazine?" she eyes me dubiously.

"Yes. Well, I glanced at it while in the line at the grocery store. The cover clearly stated that getting outside and walking is good for the soul," I say, jutting my chin out as I defend myself.

"Maybe for the soul, but not for your love handles," she says pointing to my mid-section. I instinctively run the back of my hand over my side.

"I don't have love handles!" I squeak out, disrupting a bird that was perched on the tree near us. I watch as it flies to the tree across the street.

"Not yet, you don't." She gives me her best schoolmarm look of condescension.

"Why does it have to be so hard?" I ask, feeling dramatic.

"Come on," Anna says, taking me by the arm. "We'll walk the rest of the way."

"Oh, thank goodness," I say, allowing her to actually pull most of my weight up. No need to exert unless I actually have to.

"We're going out again tomorrow," she says, her tone emphatic.

"I'd rather get a root canal."

"That can be arranged," she says, the corner of her lip pulling up.

We start the walk back to my condo. With my heart finally settling into a more human rate, rather than that of a hummingbird, I'm suddenly feeling this weird sort of euphoria. This was not expected. Does this always happen when you put your body in danger of continued existence? Or maybe my body is thanking me for not running anymore.

Whatever I'm feeling, it's not good. I mean it *is* good, and that's not good. I don't want to enjoy exercise. I want to loathe it like I always have. It's worked fine for me in the past. Why change things up? What if I become one of those exercise addicts like Brown, or my mom? Heaven forbid.

"Don't think that you can go home and nap this off, by the way," Anna says as we turn down Fifteenth Street.

"I wasn't planning on taking a nap," I snap back, scrunching my face at her in annoyance. She thinks she knows me so well. Which she does. I lied—I was planning on a nap.

"Good. Because you have just enough time to shower and get ready. We have a dress fitting at ten, a cake tasting after that, and I will make you pick out your wedding favors if it's the last thing I do." She points a finger at me, her best bossy-pants look on her face.

I let out a long, exaggerated breath, my shoulders sagging. "Okay, fine."

Not that I have a choice. Anna's the boss of me right now, like it or not. And thank goodness. She's taken this whole wedding thing over and I'm so grateful. I'd have gone mad by this point. Like, certifiable. It's not as if I was blind to it either. I was there for both Anna and Brown's weddings not even a year ago. But when it's your own wedding, it's different.

I've offered to elope, but my fiancé, Jared, won't have it. I thought that was supposed to work the other way around—the man is supposed to want to elope, and the woman wants her day as a princess. Well, I've never aspired to be a princess; I loathe being the center of attention, and I hate wearing frilly dresses. So in all, it sounds like the worst day ever. I mean, it'll be great—I'll be marrying the man of my dreams, after all. That's the part I care about the most. The rest of it is simply fluff. Bothersome fluff.

Plus there's a lot riding on a big day like that. I mean, what if I trip and fall? I successfully made it down the aisle twice last year as a bridesmaid in both Brown's and Anna's weddings. What are the odds of me making it a third time? Plus, I keep having dreams that I do, in fact, fall, and it scares me that it might be some kind of prediction of the future.

But Jared wants a wedding, and I can't talk him out of it. He wants the whole kit and caboodle. Not for him or me, mind you, but for his mother, Bobby. She only has two boys and she's been dying for one of them to get married so she can enjoy all of the hoopla that goes along with it. She probably wishes her son picked a more wanna-be-princess type, like Anna was when she married Jonathon. Actually she was more like bridezilla.

I also thought the mother of the groom was supposed to be mostly uninvolved. Not in my case. Bobby wants to be a part of everything, which is great and all—Jared adores his mom, so I know she will be a part of our lives on a regular basis—but it feels weird to have her there for so much of it. I always have to be on my best behavior, which means I can't complain and moan about everything. Like I normally do. Someday she'll get to see all my true colors — she's only seen a select few — but not until I'm legally bound to her son and she's stuck with me.

Bobby is very traditional. She wants roses, and I prefer hydrangeas or lilies — something a little different. She likes the big poufy princess dresses, and I prefer simple and classic. I want a small wedding; she's invited half of Denver. I can't even think about that part or I get physically sick.

She's been pretty good at putting in her two cents and then going with whatever I'm wanting, but one thing she won't budge on is the location of the ceremony. It has to be at a church, and not just any church, the same church her and Jared's late father got married in. She's "dreamed of the day" that one of her boys would get married there. It's a beautiful church … the carpet is a little outdated, but who am I to be picky? Plus the sentiment is sweet.

I wasn't planning on having the wedding in a church, truth be told. I'm not against it, it's just so inconvenient. Everyone has to go to the wedding at the church, then get in their cars and drive to the reception. It'd be simpler to have the wedding and reception at the same location, and I want it all to be easy. Simple and easy. But between Anna and Bobby, it's been like pulling teeth to keep it that way. Anna has seemed to chill out with all of her over-the-top wedding ideas. She's finally seeing the light, I think.

"What do you think about releasing doves when you leave the church?" Anna asks, breaking up the silence we'd been walking in.

Apparently, I was wrong. She's not lessening her over-the-top wedding ideas. At all. She was probably purposefully giving a tiny respite before she shifted back into full gear. Dang it.

"Are you serious?" I ask, searching her face for any sign of teasing.

Nope. She's serious.

"It'd be beautiful, Julia," she says, her condescending look back.

"No way. No doves," I say.

She huffs. "Okay, then what about butterflies?"

"No butterflies," I say, not believing she's truly asking me this. Doesn't she know me at all?

"Can't we just do the normal bird seed or bubbles?" I don't want anything alive jumping out at me as I leave. Plus, what if they died? That would be a terrible omen.

"Fine," she says.

Oh no. The dreaded "fine." It may sound like she's agreed (although grumpily), but I know the underlying tone in that "fine." She's essentially saying, "fine, if you want the worst wedding ever, then *fine*."

I don't want the worst wedding ever. I want a nice, simple wedding with my friends and family. Not a big ridiculous fanfare with a princess dress and half of Denver watching.

If I survive this wedding, it'll be a miracle.

CHAPTER 2

Seriously, if one more person calls me dude, I'm going to lose it.

"Your cupcakes are the best, dude," the punk with the tangled mop of hair says for the millionth time (only a slight exaggeration) as I hand him his change. His friend sniggers, probably at the reference to *my cupcakes*.

How original.

I fake smile at them both, and then watch as they stumble out of the bakery. Good riddance.

Business at the bakery these days, while great, has also been trying. Mainly on my patience. It's been nine months since my venture on *Cupcake Battles* where I took home the winning prize (ten grand, which, not surprisingly, is all spent). National television got me amazing exposure, and word has spread like wildfire. In fact, I'm going to be recognized at the Denver Local Business Gala next month, for which I've been asked to provide a gazillion cupcakes. Okay, a thousand. But trust me, when you have to make that many cupcakes it feels like an endless amount.

It's been great. Don't get me wrong. But lately I've noticed a gaggle of oddballs who like to frequent the place around closing time.

I was clueless at first, but then my employee Patti informed me that these eccentrics are of the pot-smoking variety. Apparently the legalization of marijuana in Colorado equals a bunch of people who have the munchies, and my cupcakes are the craving of the month. Or rather the last ten months, since the show aired.

I'm grateful for the business, I truly am. And I'm not judging anyone. It's just that at the end of the day when my feet are killing me, I'd like to go home. Couldn't they smoke earlier in the day, say, right around the lunch rush? That would be so much better for me. I think I'll start a campaign, or a petition ... or something. If only I weren't so tired.

I look down at my watch and am surprised that we're nearly an hour past closing time. I swear I'll eradicate that pot-smoking law myself. Maybe I'll add "running for office" on my to-do list. Which is getting longer by the minute.

"Lia," I say as I walk over to a table by the front window, "I'm closing up now." I give her a closed mouth smile that I hope nicely conveys my message to "get out."

"Yes, sorry," she says in her sickly sweet voice from behind a magazine with a burning skull on the front cover. Odd, but not really, coming from Lia. Today she's wearing a rainbow striped shirt with a non-matching floor-length floral skirt, and a peculiar grouping of beads wrapped around her short, dark red hair. She's what one would call weird, but eclectic is a kinder way to say it.

Lia is one of my regulars. She comes to the bakery every day. She's also a witch, whose card reading almost ruined my relationship with Jared. Okay, it was me that almost ruined it, but her cards definitely played a part. Needless to say, I don't do readings with her anymore, but my patrons do. They love it, actually. Once a month I let her set up a table and do readings in the bakery. I made her promise that she can only tell them the good things the cards say, and not the bad things. No doom and gloom. I want only happiness and joy oozing from my bakery, thank you very much.

"You look tired," she says, gawking at my face.

"Yes, thank you. I'm quite tired," I say as I rub my forehead with my hand, feeling the exhaustion move through me. I was up late watching my adorable nephew Liam for my brother Lennon and his wife Jenny. They desperately needed a night out, and Jenny is still not ready to hire an actual babysitter. I seem to be the only person she wants to leave Liam with, but I'm always up for it. I love that kid so much. I can't believe he's a year already.

I'm also finding it hard to sleep because I keep having that reoccurring nightmare where I trip as I walk down the aisle of my own wedding. Of course, in last night's version I was also completely naked. These dreams are so realistic I practically have to talk myself down from a panic attack when I finally wake myself up.

I'm living on Dr. Pepper and a prayer these days. Sometimes I throw one of those five-hour energy shots in, for good measure.

"Your aura is off; it has been for a while," Lia says, pointing to a spot above my head. I'm assuming that's where my aura is visible. I wouldn't know; I've never seen my aura. Or anyone's aura for that matter.

"I'm sure it is. I've got a lot on my plate right now," I say, and my eye twitches. These days it does that every now and then. I'd say lack of sleep, too much stress, and poor eating habits are the cause. Actually, that's what Google said when I looked it up.

"Would you like me to cast you a health spell?" She asks, concern apparent in her large blue eyes, which are framed with black glasses.

"Oh no," I say emphatically. "Thank you, but I'll pass." I start to walk toward the door, hoping she'll get the hint.

She grabs her things from the table and moves toward the door. "Well, if you ever need one, I'm here for you," she says, a small, thin smile perching on her lips.

"Yes, if I ever need a health spell, or any spell for that matter, you'll be the first person I call," I say as I open the door and Lia walks out.

Lovely smelling spring air wafts through the open door and for a moment, I take it all in. What a beautiful day. This is what I need, some fresh air and to simply sit on a bench in a park, if only for a few minutes. But I don't have any time to spare these days.

My phone beeps signaling a text. It's Anna.

I'm looking into pricing for a champagne fountain at the reception. Thoughts?

I have a thought—how about *hell no*. Wasn't an open bar enough? I almost didn't even agree to that. I want a short reception (or rather, no reception at all). Free alcohol will guarantee a long and drawn-out one. Not to mention the fact that the last time I had champagne, I nearly ruined Anna's wedding. But let's not go there.

Now she wants a fountain? Of champagne? What about the cost? Not that I have to worry too much there. My dad was very excited about finally marrying me off (he actually said that—though I think he was mostly joking, I hope) and said he wanted to give me my dream wedding. I told him that my dream wedding would consist of me, Jared, a beach, and whoever showed up, but he seemed to think I was just saying that to be nice. I wasn't; that's what I truly want. Now it seems I'll be living everyone else's dream wedding.

I text back a quick "no" and wait for my impending "fine" text, but there's no response. Huh. Maybe she's finally realized this is my wedding and not hers? Doubtful, but I can dream.

My phone beeps.

And there it is.

Fine.

Oh well, she can be mad. I'm putting my foot down with this one.

I lock up and turn to go to the kitchen, feeling relief wash over me that my workday is finally done. Not that I don't love my job, I absolutely adore it. I'm just so stressed with life lately, even work has felt like a chore at times.

It's also not helping that because business has been going so well, Jared is really pushing me to expand. He's even been scoping out perfect locations for a second bakery and has supposedly found the perfect spot over in a newly built-up area in Centennial that he can't wait to show me.

I've tried in so many ways—short of outright saying it—to tell him that I don't want to expand. At least not right now. I get that we should "strike while the iron is hot," or whatever, but I also don't know if having some sort of baking empire is what I truly want. Jared has visions of product lines, magazine features, and television shows dancing in his head. I love him for the faith he has in me, but really, I just don't think I have it in me. And honestly, I'm not sure I want to.

And then there's the gala. The gala that I don't want to go to or make cupcakes for. I know I'm being recognized as one of Denver's "thriving" (their word, not mine) local businesses, but can't they just come into the bakery and hand me an award with a handshake? Why the big to-do where I have to wear a gown that's sure to be itchy and breath-inhibiting? Not to mention the high possibility that I'll be sporting some Spanks as well, to hold in these extra ten—er, twelve—pounds I've acquired.

Success is not all it's cracked up to be. I think I want to go back to my lowly life of sitting in an office where no one expected me to achieve anything higher than working an eight-hour day.

Maybe not. I almost threw up in my mouth at the thought.

"Well don't you look beat up from the feet up," my employee Patti declares in her thick, southern accent as I walk into the kitchen.

"Yep," I say, with no enthusiasm. "I just had to kick Lia out."

"That girl ain't right in the head, bless her heart," Patti says, shaking her head. I internally roll my eyes. I'm convinced Patti thinks she can say anything rude as long as she follows it up with a "bless her heart" — like that's supposed to make up for it.

She's got a broom in her hand, and from the looks of my now clean kitchen, Patti's been busy, although her big blonde bouffant doesn't look affected. I often wonder how much hairspray goes into a 'do like that. Thank goodness for her and her big hair — I'd be lost without her.

"I'm concerned about ya, darlin'," she says, her squinty blue eyes peering at me over her large, round glasses.

"Yeah, you aren't the only one," I say, thinking my mom had said the same thing to me just a couple of days ago. In fact, I think Anna's the only person who's not said those words to me. But that's because she's an evil overlord.

Jared hasn't expressed concern either, but honestly I think he thinks I'm superwoman or something, and why would I want him to think otherwise?

I'd love a break, but that's not going to happen anytime soon. Definitely not until this wedding is over. And then we get to go on our honeymoon to Hawaii. Laying out in the sun, reading a book. Walking along the beach with Jared, hand in hand. It sounds incredibly dreamy, and I can't wait.

We had discussed going to Paris, but I knew that if we went there, I wouldn't be able to relax. I'd be continually on the lookout for baked goods to try and would most likely come back the size of a whale.

No, palm trees and beautiful beaches are just what I need.

"We're just wrapping up here," Debbie, another employee, says as she walks into the kitchen from the storage room in the back.

"You're life savers," I say with a worn-out smile. "Where's Kate?" I ask, looking around.

"In the walk-in," Patti says, nodding her head in the direction of the walk-in cooler.

After the whole *Cupcake Battles* thing, the work got to be too much for just Patti, Debbie, and me. So I had to hire someone, which was so much harder than I thought it would be. I figured I'd throw it out there and then have tons of applicants to pick from. While that did happen, there were very few that were qualified.

Then, as if she were Mary Poppins, Kate Bowen magically came into my life. Her resume was impeccable, her interview was perfect. Her pie crust actually brought a tear to my eye. It was *that* amazing.

She seemed to fit in well with everyone in the beginning. She just kept to herself and did her thing. But lately I've been noticing looks between Debbie and Patti when Kate says something, or a flat-out eye roll from Patti (subtlety is not her strength). Now that she's more comfortable, I've noticed that Kate can be kind of bossy. But she has great ideas. I think some of the animosity might come from the fact that I use her opinion so often. It's not that I don't use Debbie's and

Patti's, but we've been doing this for a while now, it's nice to have a fresh set of ideas.

I know I probably need to have a discussion with Patti and Debbie about it, but I've been avoiding it. I keep hoping it will all go away on its own. This is basically the theme of my life: ignore it and hope it goes away. It hasn't really worked so well for me in the past, but maybe it'll work this time.

"Did someone ask for me?" Kate asks as she comes back into the kitchen from the large walk-in cooler, her large hazel eyes searching the room. She reaches back and tugs on her tiny ponytail that her shoulder-length brown hair has been pulled into.

"Yes, actually," I say turning toward her. "Have you decided what you want to make for the dessert of the day tomorrow?"

"I'm making fruit tartlets," she states, her tone informing me that I don't actually have a choice, and frankly I don't care. I like that Kate takes initiative.

"Sounds good," I say, now thinking how amazing a tartlet sounds. If it wasn't for that dang diet Anna has me on, I'd get to enjoy one tomorrow. Now I'll have to watch as everyone else enjoys them. Or maybe I'll eat one anyway, love handles be damned.

"Well if it's okay with you, Julia, I think I'm going to take off," Debbie says. Reaching around her plump figure, she unties her apron and hangs it on a hook by the door. She takes a look in the mirror next to the aprons and fusses with her short, curly, red hair. I had to hang a mirror there after a very unfortunate incident where I waltzed through the bakery with what looked like bangs a la 1980's (the front part of my hair flying about two inches off the top of my head), made possible by some frosting. I'm not sure a day has gone by without someone bringing it up.

"Got a hot date with your man?" Patti asks, nudging Debbie with her elbow.

"Hot, indeed," Debbie says with a wink.

Gross.

Debbie recently married one of our regulars, George. Ever since they came back from their short honeymoon, it's been like perv central in the kitchen. I swear between her and Patti I've had an education that I'd rather not have had, and certainly not from either of them. I think they do it just to see how red my face can get.

It's still so strange to me that Debbie ended up with George. He's a grumpy old guy who grunted out orders and rarely acknowledged my greetings. I'm not sure how it happened, but somehow he and Debbie hit it off. Actually, much to my dismay (and churning stomach), the way I found out that they were seeing each other was when I found them engaging in a little tryst in my bakery. That picture will be burned in my brain … forever.

That aside, I'm happy for Debbie. She's finally found happiness after losing her husband over a decade ago. I've actually seen a change in her countenance since she and George got together. She's always been great to work with, but now she seems so content. It's wonderful to see her that way. I wonder if people see a change in me since I found love with Jared. Well, maybe they used to, but all this wedding planning is really taking its toll. When I look in the mirror lately, all I see are wrinkles and an over-all frazzled look.

I walk Patti, Debbie, and Kate out and lock the door behind them. Just a few things to do in the office and then I'll be out of here as well. I'm meeting Jared and his family for dinner tonight and I need time to get myself looking less like I've been working in a busy bakery all day.

I take a seat in my office, letting my head sink back into the chair. I close my eyes for a moment. It feels like I haven't sat down like this in ages. In truth, I haven't. The only time I get to close my eyes is at night when I go to bed, and even that has been a bit difficult these days with thoughts of everything I have to do running through my head, not to mention the crazy dreams. It's been a long while since I've had a good night's sleep.

My phone beeps, pulling me out of my brief break.

See you soon :)

I look at the clock on my phone. Crap! I must've dozed off! I only have thirty minutes until I'm supposed to meet Jared and family for dinner. How could I let this happen? I should've never sat down.

I gather up my things and quickly close up the bakery and run as fast as I can to my condo. Okay, I actually could only keep up a runner's pace for about a block, and then slowed to a walk. Not even being late for dinner with my future in-laws can get me to move my feet that fast.

Not that this is the first dinner we've had or anything. I've been out with the Moodys plenty of times, but tonight is the first time we all get to meet Mark's girlfriend. Mark is Jared's younger brother. He's a bit of a punk, if you ask me. Totally unreliable, runs off at the mouth, goes through women like I go through running shoes. No, that's a terrible analogy — I'm still on my first pair. More like my socks. I need to invest in some high quality socks — the kind I buy only last a month or two. Anyway, Mark has yet to bring a girl for us to meet so this will be an interesting twist for dinner. Especially since Bobby is none-too-excited about meeting her. She's totally one of those moms who think no one is good enough for their boys. Except for me, of course. At least, I hope.

I like Mark for the most part, but he's one of those people you can never take seriously. I don't even think he takes himself seriously. Maybe it's because he was Bobby's baby, and so he was more spoiled or something. He definitely plays the younger brother/baby-of-the-family well. Kind of like Anna, but even less responsible. Anna's only dumb with her spending, although her husband has nipped that in the bud. Actually, no, he makes enough money as a lawyer to keep her spending how she wants.

I'm nearly home, thank goodness. I'm not sure how I'm going to improve this catastrophic look I've got going on, but I'm going to have to try. I look up at my building as I get closer. I love this place. After living the glamorous — okay, not so glamorous—life in my parents' basement for ten years, I finally purchased my first condo. My parents' basement wasn't terrible — it was actually quite cozy — but it's a life I don't think back fondly on. I was in a rut, stuck in my ways in a dead-end job, living in my parents' basement. Call me crazy for not wanting to dream of the old days.

I do adore my little condo and am feeling a little melancholy about the fact that I'll be selling it soon. I wish we could keep it, but it's not very smart to keep a mortgage on two places, and Jared's place is much bigger than mine. My cat, Charlie, will surely love the space she'll have to run around. Jared did offer to sell his place, knowing what my condo means to me, but I told him no. I'll miss my little home, but Jared's condo is freaking awesome. The kitchen alone convinced me that we should stay there.

We haven't put my condo up for sale yet because real estate (especially condos) go quickly thanks to the new pot smoking laws in Colorado. There was another condo down the hall that sold in three weeks. So we'll put mine up closer to the wedding. Anna and Brown have been on me to sell it now and move in with Jared. But Jared and I don't want to live together before the wedding. I know that's super traditional and a little old fashioned, but we both like the idea of everything being new after we get married. Also because Jared informed me that Bobby would not approve if we "shacked up." She's apparently not a fan.

As soon as I get home, I rip off my clothing, jump in the bathroom for a millisecond shower, and race to get ready as fast as I can. I run a brush through my wet brown hair, and then hit it with the blow dryer for a minute. It's only enough to make it so my hair isn't dripping, but it'll have to do. I consider leaving it down, but I'm thinking the drowned-rat look is out of style, so I throw it up into a simple bun and then add a silver jeweled headband so I don't look so drab.

My green eyes are looking a little dull, so I throw on a bit of makeup — like the teeniest bit possible — and I quickly dress and am out the door in record time. The restaurant is only five blocks away, so as of right now I'll only be ten minutes late. Not bad, really. Well, not bad for me.

CHAPTER 3

"Julia," Bobby says my name brightly upon seeing me enter the restaurant. "You look lovely." She stands up and gives me a quick hug.

I blush and glance down at my pale pink shift dress with an off-white cardigan and give her a little smile. "Thank you," I say.

I want to add something sarcastic but I hold my tongue. I'm trying to calm the sarcasm. At least around Bobby. I get the idea she doesn't appreciate it, or she just doesn't get it. But either way, I could probably do with a little less cynicism. Plus, I only want to say something self-deprecating because I can't seem to take a compliment without adding some sort of clause for why I don't deserve the praise.

It's been tough not being so sarcastic, but around Bobby I try to keep the comments to myself. For example, when Bobby says, "you look lovely," I answer out loud with a "thank you" but in my head I'm thinking, *if you think the drowned-rat look is "lovely."* It's been working well for me so far.

"You look lovely too," I say in return. No inner sarcasm needed here. Bobby always looks lovely and put together. Her short blonde hair is perfectly styled with not one hair out of place, and she's wearing an impeccably pressed white blouse and nice jeans with simple but expensive looking jewelry adorning her ears, neck, and fingers. This is her uniform. I've rarely seen her in anything else. She, however, has seen me at my worst plenty of times. Usually with flour in my hair. And sometimes 1980's bangs, thanks to some icing (yes, she was there that day ... of course she was).

Jared stands up and pulls out my seat, ever the gentleman. "You look beautiful," he whispers in my ear, sending chills down my spine. He gives me a quick kiss on the lips before I sit down and I blush a few extra shades of red. I'm still not quite used to kissing Jared in front of his mother. I doubt I'll ever get used to it. Not that I'd ever want him to stop, mind you, because I don't think I'll ever tire of his kisses.

"Where's Mark?" I ask as I unfold a cloth napkin and place it in my lap.

"He's late," Jared says, giving me a not-surprised shrug. Mark is always late. So am I, but Mark is typically much later than I am. Which isn't a terrible thing for me.

Jared and Mark don't look much alike. They're both very good looking, but in their own way. Mark takes after his mom, with light blonde hair and brown eyes. He's got one of those dimples in his chin (which I once referred to as a "butt chin" to Jared and he thought it was so hilarious he told Mark—not the best start to a relationship with my future brother-in-law). Mark has Jared's same jaw line—that fabulous chiseled jaw—which is really the only resemblance they have.

Jared, with his dark blonde hair and light blue eyes, takes after his dad. Since Jared's dad passed away unexpectedly from a heart attack when Jared was in college, the only way I could know this was from the pictures I've seen of him. The similarities are uncanny.

"How are the wedding plans going?" Bobby asks. I could have predicted that would've been one of the first questions out of her mouth.

"Good," I say, hoping we don't have to discuss it too much. I'm so tired of wedding planning. Plus, just thinking about it gives me palpitations.

"Did your sister tell you about my champagne fountain idea?" she asks, eyebrows raised in anticipation.

Wait, that was her idea? Since when have Anna and Bobby been chatting? They usually communicate through me. I'm not sure I like them talking — things could get hugely out of hand without me bringing in the reigns.

"Uh, she did," I say, unsure of how to go about telling her I vetoed it.

"Well, what do you think?" she asks. "I saw it on that *Say Yes to the Dress* show and thought it'd be perfect. It's the big thing right now," Bobby says, and I have no gage for whether that's true or not. I'm not up on anything, honestly. I barely got on Facebook, for crap's sake — only because Jared said it would be good for the bakery. And I did it kicking and screaming.

"Sounds like a great idea," Jared interjects.

"Really?" I look up at him. "I was kind of thinking the open bar would be enough."

"I'm sure no one would complain if there were more," he says.

"I'll, um, think about it," I say hoping that my not-very-committed answer will suffice for now.

"How are things at the bakery?" Bobby asks as she picks up her water glass and takes a sip.

"Good," I say, happy to change the subject. "Busy, but that's a good thing, right?" I turn to Jared and see a sparkle in his sky-blue eyes. I love that he always seems so proud when the subject of my bakery comes up.

"Yes," he runs a hand through his hair, "It's going great. In fact, I found the perfect location for the second bakery," he says, looking at Bobby.

"Oh really?" She turns to me, and I give her a small shrug and a half smile.

Jared starts telling Bobby about all of the reasons this will be the best location and blah, blah, blah. I'm really not up for discussing this tonight. I keep to myself and hope we can move on soon.

I think what frustrates me most is that it's not like Jared or I have tons of extra time right now. With the wedding and the bakery, I'm swamped. And Jared started his own consulting company just nine months ago, which is going rather well but also keeps him crazy busy. We barely even have time to see each other. At least not every day like I'd want. I don't see how we can do it all.

My phone beeps, signaling a text. I open my purse and peer into it, trying to see who it is without being obvious. I don't want to be rude. Or make it obvious that I'm not listening.

What do you think of a candy bar for guests?

Anna with wedding stuff again. I should've guessed.

A candy bar? Like a Snickers bar for every guest? As if she read my mind, another text comes through with a picture of a table lined with jars full of candy. Hmm. That's actually kind of cute. Definitely more my style. Of course, I don't know how well it'll go with the champagne fountain, which doesn't truly fit my modern fall wedding theme. That's a bit fancier than I was going for.

Actually, the theme was one of Anna's ideas. Honestly, I was shocked she even presented it to me after all of the ridiculous antique-esque themes she had previously presented. This one had rich colors of burgundy, burnt orange, umber, and yellow. But what really got me was the splash of blue—a beautiful gray blue. It made all the difference.

"Mark's here," Bobby declares.

I look over and see Mark with a petite brunette on his arm walking toward us. She's relatively tan, with a bright white smile. Very fashion forward from the looks of her outfit. Well, not like I'd know. I know nothing about fashion and only have a decent closet full of clothes because either Anna or my best friend, Brown, have helped me pick them out. Mark's little lady is dressed rather swanky in an off-white, flowing, one-shoulder dress, and brown suede heel booties. Slightly over-dressed for the likes of this little Italian restaurant. She looks harmless at first glance. Maybe Bobby will like this one.

"What the..." I hear Jared say under his breath. I turn to him and see his eyes are about to bug out of his head. "Lisa?" he questions as Mark and the newest flavor of the month walk up to the table.

"Jared?" Mark's girlfriend scrunches her eyes at him.

"What are you doing here?" Jared asks, standing up from his seat, a broad smile spreading across his face.

"Everyone, this is Lisa," Mark declares to the table. "You two know each other?" He looks back and forth between Lisa and Jared.

"I should be asking you the same question," Jared says to Mark. "How do you know Lisa?"

"We met at a club," Mark says.

"Oh my goodness," Lisa says, her voice trailing off as she considers the situation. "Your last name is Moody?" She turns to Mark.

"Yeah," Mark says, as if it's normal for the girl he's dating to not know his last name. Actually, that *is* probably normal for Mark.

"Well, I'll be damned," she shakes her head dubiously.

"Wait," Mark says, eyes going wide. "You're Lisa … college Lisa?" He looks at her as if seeing her with a new set of eyes.

"And you," she says, pushing her index finger into his chest, "you were that punk in high school." Her eyes search his face, trying to reconcile this fact.

Huh? I'm so lost right now.

I clear my throat and Jared turns to me.

"Julia," Jared says, grabbing my hand and pulling me up to stand next to him, "this is Lisa. We dated in college. And she's apparently now dating my brother." He motions toward Mark with his hand.

Well, this is funny. Not funny ha-ha, but more like slap-you-in-the-face funny. I've always wanted to run into one of Jared's exes. And by "always wanted to" I mean *never*. Especially the one from college – the *only* one he's mentioned more than once. Jared hasn't said much about past girlfriends, but he's actually talked about this Lisa person. Not in a nostalgic way or anything, but he's also never spoken of her in a distasteful way, as I would have preferred.

"This is so crazy!" She says loud and bright, taking a few steps closer to Jared. "Come here, you!" She grabs him by the arm and pulls him into a hug. "How the heck are you?" She asks when they release from the embrace.

"Really good," Jared says, looking a little shell-shocked. "What've you been up to?" he asks, his full attention on Lisa. I'm still standing next to Jared, feeling a little strange, almost like I've suddenly become invisible.

"I'm working at the Denver Post, actually," she says. Her eyes are focused on him, almost as if the rest of us have disappeared and it's just him and her.

"So you got your dream job, then," he shakes his head, clearly impressed.

"I did," she dips her chin once, a confident smile on her face. She's actually quite stunning up close. I kind of hate her.

"Your hair ..." Jared says, pointing to her shoulder-length shiny brown locks.

"I got rid of the blonde." Lisa reaches up and twirls some strands with her finger.

"It, uh, looks nice," Jared says, as if he's not trying to compliment her at all, but still did.

Well, that's settled. That strange feeling I'm having? It's jealousy. I've only known Lisa for all of two minutes, and so far she and Jared have only exchanged pleasantries, yet I'm ready to pee a circle around Jared to mark my territory.

"That's why I didn't recognize you — your hair used to be blonde," Mark says, his face looking as if he's finally put all of the pieces of the puzzle together.

"Lisa," Bobby says from the other side of the table. I'd actually forgotten she was there, she was being so quiet.

"Bobby!" Lisa says brightly and rushes over to Bobby's side of the table and leans down to give her a side hug. Bobby half-hugs her back, the look on her face saying that she's none-to-pleased by this coincidence.

Her and me both.

"And who's this?" Lisa gestures to me, coming back to our side of the table and away from Bobby.

"Uh, yes," Jared says, slinging an arm around my waist and pulling me into him. "This is Julia, my fiancée."

"No way!" Lisa exclaims. "You're engaged?" She looks from Jared to me. "Did you get him to commit to a date? I never thought he'd commit. Definitely not with me, at least," she says, punching him lightly on the arm. "But I guess it wasn't in the cards for us, was it, Jared?"

I'm pretty sure that should be rhetorical, but from the look on her face I think she's hoping for an answer. Jared doesn't say anything, just smiles at her. I, on the other hand, am feeling the need to punch something. Like, for example *her*. I shouldn't feel like this so quickly but I can't help myself. My Spidey senses are on alert.

Now it's Mark's turn to clear his throat and Lisa finally takes her attention off Jared.

"Well, this is awkward," he says looking at Jared and then Lisa. "Shall we sit down?" he asks, pulling a seat out for her. The seat right next to Jared. Really?

"Yes, of course!" she exclaims, as she takes the seat and then places her gold clutch purse on the table. She's loud and much too cheerful for my taste. Also, I'm suddenly now regretting my quick attempt at makeup. I should've tried a little harder.

"It's so great to see you all again," Lisa says, nodding her head toward Bobby as if they've known each other for years. Of course they probably did know each other fairly well when Lisa and Jared were dating. Why does that thought annoy me so much? It was years ago.

"You as well, Lisa," Bobby gives her a small, thin smile. From the tone of her voice I'd say it's just out of manners. I can't say for sure, but from the looks of it, Bobby doesn't care for Lisa. Hmm, there must be a story there that I'll need to find out about. Not right now, of course. I'll wait until later so we can talk behind Lisa's back like grown adult women should do.

"Wow, this is crazy, isn't it? What a small world," Lisa shakes her head, looking at Jared and then to Bobby.

"Yes, definitely," Jared says, smiling, the initial shell-shocked look now gone from his face.

"So, what are we ordering?" Mark asks, rubbing his hands together as if none of this just happened. Evidently he's done feeling awkward. He's good at moving on; me ... not so much.

The restaurant we're at is Italian family style, which means we all order things to share with the table. I was looking forward to it, but now it doesn't sound quite as fun to share food with Jared's ex-girlfriend and Mark's current girlfriend. I'm trying not to be petty here, but who are we kidding. Being petty is sort of my thing.

I see Bobby glance at Lisa over the top of her menu, her lips pressed together, eyes narrowed. It was such a swift look of irritation, I'm pretty sure I'm the only one who caught it.

After a couple of minutes of mostly awkward silence as we look at our menus, the server approaches the table and takes our orders.

"So," Lisa says, after the server leaves. "Tell me how you two met." She points to Jared and then me.

"Uh," I say, ready to tell her a shortened version. No need for her to know all the details of how Jared and I came to be.

"Funny story, actually," Mark says, a big goofy smile on his face. "They met at work. Jared got her fired." He laughs a deep-throated laugh.

Well, there goes the heat crawling up my face as I turn a deep shade of red. That's just lovely. Thank you so much, Mark. Remind me to pay you back the favor later.

"No way!" Lisa says loudly, slapping Jared on the arm yet again. "How did that all happen?"

"Well, I own a consulting business," Jared starts.

"Oh, I should've guessed that. I bet you're super successful, aren't you," she says, touching his arm lightly with her hand.

Wait a second ... touching someone casually on the arm is totally a flirting move. I mean, I wouldn't know because I'm a terrible flirt, but I could swear I read it in a magazine once.

"Well," Jared says, the tips of his ears turning red. "I do fine."

"Oh, stop being so modest. I know you, Jared. You always had it in you." She touches his arm again and I consider moving my seat in between them. An obvious move on my part, but at this point, who cares. Besides, she doesn't *truly* know him. They dated years ago. My Spidey senses have moved from just on alert to extremely high alert. I do not like this chick.

"Okay so back to the story of how you met ... um ..." Lisa trails off, her head gesturing to me.

"Julia," Jared interjects quickly.

Yes, nothing says, "I couldn't care less about you" than forgetting your name within the first five minutes of meeting one another. I'm going to start making a list in my head of all the reasons I don't like Lisa. First on the list is the fact that she forgot my name. Second on the list is her stupid pretty face and her shiny dark brown hair that even *I* wouldn't mind running my fingers through. It looks ridiculously soft. Dang it!

"Yes, sorry," she gives me a super fake apologizing glance. "So back to the story." She touches Jared's arm again, to urge him on. Or to flirt. My money's on the latter.

"We met at a consulting job I took here in Denver," Jared says, turning his head toward me, a soft smile on his face. "She lured me in with her baking skills," he says, reaching over and grabbing my leg. I beam at him.

Did you see that Lisa? Huh? Did ya?

"I'm confused on the whole firing part," Lisa says, resting her chin in her hand, elbow perched on the table.

"Well," Jared laughs a little uncomfortably, and rightfully so. I mean, this is all in the past and was definitely for the best, but it's still a bit of a sore subject.

"Jared was at the company to reorganize it," I jump in. If the story is going to be told, it might as well be from me, since I was the one who got fired.

"When it came time to do layoffs, I happened to be on the list of people being let go." I don't bother going into the fact that the department I was in had fallen to shambles when it became known that my boss, the CFO, had been stealing money from the company. And also that the only real reason the president of the company wanted to keep me there was because of the cupcakes I brought in from time to time.

"No way!" Lisa says again, slapping Jared lightly on the arm once more. That has to be getting on his nerves by now. It's *definitely* getting on mine.

"It was all for the best," I say, looking at Jared whose ears are starting to turn red on the tips again. "It was a dead-end job for me, and now I own a bakery," I say. Dang it, that rhymed. I hate it when I do that.

"Yes, a very successful bakery," Jared adds. "She won *Cupcake Battles* last season."

Ha! In your face, Lisa. That look of pride was for me.

"I love that show!" Lisa says brightly. Then her eyes go wide. "Wait a sec ... oh my gosh, you were the one who threw up!" She slaps the table with her hand, laughter bellowing out of her mouth.

I blush profusely and uncomfortably push my hair behind my ear, but since my hair is in a bun and there is nothing to push back, I just look ridiculous. Throwing up on national TV was not one of my finer moments. Why can't people focus on the fact that I won? I just hope she doesn't remember the cupcake stand debacle. Please, oh please, don't let her remember that.

"And you had the phallic cupcake display!" She exclaims. "That was hilarious!"

Kill me now.

"Yes," I finally say, willing the heat in my face to go away. "That was me," I give a closed-mouth smile, wishing I could be anywhere but here right now.

"I couldn't believe you won! I thought for sure the other team would take it," she shakes her head in amazement. "They must've really wanted you to win for the ratings," she says, pointer finger resting on her chin.

Wait, was that a slight? I feel like that was a bit of a jab in my direction. Am I reading too much into things here?

"Well, I'm pretty sure it was the cupcakes themselves," Bobby says from out of the blue. She's being rather quiet, which is not like her.

"Oh sure, yeah. Of course," Lisa says, half-heartedly.

The waiter brings our drinks, thankfully. Maybe this conversation can go in a different direction now. Like Lisa feeling sick and deciding to go home. That'd be more of the path I'd like to go on.

"So now," Lisa says, eyes on me, finger tapping on her chin, "you own a bakery."

I nod my head in reply.

"It's downtown," Mark says. "Right off Fifteenth. Hey, we should go there sometime," he bobs his head at Lisa, who's looking at him like she forgot he was even here.

"Yes, definitely," she says, although her eyes are not looking like they're in agreement.

"It's a great bakery," Jared pipes in. "We're actually looking into expanding."

I give Jared a look that says shut up, and he shoots back a confused furrowed brow. I don't want to go into all that right now. And I certainly don't want this Lisa person to know about it. They may all have a past with her, but we've only just met. And also, she annoys me.

"She's also being recognized at the Denver local business gala next month," he says, clearly ignoring any of my facial expressions. I'd think that by now he'd know what my "shut the heck up" face looks like.

"I'll be there!" Lisa says extra enthusiastically. "I'm covering it for the paper."

Fantastic. Now I have even less to look forward to on that night.

"You know," Lisa says, her hand resting under her chin. "I've been looking to do a story about a local business for my column." She looks at me, her eyebrows raised. "Sort of a rags to riches type of thing. I think you might be exactly what I'm looking for," she smiles, her teeth shining white even under the dim lighting of the restaurant.

Um, I'm going to go with "hell no." First of all, it wasn't a "rags to riches" story. There were no rags at all. And honestly, there are still not that many riches. I mean, the bakery does great, but I'm no millionaire. Most importantly, I don't like doing interviews, and I certainly wouldn't want to do one with the woman that might possibly still have a thing for my future husband. I'd say I'm just being jealous, but I'm sensing something in my gut that doesn't feel right.

"That would be great," Jared says, his eyes bright with ideas. "Don't you think so, Jules?" He turns to me and nods his head.

No. No, I don't.

"Um," I say, mindlessly tucking more imaginary hair behind my ear. How do I say "hell no" in the nicest way possible? "I'm not sure I'd be that interesting to interview."

Lisa bats a hand in my direction. "Oh, I'm sure you'll be great!" she says, her voice ringing through the restaurant.

"You'd be perfect, Jules," Jared says, putting a hand on my back.

"I don't know if I'd have the time, you know with the wedding planning and all," I say, shrugging my shoulders. I'm still trying to find the right excuse that will get them to let it go. I also had to throw in the "wedding planning" part for obvious reasons. Just a little reminder for Lisa.

"Jules," Jared turns to me, a serious expression on his face, "you're being offered a fantastic opportunity here. You should take it."

"Oh yes," Lisa says. "You'd be on the front page of the business section and everything. We'll even do a little photo shoot of you at the bakery."

"I'd rather not—"

"Jules," Jared says, cutting me off. "This is great publicity for you and the bakery."

I close my eyes for a brief moment, wishing I could've feigned sick tonight. I could be lying on my couch in a junk food coma watching *Project Runway*. Of course, had I not been here, Lisa would've surely been sitting in Jared's lap by now. Her chair somehow keeps scooting closer and closer to him. Which is also putting her farther away from Mark, who is completely oblivious.

"Um," I look around the room avoiding eye contact. "Sure, that would be great," I say to appease Jared and Lisa. I'll have to find another time to come up with an excuse to get out of it.

The server arrives with our food and the conversation stops for a bit while we pass the plates around and load up our own. I look down at mine and apparently I've been mindlessly dishing up everything. The plate is starting to overflow. Clearly I'm stress eating. Or I'm using food as a crutch so I don't slap people. Even Jared's on my list right now.

Mark takes over the conversation from there, bringing up stories from the past. Lisa adds some of her own from when she and Jared were dating. They all laugh and add comments as they reminisce. Bobby is pretty absent from the conversation, just a few head nods here and there. I'm the odd man out here, that's for certain. Not because of anything Jared's doing, mind you. He looks directly at me when relaying his part of whatever story they're telling. His hand moves from holding mine, to settling on my leg.

Mark tells the story of how he and Lisa met at the club they were both frequenting. He gives her flirty winks as he talks, and she flirts right back. I wonder if Lisa knows what a player Mark truly is. I'm definitely looking forward to when he moves on from this one.

Every once in a while, Bobby throws a quick non-approving glance in Lisa's direction. I'm *so* going to find out the reasoning behind that.

The rest of the evening goes on without much merit, thank goodness. Lisa has seemed to return her attentions to Mark, now touching his arm when she talks instead of Jared's. Well, she does touch Jared's arm every now and then. It dawns on me that Jared hasn't taken notice nor has he ever reacted to her touch. That bodes well ... for Jared. Otherwise he'd be getting a mouthful from me.

"It was so fantastic to meet you, Julia," Lisa says, her voice overly happy as we walk outside of the restaurant.

"And you," I say, fake smile on my face. Two can play that game.

I shiver a little in the late May night air and Jared immediately takes his jacket off and places it around my shoulders.

"You always were so thoughtful," Lisa says to Jared, noticing the gesture.

I hate that they have a past I know only bits and pieces about. I hate that Jared was ever thoughtful with this woman, or cared for her. It's childish, I realize, but I can't help myself.

Lisa says goodbye to Bobby, who barely acknowledges it (I think I like my future mother-in-law even more now), and Mark makes his goodbyes as well.

After getting Bobby settled in a cab, Jared walks me to my condo.

"Have I told you," he says as he makes himself comfortable on the loveseat after we make it back to my condo, "how beautiful you look tonight?"

I sit down next to him, and he puts an arm around me, pulling me into him.

"You did, but I don't mind hearing it again," I say as I look up into his eyes. He leans in and kisses me softly.

"So that was crazy," I say when he pulls away, "running into your ex-girlfriend."

"Hmm?" He asks, his fingers playing with my headband. Almost as if he's forgotten that we just had dinner with Lisa. "Oh yeah," he says.

"She seems ... nice." I use the word "nice" tentatively. That's not really how I'd describe her; more like a word my mother has asked me repeatedly not to use, the one that starts with a B.

"You know," Jared says, pulling me even more into him, "I don't feel like talking about her right now." He starts kissing a trail from the corner of my mouth to the spot right by my earlobe. The spot that gets me every time. A chill runs down my spine, and not the cold kind.

"You don't?" I question, feeling suddenly breathless. I want more information on Lisa, but maybe right now isn't the right time as his lips have traveled down my neck and to my collarbone.

"No, I don't," he says as he reaches his hand to the back of my neck and then claims my mouth like I'm the only person in the world that matters to him right now.

As if like magic—as always with his touch—my brain turns to mush and I completely forget what I was thinking about. All I can think of is him.

Lisa who?

CHAPTER 4

"I need a pastry," Brown declares as she enters the bakery.

I nearly choke on the drink of water I just took. Brown needs a pastry? I'm not totally positive, but I don't think those four words have ever come out of Brown's mouth in her entire life. I look over at Debbie who's behind the cash register, and she gives me a questioning glance.

"Seriously, Jules, give me something good and full of calories." She walks hurriedly over to the display, her long, straight, blond hair swinging dramatically behind her as she eyes what little baked goods I have left after another busy day.

"Whatcha got for me?" her eyes search the display as if she's a crackhead who needs a hit.

I feel as though I might need to check her temperature, or ask her questions that only she'd know so that I can rule out a body invasion. I've known Brown for over six years and have never seen her eat a pastry. Or sugar, really. She's a health and exercise fanatic. She actually eats kale chips as a treat. I'm sorry, but kale, in any form, is *not* a treat. It's a form of torture.

"Betsy Brown, are you feeling okay? You are Betsy Brown, right?" I use her full name since I think I'm leaning toward the body-snatching scenario. That seems most plausible at this point. I could use her full married name — Betsy Brown Whitehead, but she hates her new last name, so right now is probably not the time to use it.

"Yes!" She snaps at me. "Now give me some sugar!" She demands, and the remnants of customers we have in the store all turn their heads to look at her. She doesn't seem to notice or care.

I come around from the back of the counter to the front and look her over. She doesn't look sick, although her blue eyes do look bloodshot, like she's been crying. Also not a norm for Brown. What's going on?

"Is this one of those best friend tests where I'm supposed to talk you down from eating something bad?" I ask, eyeing her suspiciously.

"No," she snaps again. "I'm stress-eating. Now please, Julia, get me something and come sit with me. I need to vent."

After finding her something (a lemon bar so at least there was an element of a fruit in there — that's how I justified it anyway), and grabbing her a coffee, we take a seat in the back corner of the bakery.

We sit in silence for a minute as she nibbles on the lemon bar. Honestly, if she didn't look so panic stricken, I'd probably have to snap a picture of this momentous occasion. Brown eating a pastry. I'll just have to settle for a mental picture. I never thought I'd see the day.

I haven't had a long conversation with Brown in a couple of weeks because we've both been so busy. I so want to tell her about Lisa and the most eventful (read: annoying) dinner that happened last week, and the impending interview happening tomorrow that I haven't been able to get out of. But I'll have to save that for later. She needs me, and to be perfectly honest, it feels nice to be needed. This is a big role reversal here.

"What's going on?" I finally ask, eyeing her with concern.

"I killed them," she says, a sob escaping after her declaration.

My eyes go wide. That was not what I was expecting. I was thinking more along the lines of trouble at work. But that's not likely with Brown. She's good at what she does. She works in sales for the company I used to work for which also happens to be the place I met Jared. Maybe trouble at home, but that also seems unlikely. Her and Matt have been married for a year, but have been together for much longer.

Killing was not on my scope with Brown. Anna possibly, but not Brown. Brown has always been the epitome of calm and collected. Unless you count last year when she nearly had a nervous breakdown before her wedding. But even the most even-keeled person can lose it over a wedding, I'm sure. Actually, I'm positive.

"Okay ... who did you kill," I say slowly and softly, as to not make her mad and therefore become her next victim.

"No," she bats a hand at me. "I didn't kill anyone, I just—" she cuts off with another sob, a tear forms at the corner of her eye and then travels down her cheek. She puts the lemon bar down and puts her face in her hands, and this time I can see her shoulders shake as she really lets go.

"Brown," I say, scooting my chair closer, I start to rub her back. I'd hug her, but Brown isn't a huggy person. I grab a napkin and hand it to her and she blows her nose into it, not caring that everyone around can hear her.

"Okay, start from the beginning," I say, once the blubbering begins to subside.

"Yes, okay ... good. I need to talk this out," she says through sniffles.

"Yes, talk it out. This is a judgment-free zone here," I say. Although, if there truly was killing then I'm not certain I can guarantee that.

"So we had an appointment with the fertility clinic today," she says as she dabs her eyes.

Right. The fertility clinic. I should've known. The breakdown Brown had at her wedding actually had something to do with that. She freaked out because her soon-to-be husband informed her that he didn't want to wait to have kids, and she wasn't sure if she was ready for that. But after the wedding, something snapped in Brown and she decided to get on board with the whole baby thing. In fact, she went into full beast-mode. She read nearly every book on it, bought ovulation tests, kept a calendar, took her temperature ... she was going to make this happen.

Only, it didn't. Nearly a year after their wedding, and months of negative pregnancy tests (of which she would take four or five, just to make totally sure), they finally decided to seek help.

"So what happened?" I ask, coaxing her to talk. She was still tearing up at this point.

"We had our post-coital test," she rattles off like anyone in the world would know what that is.

"Uh, post-coital test?" I ask, narrowing my eyes. I'm not sure I actually want to know.

"Yes, a post-coital test. It's a test where we do the deed the night before and then within twelve hours the doctor does a swab of my cervix to test it." She says it so matter-of-fact, like this is normal procedure.

I, on the other hand, am slightly mortified. Okay, mostly mortified. I can't imagine having to go to the doctor and sit in a room where they swab me knowing full well what I did last night. I can feel the heat in my face at the very thought.

"Oh Julia," Brown rolls her eyes. She knows exactly what I'm thinking without having to say anything. "It's all medical at that point."

"Right," I shake my head, face still burning.

"Anyway," she turns her head away from my red face, "so after they swab you, they put it under a microscope connected to a big screen so everyone can see it and so the doctor can explain things as he sees them." Brown sniffles loudly.

"Okay, so what happened?" I ask, nodding my head.

"They were dead. All of them," She says as more tears start to trickle from her eyes.

"What was dead?"

"Matt's sperm—his little swimmers," she makes a swimming motion with her hand. "I killed them all. Apparently I have what's called a 'hostile environment,'" she says using air quotes. "I'm a sperm killer."

Now, I do realize the severity of the situation. If the "little swimmers" can't even make it to the egg, then how can you conceive? But for some reason, the sperm killer thing sets me off and try as I might to stifle it, a giggle escapes my lips. I mean, I knew Brown could be hostile at times, but I didn't think even her uterus could be.

"Julia!" Brown says, looking incredulously at me, "are you laughing?"

"No!" Another giggle escapes. Dang it!

"Julia! I'm having a crisis here. This is *not* funny," she says, her eyes wide.

"I'm so sorry, Brown. It was just the sperm killer comment," I say, and then I can't help it. I start laughing.

"I hate you so much right now," Brown says, but I can see her trying to hold back a smile and it's not too long before she's laughing with me.

"Okay, fine," she says after the laughing subsides. "I guess when you say it out loud it is kind of funny, but it wasn't at the time. I mean, Jules, you should've seen Matt's face when he looked at the screen. He looked sick, like he was going to throw up. 'They're *all* dead?' he kept asking the doctor."

"Wait, was he mad at you?" I ask, feeling suddenly defensive for my friend. I mean it's not like she made her uterus a hostile environment on purpose.

"No, no," she says, batting the question away with her hand. "I mean his initial reaction was shock, and — I don't know — a bit horrified. But it didn't take him long to recover and then he went back to typical Matt, jumping right into asking questions about what we can do next."

"So what do you do next?"

"There are a few options, but I think we've decided to try IUI," she says.

"IUI?" I don't know why she keeps using terminology that I have no clue about. It's like she thinks the whole world is in the know when it comes to infertility. Those of us that have never been through it have no idea.

"Intrauterine insemination, or some people call it artificial insemination." Still seeing the blank look on my face, she continues. "It's where the doctor takes Matt's sperm and places them near the egg so they don't have far to go, completely bypassing my hostile cervix." She sniffles dramatically.

"So that sounds like a good plan then," I say, still not sure why she's as devastated as she is.

"I guess so, it's just that—" she looks down at her hands.

"It's just that what?"

"I just feel like I've failed, you know?" She says as tears quickly gather in the corners of both eyes and trickle down. It's not a hysterical cry, it's a heartbroken cry. *I'm* feeling heartbroken, and it's not even happening to me. I've never seen Brown like this. She looks fragile almost. And that's not an adjective I'd ever use for Brown.

"Brown," I say, avoiding a tone that might be taken as pity. "You haven't failed."

"I know. I know it sounds like a stupid thing to say. But I've never really failed at anything. When I set my mind to it, it happens. This time though, I couldn't make it happen." More tears form and fall.

"But this isn't the type of thing you can make happen," I say, bringing my hand up to touch her arm for emphasis. "Does Matt feel the same?"

"Matt?" She scrunches her face at me, confused by the question. "No," she shakes her head when she finally understands my question. "He keeps telling me that it'll happen, even if we have to buy our babies."

I give her a half smile and she returns it. Matt truly is perfect for Brown.

"Julia," Brown says, looking down at her hands, "what do I do?"

This is quite the awkward question coming from Brown. I don't know if she's ever asked me for advice like this. There's a lot of firsts going on with Brown right now.

"I think you should do what you do best. Attack this intra-insemi-thingy like a boss."

Her lips curl into a small smile at that. "Yeah, you're right."

"I don't know if you've ever said I was right in our entire friendship. I think I should write this in my journal," I say, and her smile broadens a touch.

"It's going to be fine, Brown. I know it," I say, and truly mean it. I can picture Brown and Matt with their children, looking like they stepped out of a magazine (they're beautiful people so obviously their kids will be gorgeous), hosting neighborhood barbecues, and rocking sporting events. They'll be the epitome of the perfect family.

"Thanks, Jules," she says, reaching over and grabbing my hand.

"Anytime," I say giving her hand a little squeeze.

~*~

"You better never say anything," I say to Jared on the phone as I lay in my bed. It's the only time I've gotten to hear his voice today. I've just filled him in on the Brown fertility drama that happened earlier.

"Of course not. What would I say? 'So Matt, I heard your wife killed your swimmers,'" Jared replies, the sarcasm thick in his tone.

I snort-laugh, which used to embarrass me around him, but not so much these days. He put a ring on it. He's stuck with me.

"It got me thinking, though," I say, feeling a little shy about bringing this up, but it's never truly been discussed. Sure, there's been the mention of it, but never anything serious.

"Yeah?" he asks.

"I know we've both said we want kids, but I've never asked you how many you want," I say, wrapping a tendril of hair around my finger. I begin to twirl it nervously.

"Seven," he says without skipping a beat.

"Seven? Seven kids," I say, my voice rising slightly. "We're too old to have seven kids. I'd have to get pregnant every year in order to have them all before my eggs start to rot." I'm not certain my voice is conveying the anxiety I'm feeling right now. Seven kids? Really?

"You're right. I should be marrying someone younger," he says, laughter in his tone. He's teasing me.

"You jerk," I say, and if he were around, I'd throw something at him and then probably kiss him. I can never stay mad at the guy for long. He's too dang cute.

"How about we start with two and go from there," he says, still not taking back the previously mentioned amount.

"I'm just telling you right now, this uterus isn't having seven kids, so don't get your hopes up."

He laughs at that. I love that laugh so much.

"I think we'll have one boy and one girl and we'll name them Jared Junior and Julianna," he says, humor still oozing through his voice.

"That sounds lovely. They won't resent us at all," I say cynically.

Picturing Jared and me with children makes butterflies fly around in my stomach. I can just see us in a beautiful, two-story brick house in the plush area of Cherry Creek. Maybe we'll even have a white picket fence (although I've never pictured myself as a white-picket-fence kind of gal, but thing's change). The kids will be running around outside, chasing Charlie in our beautiful landscaped yard. Jared, his arms around me as we look at our lives, pure contentment on our faces ... it's going to be amazing.

I seriously can't wait to start a life with Jared.

"How long should we wait to have kids?" I ask, remembering how upset Brown was when Matt sprung it on her that he didn't want to wait.

"Why put a date on it?" Jared says. "We'll know when we're ready."

"You know what I think?"

"What?"

"I think I just fell in love with you even more. I didn't think that was possible."

"I love you, Jules," he says and I swear I'll never tire of those words. "Now, get some sleep. You have your interview with the newspaper tomorrow."

"Don't remind me," I say grudgingly.

"Jules, you'll be great," he says. The confidence he has for me almost makes me believe him. Almost.

"I'll be great as long as you're there to make sure I don't snort when I laugh." He chuckles.

"I'm afraid I can't help that, but I promise I'll be there," he says, making the nervousness in my stomach dissipate some. I'm *so* not looking forward to this.

"Just think of how great this will be for the bakery," he says.

"That's the thing. I mean, it's not like we need it," I say.

"Of course you do, Jules. Marketing is always good," he says. "Besides, I'm not just talking about the bakery. I'm talking about other bakeries."

Right. The expansion. Crap.

"You know, I'm not so sure — "

His yawn of enormous proportions cuts me off.

"What was that?" he asks, on the tail end of his yawn.

He's tired. I'm tired. This probably isn't the best time. I'll find another time to tell him that I think we should wait.

"Sounds like you need sleep as well," I say.

"I think I do. Goodnight, Jules," he says, groggily.

We hang up and I roll over on my side, snuggling into my pillow. I know I need to talk to him about how I'm truly feeling about the expansion. But I don't want to let him down either. Maybe if we slowed it down a bit. I'll definitely talk to him tomorrow after I have this interview behind me.

As I start to drift off I think about how soon I'll be snuggling up to Jared every night of my life instead of this stupid lumpy pillow.

My days of sleeping as a single woman are numbered. And I can't wait.

CHAPTER 5

Jared is a big fat lying liar head.

I'm so ticked right now, I can't even see straight. First of all, my alarm didn't go off when it was supposed to, so I slept in. And I had a rough night of sleep as it was. I had that stupid recurring dream where I was walking naked down the aisle at my wedding, only this time Lisa was there with a notepad taking detailed notes of my naked wedding to put in her newspaper article. It went on and on all night.

So my plan to actually look presentable today didn't happen. I was smart enough to iron the light pink polo shirt with my logo on it last night, so at least I have that. Although Charlie decided to use it as a pillow, so it was covered with cat hair this morning. That was super fun to try to get off. I was in such a hurry I threw on jeans that were dirty because I forgot to dry the jeans that I'd washed last night. Then there's the disaster that is my hair—which is in a messy knot on the top of my head. And to complete my look, I went all-natural by wearing no makeup whatsoever. I brought makeup with me, but there's no help for my hair.

My appearance was bad enough that Patti, upon seeing me, said that I looked like I'd been "rode hard and tied up wet." Which I completely misunderstood and took to be something pervy. She laughed until she cried. Her and her crazy southern sayings can stuff it.

Then, to make matters worse, Jared called to tell me he has some "fire" with his company happening on the East Coast that must be taken care of immediately. He swears he'll make it to the bakery at some point during my interview, but now it won't be as I pictured it, with him sitting near me and making me feel more confident. Now I'm on my own and who knows what I'll say. Left to my own devices I've said some stupid things. Like, ridiculously stupid.

Holy crap, I'm freaking out. I think I'm actually having heart palpitations. I've never had a panic attack, but I think one's coming. I've also developed an award winning eye twitch. It can actually be seen from space, it's so bad.

I don't have time to do anything about my look right now because it's nearly opening time. Luckily Debbie, Patti, and Kate had things happening before I got here. At least that part is going well for me. My staff knows how to run my bakery with or without me. Maybe I can get Lisa to take a picture of them instead of me ... and have them do the interview, as well. Heaven knows Patti would be much more entertaining and better suited for it.

"What's going on with your eye," Kate asks me as I enter the front of the bakery from the kitchen. She looks wide awake for this time in the morning, her brown hair pulled back into a slick looking ponytail. Must've been nice to not oversleep. It's not her fault I'm having a crappy morning, but I'm looking for someone to blame. Maybe Jared is the better option since I'm already annoyed with him.

"Eye twitch," I say as I open the door to the display case and slide in the tray of raspberry almond scones that I was carrying. Everything looks ready to go, which is a good thing since it's time to unlock the doors.

"Yikes," Kate says, moving her face up close to mine. "That's a terrible one. You look like you have Tourette's."

Well, if that isn't offensive on many levels, I don't know what is. I make the conscious decision to not even reply to that. Plus, I saw the twitch myself in the mirror earlier, and thought the exact same thing. But unlike Kate, I usually keep non-politically correct declarations, such as that, inside my head where they belong.

"Also, you've got something in your hair," Kate says as she grabs a set of keys from a drawer under the cash register.

"What?" I say, and then reach up to my hair.

"I think it might be frosting," she moves her head up close to mine again to inspect. "Yep, it's frosting."

"Seriously?" I feel around my head until my fingers land on what feels like a greasy blob on the right side of my head. I pull a little off with my fingernails and inspect. Oh, not frosting again! And this time it's hot pink.

The frosting was a mishap to begin with. It was supposed to be a soft pink, but I accidently put too much coloring in and it turned into a fuchsia color. Instead of diluting it out, I just thought I'd run with it.

I let out a long sigh, grab a napkin and start blotting the frosting out.

Of course, trying to get frosting out of your hair isn't easy. And I would know, as this isn't my first mishap. The 1980's bangs episode was also not my first mishap. Yeah, it's happened a lot. So now, along with my messy hair and no makeup, I also get to look like a grease ball. A hot pink one. Just fantastic.

"What else can go wrong?" I ask aloud, and then quickly clamp my hands over my mouth.

Holy crap I've just unleashed the deadliest of questions, which is never to be spoken aloud, lest you want to find out exactly what else can *actually* go wrong. I need a take-back. Or some holy water and a priest. I need anything that might scourge the question from history.

Kate unlocks the main door to the bakery as I try to work the frosting out of my hair. Customers who had been waiting outside in the brisk morning start filing in.

Here we go.

"Hello, Julia," a sickly sweet voice says from the other side of the counter.

"Hi Lia," I say and start to grab her normal breakfast order. "You're here early," I state as I place a blueberry streusel muffin on a small white ceramic plate.

"Yes," she says, eyeing me as I grab her a cup for coffee.

"What is it?" I ask as she looks at me. "Is my aura off again?" I'm sure it is. When has my aura ever been on?

"Not that, I mean—yes, it's off—but I'm actually talking about your hair," she says pointing to the top of my head.

"Oh right. That's icing," I say, reaching up to feel my greasy hair.

"Oh," she says, not convinced. What the heck else would it be? "Can I get some orange juice today?" she asks just as I've poured her some coffee.

"Uh, sure," I say setting the cup of coffee aside. I go to the tall glass-front cooler and grab the pitcher of orange juice and pour her a cup. I go to set it on the counter in front of her just as she goes to grab it, and within a millisecond, orange juice is dripping down the front of me.

"I'm so sorry!" Lia says so loudly, everyone turns to look at me.

It's at this point that I realize in my haste to get everything ready after starting late, I never put on my apron. Now the entire bakery can see my lacy white bra through my shirt.

It's official. I've jinxed myself. I think what would be best right now is if I went home, back to bed, and hope that this is all a nightmare and I can get a do-over.

I make a beeline for the back and send Debbie to the front as I'm trying to pull the orange juice covered shirt away from my skin as it has suctioned itself to me. Why couldn't it have been water? Of course it had to be sticky sugar-filled juice.

In my office I have a spare T-shirt—no logo on it—but it'll have to do. I grab it and a clean dishtowel and head to the bathroom to clean up.

Donned with a clean shirt (well, it wasn't as clean as I had hoped, but it'll do) and mostly sticky free, I head back up to the front. At least this time I remember my apron. Stupid hindsight.

The line has gotten quite long since the orange juice debacle. I'd briefly debated running home and attempting to hose myself off, but the bakery is extra busy this morning so there's no possible way for me to leave. I'll have to make do with what I have.

Despite my morning of turmoil, I somehow survive the breakfast rush without any further misfortunes. Lia was overly apologetic and cast some sort of light spell on the bakery to make up for the spill. I'm not even sure what a light spell is, but I didn't have time to ask. Let's just hope it reverses the jinx I put on myself.

Before I know it, it's nearly nine o'clock and I only have a half hour until Lisa gets here with her photographer. I head to the bathroom in the back and inspect myself. There's no helping my look today. Although I took a stab at the pink frosting in my hair after I cleaned up the orange juice mess, I didn't have time to do a decent job. Now as I take a towel and try to clean it up, I see that the pink has stained my hair. This could be cool, if I were fifteen. But since I'm not, it's just a tacky pink streak in the front of my hair. Not somewhere easily hidden of course … Of-freaking-course.

Giving up on my hair, I slap on some makeup. The lighting in the back bathroom is dim, but I do my best to give my pale appearance some color. The bags under my eyes couldn't be more obvious, so there's not much I can do there. Good heavens, I look like I haven't had a good night's sleep in ages. That's actually fairly accurate. I suddenly wish I'd purchased that under eye treatment I saw on the home shopping network ... when I couldn't sleep last week. I'm aware of the irony there.

"Julia," Patti yells from the other side of the bathroom door. "How're ya doing in there?"

I open the door and by the look on her face, she's not impressed by my appearance.

"Bless your heart, you're a right mess," she says eyeing my face and my hair. I'd pulled my hair out of the messy bun when I tried to get the frosting out. I thought I'd done a decent job of fingering through the tangles — I'd forgotten a brush — but apparently not.

"I *am* a mess," I say, my shoulders slouching. *In so many ways*, I want to add, but that would be moot.

"No worries, darlin', let Patti help ya," she says, referring to herself in third person.

She leaves me standing in the doorway of the bathroom as she runs and grabs her purse. I'm too tired right now to fight her. Besides, anything she can do will probably be better than what I've been able to accomplish. I only have fifteen minutes until Lisa gets here; I basically need a miracle.

"We got ourselves an emergency, Debbie," I hear her yell out to the front of the bakery where Debbie had gone to help Kate while I tried to fix myself.

It's not long until I hear both Debbie and Patti, feet shuffling, as they come toward me. Patti must've informed Debbie of the hot mess that I am because she doesn't even give me a once over.

Debbie pulls the rolling chair out of my office, and Patti pushes me into it. And then they go to work. They tug and pull as they work on my hair and then once they both agree that's in order, they spray it to oblivion with terrible smelling hairspray. Then they get to work on my face.

"Dear heavens, what in tarnation is going on with your eye?" Patti asks as she tries to apply mascara.

"I have a twitch," I say, reaching up to touch my eye. She bats my hand away with hers.

"That right there isn't your run-of-the-mill eye twitch. You look like you're havin' a seizure," she says, pulling the corner of my eye taut so she can try to keep the twitch at bay as she applies mascara.

Lovely.

Once the mascara is applied as best as it can be, they go to work on the rest of my face. I flinch a few times when I see the bright red blush and lipstick Patti pulls out of her bag. I'm sure she knows what she's doing ... I hope. Maybe I should start praying.

"Okay, whaddya think, Debbie?" Patti asks, and they both stare at me for what seems longer than necessary. I'm hoping it's passable because we're nearly out of time.

"I think it's the best we can do under the circumstances," Debbie shakes her head with pity.

"It's much better than the disaster she had going on before," Patti says, nodding her head toward me.

"You know I can hear you, right?" I ask, as if they forgot I was a real person.

I stand up and go into the bathroom. The anticipation of seeing what might reflect in the mirror is making my anxiousness move to a fever pitch.

I close my eyes as if I'm being presented to myself, face the mirror, and open them.

Oh my holy crap, mother of hell.

I look like the wife of Colonel Sanders. And to be honest, I'm not even entirely sure what his wife looked like, but this must be it.

Let's start with my makeup. It's so overdone, I hardly recognize myself. Bright red blush adorns my cheeks and dramatic blue eye shadow on my eyelids. They've outlined my lips to be slightly bigger than my actual lips (not really necessary since they weren't thin to begin with) and the bright red lipstick they filled in with makes me look like a prostitute with clown undertones.

Then there's my hair. So backcombed on the top, it's almost as high as Patti's hair. It's been sprayed to the max, and I'm fairly confident that even a tornado couldn't bring this 'do down. Plus, the pink frosting streak is even more obvious now.

"You guys," I say, turning to Debbie and Patti. "I can't go out there like this!"

"Well why not?" Patti asks. "It's a far cry better from what ya looked like before," she says, squinting at me through her glasses.

I suddenly realize that I can't say anything because if I insult any of it, I'm vicariously insulting Patti, since this is basically her look. Only it works for her. But it most certainly doesn't work for me.

"The newspaper's here," Kate yells over to us as she walks from the front of the bakery into the kitchen. She takes one look at me, eyes bugging out of her head, and turns around and goes back out front. She's literally speechless.

Oh no. What the heck am I going to do? I can't get this off me without rubbing my skin so raw, I'll look even more clown-like than I did with the makeup on.

"Just give me a second," I say to the ladies as I shut the door the bathroom and try to think if there's anything I can do.

Carefully, I run my fingers through my over-sprayed hair, trying to untangle the backcombing. It's mostly a futile effort, but I'm able to bring it down a few inches. Then I blot my lipstick off on some toilet paper until it resembles a lighter shade of red. Using some of the makeup I brought I add a nude shade of lip gloss to the top, making the red look almost a decent shade of pink. Not a color I'd normally. wear, mind you, but better than the bright red. I can't do anything about the liner that has made my lips look only slightly smaller than Mick Jagger's. But with the nude added to the red, it's passable ... I hope.

I grab some more toilet paper and try to dampen the blue on my eyelids. Grabbing my favorite light neutral, I put some on top of what's left of the blue. It helps me to venture out of the 1980's and into the late 1990's. Still more than a decade behind, but maybe that puts me ahead of the times.

My phone beeps, signaling a text. Probably Jared sending me a text to grovel. Or maybe to tell me he's on his way. Oh please, oh please, oh please...

Save the dates need to go out next week.

It's Anna. This is *so* not what I need right now. I thought I nixed the save the dates in hopes that Bobby's massive guest list wouldn't be able to come because they had so little warning. I knew I wouldn't get away with it, though. I just hoped.

I don't have time to go into it right now so I text back an "okay" to hold her off until we can actually talk in person.

There's a knock at the bathroom door. "Did ya fall in?" Patti asks through the door.

I wish.

I stand back and look in the mirror and assess. Hair less teased? Check. Makeup less scary? Check. Eye twitch? Check.

My look still ventures on that of a prostitute, but at least it's not as bad as it was. I take a deep breath, square my shoulders and open the door to the bathroom. Debbie and Patti are both waiting for me on the other side of the door.

"Your hair," Patti purses her lips and shakes her head. "It's all flat now."

Good gravy, this is what she considers flat? I'm still teased to Timbuktu.

"Sorry," I say, looking at both of them. "I'm just not used to seeing myself like that. I only messed with it a little." I look apologetically at them.

"You look lovely," Debbie says, though I can tell by her eyes that she's mostly lying.

"Thanks," I say, and then swallow hard. "Okay, let's get this over with."

"You got this," Patti says, giving me a quick pat on the shoulder.

I'm pretty sure I don't, but I'm going to fake it as best I can.

CHAPTER 6

"Okay, let's get started," Lisa says, sitting across from me at a table in the corner, lemon muffin in hand, her dark brown hair looking glossier than ever. I really need to find out what products she uses.

Unlike Brown, Lisa is apparently a connoisseur of baked goods and eats them on a regular basis. Hard to believe by her tiny waist, but there are those people who can eat and never gain weight. I know—I was one of them … until I bought the bakery. Luckily, by the expression on her face and the moans of delight that come from her mouth, she's thoroughly enjoying the muffin.

She's one of those noisy eaters that irritate me so. Good thing the café is quiet right now. We have just under two hours until the lunch rush begins.

I guess Lisa has never worked in the service industry because some of the first words out of her mouth upon seeing the almost-empty bakery were about how quiet it was and that maybe business "isn't going so well." Her look of pity was palpable. I internally rolled my eyes, but I didn't let my irritation play outwardly … I hope.

The photo shoot was first. I tried desperately to get out of it, giving Lisa the shortened version of my morning from hell, but she said I looked great and that the picture would be black and white anyway, so I had nothing to worry about. Of course the comment about the picture being black and white did make me realize that she must've thought I was a bit overdone. That's the understatement of the century.

"So," she starts, pen to a pad of paper, recording device on the table, "tell me how this all came to be," she gestures to the bakery with her eyes and a sweep of her hand.

"Well," I say, wondering what else she needs to know that wasn't already told to her at dinner. Of course it had been more than a week since we went to dinner, and considering how she had forgotten my name in the first minutes after meeting me, I'm going to venture that Lisa doesn't have the best memory. Especially for things she doesn't truly care about.

"First, I have to tell you that I love what you've done with the place," Lisa says before I can even go into the story of how I became the owner of a bakery. "It's quaint, you know?"

"Um, yes, that was what I was going for," I say looking around the room. It's quaint, but not in a homey way. It's more of a contemporary look with bright colors and straight edges. I'm not one for doilies and floral patterns.

"You've done a great job of keeping it simple, and sort of plain, you know?" She nods her head at me.

I'm not certain how to respond to that. My eye does though; it does a double twitch. I pray she doesn't notice. I don't think the space is plain at all. Lisa has a very interesting way of insulting me without thinking she's actually insulting me. Or maybe she does?

"Sure," I finally say.

One thing's for sure. Each underhanded comment has made my eye twitch even harder. I didn't think it was possible. I'm also slightly starting to freak out that it will never go away and this is how I'll have to live my life forever.

"Okay, so back to the question, give me a little history on this old place," she sits back and takes a sip of her Diet Coke. The Diet Coke she insisted on having at nine in the morning. It's her "coffee" since she said she doesn't drink coffee because of all the issues it causes her stomach. As if Diet Coke is a better option. Who am I to judge though, really? I could totally go for a Dr. Pepper right now.

I'm trying super hard to not be Judge-y Mc-Judging-pants, but it's incredibly hard to do.

I begin by telling her about the previous owner, Beth, and how I came to work here after my dad had brought some of my baked goods into work (Beth's husband worked at the law firm with my dad, but is now retired). I tell her how this was supposed to be a temporary stop between jobs, but once I started working here, I knew I could never leave. Then when Beth decided to sell, and with the help of my family and a much needed nudge from Jared, I took a leap of faith and purchased the place.

Writing notes as I speak and inserting a few "uh-huhs" into the conversation, I get the sense from her body language that Lisa is bored to tears.

"And this all came to be because Jared got you fired from your job," she throws out there, like it's part of the story. I mean it is, but will that be going into the article?

"Yeah," I say, shortness to my tone.

"How did you get over that?" she leans toward me, tucking some of her shiny dark locks behind her ear.

"Well, it took a while," I say.

"I'm sure it did," she smiles, twinkle in her eye. *Twitch.*

"I guess it didn't take me too long. Maybe a month before he came groveling to me." I give her a tight, smug smile when I see the shock in her eyes.

"He groveled? Jared Moody groveled?" she asks, completely taken aback by this bit of info.

"He did. He came here to the bakery every day for two weeks until I agreed to go out with him so he could explain," I say. By the look on her face, this was not expected information. There's something else there too. Could it be jealousy?

She clears her throat, and with it, her facial expression. "That's interesting," she says, her tone and eyes indicating that she doesn't really find it interesting at all. Or, at least, she doesn't want to.

"Tell me more about the bakery," she says, eyes downturned, changing the subject as quickly as possible.

Glad to be off the Jared subject, and away from the venom that seemed to pour from her eyes the more I talked about it, I tell her more about my experience on *Cupcake Battles* and how business has been crazy busy ever since (the look of uncertainty as she glanced around my empty bakery did not go unnoticed).

"Do you love it?" she asks, writing something down on her notepad.

"The bakery? Yeah, I do. It can be stressful at times, but I could never go back to a desk job after working here," I say, looking around the room, a welcomed feeling of peace in my stomach as I realize I'll never sit at a desk again doing accounting. Unless you count my desk in the back that I do all the accounting at … which doesn't count to me.

"So when's the wedding?" Lisa asks after scribbling some notes on her pad of paper.

"Huh?" I ask, not sure what this has to do with her article and my bakery, but neither did the conversation of how I snagged Jared. She's kind of all over the place.

"Your wedding to Jared?" she questions me with brows creased as if she thinks I need a reminder about my own wedding.

"Oh, uh, September fourth," I say with a quick nod of my head.

"So less than three months," she states, looking as if she's doing some sort of calculation in her head.

"Yep," I say, sitting back in my seat. "I'm sorry, what does this have to do with the bakery?" I ask, trying to get her back to the conversation at hand. I have a lunch rush to get ready for. And prostitute/clown makeup to scrub off my face.

"Oh, no reason," she says, batting her hand in the air as if it's not a big deal. "I was just curious. It's just so crazy—Jared, *my* Jared—finally getting married." She shakes her head in wonder.

Her Jared? Seriously? He hasn't been hers for over a decade.

"It probably took him a while to ask you, right? He was always so slow." She purses her lips in a smug, all-knowing way, and sits back in her chair, arms folded.

"Actually from the time we started dating to the time we got engaged was just around a year," I say. I feel a pinch of self-satisfaction at that statement. I want to throw in something about how obviously when he knew it was right, there was no need to go slow, but I'm trying to take the high road here.

"Impressive," she says, her tone ringing of conspiracy, like I'd somehow tricked him into it.

"Uh, thanks?" I say, unintentionally turning my voice up in the form of a question.

"Back in college he wanted to marry me, you know," she says, her eyes looking directly at me, seeking the surprise she was looking for.

She found it. I'm quite taken aback by this bit of info. My eye gives a little twitch in surprise as well.

"He did?" I say, trying not to sound disbelieving, but failing miserably.

"He did. He asked me more than once," she says, clearly enjoying the upper hand she thinks she has right now.

"You were engaged?"

"Yes … well, not for very long. I broke it off with him." She tilts her head to the side inquisitively, a smirk on her lips. "He never told you anything about it?"

She can obviously tell by the shock on my face that he didn't.

"Yes," I lie out of the blue, "I mean, I'm sure he did. I must've forgotten." Oh gosh, I'm sinking to her level with the underhanded jabs. It doesn't matter because from the look on her face, she can tell that I'm lying.

"Oh, that Jared," she shakes her head slowly from side to side, "he was never very good at being open about the past. I guess things haven't changed."

A sinking feeling hits my stomach. My heart is telling me not to make a big deal out of any of this, but my mind is racing.

"Why did you break up with him?" The words pour out of my mouth before I can take them back. By asking this, I'm acknowledging that I believe this crazy story.

She looks to the side as if deciding how she wants to explain. "Things got complicated," she finally says and then moistens her lips with her tongue.

"Complicated," I echo.

"Yes, complicated," she repeats again. I get from her tone that this is all she plans to offer to the conversation. I want to dig deeper, but I also don't want to add more fuel to the fire — the fire being this conversation, and the growing pit in my stomach.

We sit there in silence for a bit, me dying to ask more but not allowing myself to, and her looking as if she wants to say more. I'm not giving her the satisfaction.

"Well, I think I have enough for the article," she finally says, and then starts to load her pad of paper and recorder into her black leather satchel.

"Okay," I say and stand up from the table.

"Thanks for humoring me today, Julia," she says, her fake smile plastered back on.

"Uh, thanks for interviewing me," I say, but not really thankful at all.

I walk her to the door and we say quick goodbyes. I have no plans to dilly-dally at the door.

I have a phone call to make.

CHAPTER 7

"Jules, it's not that big of a deal," Jared says, his tone indicating that he's tiring of this entire phone conversation.

"Uh, it kinda is," I say, not fully accepting how he's downplaying the whole thing. "You wanted to marry her. Don't you think that's an important thing to tell me? That you were engaged once?"

"It would be important, if it were important," he says, his tone quiet but earnest.

"What's that supposed to mean?" I ask, confused.

"I mean, don't you think that if it were a big deal, I would've told you?" he says, sounding insulted that I'd doubt him at all. "Besides, the engagement was like a millisecond long. It was foolish and stupid. We were both young."

"Were you in love with her?" The question slips out of my mouth before I have the sense to stop it.

"Oh geez, Jules. No. No I wasn't in love with her. I mean, I thought I was. But I was young and naïve and … no, it wasn't love."

"I just wish that I would've known. I felt so dumb, and she really rubbed it in, saying something about how you were never good at revealing your past. My mind started wondering about other things you might've never told me," I say.

"Don't worry about Lisa; she's harmless," he says. And I roll my eyes. He's obviously clueless about that one. "And as far as my past, why don't you assume that everything you don't know is probably because it's useless information that I'd rather not waste our time together on. Okay?"

I sit in silence, nibbling on my bottom lip.

"Yeah, okay," I say, realizing that he's right. I mean, it's not as if I've filled him in on all of my past escapades. Mostly because there are so few it's almost embarrassing. I truly had such a dull life until Jared waltzed into it.

"Do you want to know how I know that I wasn't in love with Lisa?" he asks, his tone soft. "I had no idea what real love — true love — was, until I met you."

Good gravy, how do I ever doubt this man? There must be a serious chemical imbalance in my brain.

"You see? It's those kinds of comments that make it impossible to be annoyed with you," I say, a lighter tone to my voice.

"Then my evil plan worked," he quips.

"Why don't you and your evil plan come over so we can kiss and make up?"

"I'm already walking to my car."

How did I let myself get caught up in all of this in the first place?

~*~

"Well, if I were you, I'd be madder than a wet hen," Patti says, nodding her head like I have a clue how mad a wet hen could be.

I'm going to assume that's really angry. Here's the deal though: I'm not.

"I'll have a talk with her," I say, hoping to appease her for now. I don't want to have a talk with Kate, but I know it's inevitable.

"Look, I'm not tellin' ya how to run yer business, but I think she's stepping all over everybody's toes, and I'd do something about it now before it gets worse," Patti says, her pointer finger jerking in my direction and her other hand wrapped tightly around a broom.

"I just don't think it's that big of a deal. So she ordered a few things we needed without asking me," I shrug my shoulders. "It was stuff we needed."

"And she changed our coffee supplier," she says, eyebrows higher than would seem humanly possible.

"Our other supplier raised their prices."

"She also changed our napkin supplier."

"She did? Well, maybe she got a better price."

"She made a bathroom schedule for us to take turns cleaning."

The look on Patti's face would indicate that this may have been the straw that broke the camel's back.

I let out a big long breath.

"Like I said, I'm not trying to tell you how to run your business, but I'd be worried about that one," she says pointing toward the front of the bakery where Kate is helping customers.

"I'll talk to her," I say, hoping that will appease Patti for now. I don't want to have a conversation with Kate. I hate confrontation. But if Patti thinks I should, then I probably should.

Patti sniffs dramatically and goes back to her sweeping.

I walk out to the front. Maybe I should just take care of this now. Rip the Band-Aid off super fast. That's the best way to do things, so I've heard. I wouldn't actually know. I put off and procrastinate until it all pops like a huge blister. A trait that actually gets on my own nerves, but I can't seem to change.

Okay, so I'll do it now. I can do this. Just a quick little chat with Kate, and everything will be fine. It'll be easy. So why is my heart beating faster and why do my palms feel sweaty? Dear heavens, I really do hate confrontation.

"Kate," I say as I walk up to her. She's squatting down behind the display unit counting what we have left from the morning rush so we can make sure we have more for tomorrow since it's Friday. Fridays are notoriously busy.

"Yes," she stands up from looking in the display case.

"I need to talk to you," I say just as the bells on the door chime signaling someone has come in.

Oh please no. What's she doing here?

"Hi Julia," Lisa says in a bright, fake voice. My eye twitches in response. Dang it. I was hoping I was done with the twitching; it had been a while.

"Hi Lisa, can I help you?" I ask, trying not to convey the annoyance that she's here while trying to make it clear that I'm busy. It's not easy to do, and I feel my face moving from eyebrows raised to furrowed brow, back to eyebrows raised as my face fights expressions. I probably look like I'm having a seizure.

In any case, Lisa doesn't notice, or doesn't really care because she waltzes right up to the counter and peers in.

"I was in the neighborhood and thought I'd drop by and see if you have any scones left. I never got to try one the other day," she says, her perfect white teeth displayed through a huge, over-the-top smile.

"Yes, I think we have one left," I say, hoping to hurry her out. I'm not in the mood for any more Jared surprise stories.

I put a scone in a white paper bag and hand it to her. She reaches into her purse for her wallet.

"On the house," I say, holding a hand out to stop her from paying.

"Thanks," she says brightly. She didn't even try to argue with me. Figures.

"How are things going with the wedding planning?" She asks, opening up the bag and breaking off a piece of the scone.

Lovely. I was hoping she'd grab her scone and go. Apparently that was not her plan.

"Things are going great," I say as happily as I can muster. I still need to talk to Kate, so this chick needs to skedaddle.

"You don't seem that excited," she says, head tilted in mock concern.

"I don't?"

"I mean, you don't give off that typical glow most brides have."

Twitch.

"Well, you know, I have more going on besides the wedding," I say, feeling defensive.

"Oh I'm sure! I just would've expected someone at your age to be super excited about the whole bride thing." She nibbles a bite of pastry.

Twitch.

"Aren't we the same age?" I ask, realizing the dig right away.

"Oh sure, that's why I'm saying it. I can relate. If I were marrying Jared, it would be consuming my every thought." She gives me a thin smile.

"Well, I guess I have other things that need part of my brain," I say, oozing irritation. "Like running a business." I hold my hands up motioning around me. "But I guess you wouldn't have a clue about that." I can feel the heat rising up my face.

She holds up a hand. "Oh no, sorry! I didn't mean to offend." Her sincerity is about as transparent as plastic wrap.

"No," I shake my head. "Sorry, it's been a stressful morning. I'm a little tired," I say, feeling stupid for getting so defensive so quickly. "I think I'd be better off eloping," I say, trying to lighten the conversation a bit.

"Oh, I'm sure," she says, and for a moment I feel like she's truly trying to understand me. "I'm really sorry if I upset you, Julia. Honest."

"Don't worry about it," I wave the unnecessary apology away with my hand.

"Hey, we should do lunch sometime! I'd love to get to know the girl that's marrying Jared Moody. I'm dating his brother, so, you know, we might be family someday." She gives me a little wink.

Yeah, that's pretty doubtful. I should feel sorry for Lisa — her days are numbered with Mark. He'll toss her to the side soon enough just like all the others. If I weren't petty, I'd feel sad about that. But … well … I'm petty.

"Well I better take off." She grabs a napkin from the dispenser on the counter.

"It was nice to see you, Lisa," I lie.

"You know," she says as an afterthought, "I really like the messy bun thing you do with your hair. I wish I could just go with the flow and not care what my hair looks like." She winks at me again. "Anyway, take care!" She says with way too much enthusiasm as she walks out of the bakery.

Twitch.

"Well, she's a ray of sunshine," Kate says sarcastically.

"Yeah, isn't she?" I roll my eyes.

"How does she get her hair so straight and shiny?" she asks, looking out the door as Lisa basically glides down the sidewalk.

"I have no idea," I mutter, staring after her as well.

Stupid Lisa and her stupid locks. I need to make sure I ask her how she gets her hair like that before Mark gives her the heave-ho.

Glossy, commercial-perfect hair aside, the more I'm around Lisa, the more I don't like her. Her underhanded jabs are starting to get to me. Maybe I'll say something to Jared. Although I'm not certain what that would do. He'd probably tell me to not even give her a second thought. Which is great advice, actually.

Thank you, subconscious Jared, for your well thought-out guidance.

With that, I turn to Kate to get this chat over with. Just as I open my mouth, the doorbell chimes.

"Well hello, Lia," Kate says before I can greet her. I turn and look at Kate. She has a genuine smile on her face, and Lia is reciprocating. How refreshing that she's making connections with the regulars already. Patti was here long before I was, and she still can't seem to muster up a smile for anyone. But then again, Patti's not really the smiling type. That's why she stays in the back and the rest of us work the front.

"Hi Lia," I say, actually glad to see her. Her face is a welcome sight after Lisa.

"Hello Julia," Lia says in her face full of concern. "You—"

"I know," I interject quickly. "My aura's off." I can't see it, but I can pretty much guarantee it.

"No—I mean, yes it is—but I was actually going to say that you look tired."

"Yes, I'm that too." I give her a thin smile. It's all I'm capable of mustering.

"Well you should get some rest," she says, nodding her head. "I had a dream about you the other night and I'm a bit concerned."

"Rest would be nice," I say, purposefully not asking her about the dream. I don't really want to know. "But unfortunately, it's not in the cards for me right now."

"Oh! Do you want me to give you a reading?" She asks, excitement in her voice at hearing the word *cards*.

"No!" I say a little too loud. "I mean, er, no thanks, Lia. That won't be necessary." I really don't need to see my future right now. I can't even handle the present.

"Well, I'll take a muffin then," she says, peering down into the display case.

I look over to Kate. "Can you take care of Lia? I have some work to do in the back."

Kate doesn't even reply. She just gets right to work. Why was I having a conversation with her again? I mean, she's a stellar employee and as far as I'm concerned, she's doing stuff that needs to be done that I don't have time to do. And I know Patti will hate this, but we actually do need a bathroom schedule.

No, I think Kate Bowen is doing just fine.

CHAPTER 8

"Julia!" Anna yells as she sees me crack a soda. I was trying to hide it, but then I thought about the fact that I'm a grown woman and I can do whatever the hell I want, and so I just opened the darn thing.

"You said you gave up that junk." She tilts her head to the side, eyeing me through squinting, judging green eyes.

Brown, Anna, and I are sitting on the floor of my condo going over wedding stuff, of course. What else would we be doing? When not doing bakery stuff, I live, breathe, eat, and drink wedding stuff. I'm trying not to be over it … but I *so* am. Why won't Jared elope with me already?

"I did give it up," I say as I take a sip, the beautiful liquid instantly perking up my taste buds. I'm not lying. I actually gave up soda for nearly a day and a half, and along with it, my will to live.

"I thought you wanted to lose weight before the wedding," Anna says disapprovingly.

"I do. I just want Dr. Pepper more," I say, taking another delicious swig.

"I can't believe you still drink that stuff," Brown pipes in after she ends a call on her smart phone. "It's terrible for you."

This coming from the woman who quit smoking just over a year ago. I don't point that out, though.

A purring Charlie plops herself in my lap and I instinctively start to pet her, taking time to scratch her behind the ears, which she loves.

"Have you picked out a dress for the gala?" Brown asks as she reaches over and pets Charlie on her back.

"Not yet," I say, wishing that stupid gala was not on my to-do list.

"We can go together," Brown says, a smile spreading across her face.

Spectraltech, the company I worked for before the bakery, will be featured at the gala as well. They were recently given the key to the city by the mayor for economic growth over the past two years. Kind of funny, since they laid me off just before that.

"Julia, we need to focus. We have a huge list of things to go through for this wedding," Anna says, pointing to the checklist in front of her.

"So you're still going through with the marriage?" Brown asks, eyebrows raised, nudging me with her elbow.

"Yes, everything's fine," I say and then roll my eyes at her.

"Oh please, you totally overreacted to that," Anna says, referring to the Lisa and Jared situation. Ew. I don't even like to think of their names with an "and" between them. Or that there was ever a situation there in the first place.

"What did Jared say?" Brown asks, angling her body toward me.

I lean back against the base of the couch. "He downplayed it, of course. But honestly, I was jumping to conclusions. I mean, it was over a decade ago. He said they were young and naïve."

"Yeah, I can't imagine how things would've ended up if I'd married my college boyfriend." Brown shudders at the thought.

"Me neither," I add, but then scrunch my face. I have no idea why I said that.

"You never had a college boyfriend," Anna says all too quickly.

"How do you know? You were ten when I was in college," I say, giving her a major smirk.

"Because, Julia, I may have been ten, but I watched you like a hawk," she says and tinges of guilt fill me as I remember how I pushed her away all of those years, but she still looked to me as a big sister. It's in the past, though, and I feel like we're doing a pretty good job of making up for it. Anna has become a necessary part of my life and I don't know what I'd do without her. I'm not going to say that out loud or anything. We don't do cheesy.

"Well, I dated plenty of guys I'm glad I didn't marry," I say, and that's the truth. Although marriage was never on the table, so I never had to go there.

"Back to the wedding, Julia," Anna says, evidently done with this conversation. "Would you just make a decision already?" She points to the five color samples I have to choose from for the tablecloths at the reception.

"But I like them all. You decide," I say turning to Brown. I'm not going to give Anna the option because she'd jump all over it. She's making too many decisions in my life right now as it is.

"No way, this isn't my wedding. Jules, you're making it too hard." She tilts her head to the side, annoyed look on her face.

"I know," I say and sigh heavily. I do realize I'm not good at making decisions.

"Fine," I say, "I think I'd like the cream ones." I point to the sample.

"Are you sure?" Anna asks, uncertainty to her voice.

"Seriously, Anna? Of course I'm not sure. I'm not sure about anything. I'm only sure that I want to marry Jared and live my life with him and that's it." I lay into her, my anger setting in quickly as my tone gets louder with each word.

"Okay, sheesh. Sorry. The cream is fine," she turns her head from me, but I catch the eye-roll. I'm not going to acknowledge it, even though it's at the tip of my tongue.

"Did you just roll your eyes at me?" I ask, the acknowledgement slipping right out of my mouth. I'm too tired to fight even myself.

"Yes, because you're being ridiculous," she says, folding her arms and sitting back against the base of the couch, her legs tucked under her.

"Anna," Brown chastises with her voice and a silent conversation happens between them with only their eyes. This isn't the first time they've done this talking without talking thing.

An unexpected bit of jealousy goes through me. I think my sister has stolen my bestie. And I'd point that out if we were in the fifth grade. But since we're all adults here, that probably wouldn't fly. It's along the same vein as telling Anna that she's not the boss of me. Which I have actually said, more than once.

"Fine," Anna says, conceding to Brown. She looks down at the list. "Okay, now that's settled. Let's move onto the music."

"I only want jazz," I say and then take a chug of my pseudo-poisonous soda.

"No," Anna and Brown say at the same time.

"Why not?" I ask, insulted by their emphatic tone. Last I remembered this was *my* wedding.

"Because that's boring, Jules. And I know you don't dance, but the rest of us do. We want some booty-shaking music," Brown says, doing a little shimmy.

"Oh gosh," I say, thinking of all the things I'm going to be forced to do at this wedding. I have to stand in front of a huge crowd, which I hate. Then go around and smile and try to be interesting at a reception that I don't want. And now I'll have to dance with a bunch of people I don't truly know?

Why won't Jared elope with me, dang it? I'm not asking much here. Just him, me, and a beach. That's all I want.

"Stop dreaming of eloping. Jared doesn't want that," Anna says, reading my mind.

"Fine," I say, sounding very much like Anna, "you can have your stupid booty music."

"Yes!" Brown says, clapping enthusiastically.

"Just know that I won't be doing any lame line dances," I say. Debbie and Patti had already put in a request for the *Electric Slide*, which I turned up my nose to immediately. Then they spent the rest of the day showing me stupid dances and trying to get me to do them. Although it was pretty hilarious, I still wouldn't acquiesce.

"You're no fun, Jules," Brown says, teasing me.

"Can we be done now?" I ask, feeling exhausted. Not even caffeine can rescue me from my sleepiness. And I've drunk my weight in caffeinated soda today, so I would know.

Anna runs over her lists, putting checkmarks next to the things we did tonight. I take a peek at the list and internally groan at the amount of things still left to do.

"How goes the baby making?" Anna asks Brown once she's finished running through my wedding to-do list.

Brown sighs, a look of sadness washing over her. I think she was hoping to avoid the topic.

"It's not," she says, her eyes crestfallen.

I reach over and rub her back for a moment, trying not to be overly comforting. It's not my forte and Brown isn't all that receptive to it anyway.

"What's going on?" I ask.

"I'm just wondering if we should skip IUI and go straight to in vitro," She says, looking at her hands now twiddling in her lap.

"Why?" I ask.

"Because we're already spending money on the IUI; why bother if it might not work? Why not put our money toward something a little more guaranteed?" she says.

"So why doesn't Matt want to?" Anna asks.

"There's just a lot more worry with that. IVF involves a lot of hormones and increased risk for multiples too."

"Multiples," I echo with a slight shudder. Brown could probably handle more than one baby because she's organized and when she puts her mind to something she can pretty much do anything. She has strong determination. Me? I'd end up in a straitjacket.

"So what're you going to do?" Anna asks.

"I don't know," she says with a small shrug. "We've been fighting a lot about it lately."

"Well, maybe you should try the IUI first?" I say and rub her back again.

"Yeah, maybe. I guess it wouldn't hurt," she sniffs and then gives me a half-hearted smile.

"You'll get through this," I say like the cheerleader I am. But I'm not just saying it. I have full faith in Brown. She *will* come out of this with flying colors.

"You know," Anna says, "all this baby stuff has got me thinking about it."

"What?" Brown and I say at the same time.

"Jonathon and I have been talking about it. Think of it, Brown—we could be pregnant at the same time." She bobbles around on her knees, excited at the thought.

"Oh that would be fun," Brown says, smiling. The smile quickly falters. "That is, if I ever get pregnant."

"Yes, first things, first," I say, trying not to feel annoyed that my best friend and sister are now planning babies together. "Let's get Brown pregnant and then worry about you," I say, nodding my head toward Anna.

I want to start into the fact that Anna is still so young, having had a whirlwind courtship with Jonathon, they both need time to enjoy each other before adding children into the mix. But with Anna, that would only push her toward the decision. I also can't have Anna getting pregnant before me. I mean, I'm the firstborn of the Dorning children and the last to get married. I can't be the last to have kids. That just seems wrong. And totally unfair, in my very petty opinion.

"Yeah," Brown says, sadness in her tone and expression. "I hope it happens."

It's so hard to see Brown this way. And I can't do or say anything to help the situation. I feel helpless as her friend.

"Okay, so Julia, are you sure about the cream tablecloths?" Anna asks, changing the subject back to me, clearly as uncomfortable with this new side of Brown we're both seeing.

I pick up a throw pillow and toss it at her head. Brown laughs and just like that, the serious tone that was blanketing the room changes.

I guess right now I should be thankful for Anna and her obsessive-compulsive disorder over my wedding. But only in this instance.

CHAPTER 9

"Can I have a word, Julia?" Bobby asks from the display counter.

It's a week later and things seem to be going smoothly, which means everything's about to blow up in my face.

"Of course," I say cheerfully. "What can I help you with?"

She looks around her, seeing the other eyes and ears in the room with us (basically Debbie and Kate). "Can I talk to you alone?"

"Sure," I say, my eyebrows pulling together as a feeling of uneasiness spreads over me. Bobby's look is a mix of worry and irritation.

I walk out from behind the counter and into the main dining area. We grab a seat at a back table.

"How are you?" I ask happily, trying to kick this conversation off on the right foot. Which is stupid, because how can my tone instantly change someone's mood? But I try, regardless.

"Well, I'm a little concerned," she says, looking directly into my eyes.

"Concerned? About what?" Oh dear, what have I done. I start thinking of things in my head. With me, there could be so many possibilities.

"Well, I spoke with Mark yesterday and he said that Lisa told him that she spoke with you and that you indicated that you weren't excited about getting married."

"What?" I say, surprised. Which isn't a stretch, I'm truly stunned. Also, at the mention of Lisa's name my eye does a little twitch.

"She said she came into the bakery to grab a treat and that you just started telling her how you felt overwhelmed and stressed and that you weren't sure you wanted to get married at all," Bobby says.

"I never said that!" I say, louder than I intended.

"Well why would Mark just make that up?" Bobby says, confusion in her countenance.

"I don't know. I mean, Lisa did come here last week. But she was the one who assumed that I wasn't excited. Yes, I'm a little overwhelmed — with the bakery and the wedding planning — but I most definitely want to get married to Jared."

Twitch.

Dang it! Why is it anytime Lisa is mentioned my eye twitches? My eye must really hate her.

"Oh," she looks to the side, as if contemplating what I'm saying. "Well, that's good," she says, not sounding entirely convinced.

"Bobby," I say, reaching across the table and covering her hand with mine — an odd gesture for me, but I'm rolling with it. "Trust me. I want to marry your son. I'm excited about it. I may not be thrilled with doing the whole wedding hoopla and would rather elope, but I'm..."

Oh crap. What did I say? The color in Bobby's face has drained and she swiftly removes her hand from underneath mine as if my touch has burned her.

"You'd rather elope?" she says, her eyes wide with disbelief. "After all of the work we've done?"

"No!" I say quickly. Holy crap, I'm so awesome at making things worse. Really, it's a talent. "Of course I want a wedding and all of that; the eloping is more of a silly dream." I smile, hoping to convey that the eloping thing was not something I seriously considered, which is a total lie, of course. But no matter, I can tell by the look on her face that she's not buying it.

"Well," she rubs a temple, "I wish I would've known that you prefer to elope so then we could've avoided all this planning."

Wow, she's ticked. I'm going to kill Lisa. Like actually kill her—not just saying it. My eye is twitching at a rapid pace now.

"No," I say emphatically. "I want a wedding. I'm just not a big wedding kind of gal. I don't like a lot of fuss."

"What are we supposed to do? Uninvite people? Save the Dates have already gone out," she says, her voice stern. I don't think I've ever seen Bobby like this before.

"Of course not," I say. "The wedding is planned, the guest list is made. It's going to happen no matter what I prefer."

Hello foot, welcome to my mouth.

"Well, maybe you should elope, then, if it's what you 'prefer.'" She spits out the last word and starts to stand up to leave.

"Bobby, no—that's not what I meant. I'm sorry, my mind is a bit foggy. It's been a busy morning. What I mean to say is that I want to have this wedding, I want to marry Jared, and I want it to be a wonderful day for everyone. Okay?"

It's barely readable, but her eyes do soften a touch when I say this.

"Well, okay then," she finally says, and my stomach relaxes slightly.

"Can you do me a favor and not believe anything Lisa has to say?" I ask.

She laughs. "I'm a little shocked I believed anything out of that girl's mouth. Especially after what she did. I should've known..." she trails off, looking down at her diamond-ring adorned hands, resting on the table.

"What did she do?" I ask. I knew there was a story there!

"Oh, it was nothing," she says, batting the question away with her hand. "I mean, at the time it was a big deal, but that was a long time ago. I'd hoped that she'd grown up. But apparently she hasn't."

"Well, Mark will kick her to the curb soon enough, I'm sure," I say, wishing I could know more, but I know Bobby well enough to know that if she wanted to tell me, she would. Maybe at some point I'll get it out of her.

"I'm not so sure," she says, her lips forming a flat line. "He's asked if she can be his plus one at the wedding." She shakes her head.

"He has?" I can't hide my disdain. That sucks. I don't want her at my wedding. "But it's still over two months away. How does he know they'll even be together? His track record isn't fantastic."

"That's what I asked him, but he told me he had 'a feeling' about this one," she says, a glint of frustration in her voice.

"Well has he ever had a feeling before?"

"Not that I know of. At least, not that he's mentioned." She sighs a big frustrated sigh, and I echo her.

"Well, I guess we can only hope he'll un-feel the feeling before then." I just really really really don't want Lisa at our wedding. I can picture her looking at me with that smug face of hers, her eyes indicating that Jared is only settling for me.

Suddenly, when I picture myself in my wedding dress I feel frumpy. I need to go for a jog. I can't have Lisa one-upping me at my own wedding, which she most assuredly will try to do. She might even flirt with the groom, since she's pretty good at doing that as well.

"Well, don't you worry about Lisa," Bobby says. My face must've been revealing my thoughts.

"I'm not," I say a little too quickly, indicating that I'm probably more worried than I should be.

"I've got to run," she says, standing up, her purse in her hands. "If I haven't told you, Julia, I'm glad you're marrying my son." She turns and heads toward the bakery exit.

My eyes unexpectedly well up at that. "I'm glad to be marrying your son too," I call out after her, other patrons turning my way at my declaration. I totally ruined that moment, but who cares. She's "glad" I'm marrying her son. How would Lisa like that, huh? Too bad she wasn't here to hear it. Although if she were, I would have pummeled her. The nerve of that girl.

~*~

"Julia!"

"Huh?" I say, waking up. I didn't even know I'd dozed off. I'm sitting next to Anna on my couch and she's got my wedding binder opened. We were going over the things we needed to get done this weekend … I think.

"Did you seriously fall asleep while I was talking to you?" Anna accuses, her eyes squinting in disgust. "And you said you were going to 'cut me'?"

Did I say that out loud? Crap.

"Sorry," I say, rubbing my eyes. "I'm just so freaking tired."

"Well, you'll have time to sleep after the wedding," she says, no indication of sympathy in her voice. "You're not even doing all the work. I am."

She does have a point. I think it's the combination of running the bakery, the upcoming gala and all that entails, and the wedding that's draining me of my livelihood. Good heavens, what if I didn't have Anna? I'd surely be institutionalized at this point. Even with her help, I still could end up there.

"I was watching Liam until late last night," I say with a yawn.

"It's so unfair," Anna pouts. "I've offered to watch Liam so many times and Jenny always asks you. Why is that?"

Because Jenny doesn't trust you is what I want to say, but I hold my tongue. Instead I shrug as if to wonder the same thing.

"I need the practice too," she says, putting a hand on her stomach.

Oh no. My stomach falls.

"Wait … are you?" I ask, trying not to sound panicked. Anna can't be pregnant now. I'm not ready. And of course, her getting pregnant is *all* about me.

"No, not yet," she says. "But not for lack of trying." She gives me a quick double eyebrow raise.

Gross. A picture of my sister and her prim and proper husband, Jonathon, getting busy and I'm about to up-chuck my dinner.

"Are you really… um … trying?" I ask, my voice sounding rather sickly.

"Well, not yet. I guess you could say we're practicing," she says, her hand back on her stomach. Is she practicing that too?

"Is Jonathon ready for children?"

"Yes … I think he is," Anna says, avoiding eye contact with me.

"You think he is?"

"I mean, we've only discussed it briefly," she says, still avoiding eye contact.

"And?"

"And he said he didn't want to rush it."

"So how does that make him 'ready' then?" I question. This is so typical of Anna, once she's made up her mind it's as if no one else has an opinion. Even her own husband, who'd be the father of this future child. I'm no psychologist, but I'm pretty certain there's a lack of communication going on here.

"Don't you worry about that," she says, a sinister smile spreading across her face.

I take in a quick breath of air. "You're not going to pull one of those soap opera story lines where you stop taking birth control without his knowledge, are you?" My eyes go wide at the thought.

"No," she says, rolling her eyes. "The power of persuasion from a wife can be very convincing. *You'll see*."

Oh yes, "you'll see," my two least favorite words in the dictionary these days. I swear Anna is always rubbing it in that she got married before I did. Her and Brown love to talk like they're part of a special club and say things like "just you wait until you're married, Julia. *You'll see*." Or, "this is just what married people do, Julia. *You'll see*." Or, "that's totally a husband thing to do. *You'll see*, Julia." Mind you, I'm older than both of those wenches. Although I've never been married, so I guess I *will* see. Whatever.

"Well, make sure you keep Jonathon in the loop," I say, recalling how she was totally controlling when she got married and it almost caused them to break up the night before the wedding. I may or may not have aided in that, due to a little too much champagne. So, more "may" than "may not." But I was also the one to fix it all, so you could say I saved the day … after nearly ruining it.

"Duh," she says, giving me her best snooty-duck-lips face she does so well. "Anyway, back to the list," she brings my attention back to the binder in front of us.

"Yes, the list," I say with a yawn.

"No falling asleep," she scolds.

"Yes, master," I say, and yawn again.

CHAPTER 10

"Bakery owner Julia Dorning knows how to bake a pastry. Don't let the dowdy look fool you. Underneath that disheveled hair and over-the-top makeup beats the heart of a true business owner. She epitomizes the growth and spunk of the local Denver businesses that are coming on the scene with a punch..."

Holy hellfire and brimstone.

I'm staring down at the article that Lisa wrote and printed on the front page of the business section of the *Denver Post*. And I'm quite suddenly feeling homicidal. Yes, that describes my feelings perfectly at this moment.

I can't say I was excited for this article to come out and I most certainly wasn't thrilled to see my picture in the newspaper, but this ... this goes beyond all my fears. I'm seriously hoping this is a bad dream and at any moment I'll wake up. Please oh please let it be that.

The article is full of jabs, but to the average reader, I suppose they would look past all of that. But the picture? Oh dear heavens ... the picture. Apparently it was caught mid eye-twitch. So not only do I have backcombed hair and overdone makeup, I also have a shadow of a double chin and a lazy eye. I look like a southerner with Quasimodo undertones.

"Jules, it's not that bad," Jared says as he reads the article. We're sitting in my living room. He surprised me this morning with buttermilk donuts from Amerigo Delicatus (my favorite) and the newspaper. He wanted to read it together. I reach over and poke him with my finger and he gives me a confused look.

Nope. Not a dream. Damn.

"Not that bad? Are you reading the same article?" I ask, incredulous look on my face. I don't dare bring up the picture. I can't bear him to acknowledge it out loud.

"*'Don't let the dowdy look fool you,'*" I quote the article with my best Lisa imitation—which sounds more like the Wicked Witch of the West. "She basically said I'm not one of those girls who care about my appearance."

"Well, you aren't one of those girls," Jared says, his tone implying he thinks he's complimenting me.

"Oh my gosh, you think I'm dowdy?" I say, louder than I meant to.

"No!" he interjects quickly, and good thing he did. He was about to lose a limb. One that he'd be very sad without.

"I mean, you're easy," he says, and then his eyes bulge out at the realization of what just came from his mouth.

"I'm easy," I deadpan.

"No! I mean, you're just ... you know ... you." He nods his head, acknowledging that I am, in fact, me.

"I'm not sure how to take that," I say with little inflection in my voice.

"You should take it," he says, putting the newspaper down on the coffee table and pulling me into his arms, "as a good thing. I like you just as you are."

"Keep talking," I prod.

"You're the most interesting, intelligent, beautiful person I know." He swipes a lock of hair that's fallen in front of my eyes and pushes it behind my ear.

"Uh-huh," I close my eyes and lean into him.

"You don't even need any makeup." His lips touch mine briefly.

My eyelids flutter back open. "Now you're patronizing me." Obviously, I look like I've come back from the dead when I go without makeup. Actually "you look like you've come back from the dead" was a direct quote from Lia the witch. And she would probably know. She's familiar with talking to the dead (or so she claims).

"You certainly don't need makeup like you had on in that picture," he points to the newspaper.

I knew I was delusional to think that I could get away with no comment about the picture.

"That was all Patti and Debbie," I say, trying to pull away from him, but he tightens his grip around me.

"The hair too?" he asks, running his fingers through my hair.

"The whole freaking thing. Actually, it was worse. I tried to fix it but clearly I wasn't able to," I say, nodding my head toward the offending newspaper. "It's all your fault, you know. You should've been there." Not that much would've changed if he were. All of the disasters happened before he would've even shown up.

"Sorry, Jules, I wish I could've been there. Anyway, don't get worked up about it. The article was good. It'll be great for business," he says, and then brushes my lips with a sweet kiss. Yes, of course he'd think that. This is all going to be good for the expansion that I still haven't told him I don't want to do.

"That's the thing, though," I say, pulling back. "What if I don't want business to be better?" I ask.

"What do you mean?" He furrows his brow.

Say it now, Julia. Just do it now before it gets too crazy. You can do this.

"It means that I—"

Jared's phone rings, interrupting me. He looks at me, questioning with his eyes as to whether he should answer it or not. I give him a quick nod.

"Hey Bobby," he says when he puts the phone up to his ear. I still can't get used to Jared calling his mom by her name. If I ever tried that with my mom, she'd flip.

I move away from him and grab a donut to munch on while he chats with his mom. This is the right time to tell him, it has to be.

"I've gotta run," Jared says, standing up quickly from the couch after he ends the call.

"You do? Why?" I ask, disappointment obvious in my voice.

"Bobby had some sort of pipe burst in the basement. She wants me to come and check it out." He reaches down and pulls me up to standing, then pulls me into him and kisses me softly. "Mmm, buttermilk donut," he says as he tastes the donut that I was just eating on my lips.

"I'll call you later," he says as I walk him to the door. He gives me another quick kiss before he leaves.

I guess I'll have to save the conversation about the bakery expansion for another time. It needs to be soon, though, before I get stuck too deep and can't get out of it.

~*~

"What's going on here?" I ask as I look in the mirror, investigating my arms. I'm in a floor-length plum halter dress by Badgley Misch-something. It's been the top runner of dresses for the gala so far. And a great designer according to Brown. I'll have to take her word for it.

"What do you mean?" Brown asks. She's seated in the corner of the dressing room looking at her phone. We're shopping for a dress for the gala. She's going to the gala too, since Spectraltech is being featured as well, and she was their top salesperson last year. But of course, Brown found her dress months ago because that's what Brown does. I, as usual, like to wait until time is crucial. Because that's what I do.

"Look at this," my eyes widen as I take in the dangling skin that's hanging from the underside of my upper arms.

She looks up from her phone at me staring the mirror at my arms. "Batwings," she says simply.

"Batwings?" I say, horrified.

"It happens when you get older and you haven't worked out enough," she says this very matter-of-fact like.

Information that would've been useful a decade ago.

"You do realize you just insulted me twice," I say, turning around to look her in the eyes. She gives me a look like she's not following. "You said I was old *and* didn't work out."

"Jules, you know what I meant." She stands up and comes over to the mirror to inspect me closer. "Anyway, you don't have true batwings ... just, you know, the beginnings of them."

"You're not making it better," I say, my mouth forming into a pout. "Look!" I say and start waving in the mirror, watching the skin on my underarm jiggle around.

"How much waving do you plan on doing at this gala?" Brown asks. "It's not like you're royalty."

"That's true. And if I just keep my arms down at my sides like this, no one will see them." I start walking around the dressing room, my arms plastered to my sides.

"That looks totally natural," she deadpans. "Jules, you'll be fine. This dress is perfect on you. You look like a million bucks."

I stop my robot walking and look in the mirror. This is by far the best dress I've found. I'm so sick of trying on dresses, especially gowns. Ball gowns, wedding gowns—it's exhausting. The most draining part is squeezing myself into the Spanx. Thank goodness for them, though. They hold me in, in all the right places. I just have to be careful not to breathe, or sit down, or use the bathroom.

"Did I tell you Lisa will be there?" I ask, looking at myself in the mirror.

"Yes, you did," Brown says. "How are you feeling about all of that?"

"About her coming to the gala, or the article?" I ask.

"Both. But mostly the article," she says.

We haven't discussed the article yet. I texted her before we met up to go dress shopping and said I didn't want to talk about it. I knew I wouldn't get away with not talking about it with Brown.

"Not much I can do about that stupid article," I say, examining the small train on the back of the dress in the mirror.

"Uh, you could say something to her," Brown says, looking at me in the mirror, her eyebrows pulled together.

"Yes, because I'm so good at that," I say, and Brown nods her head in agreement. "Besides what can she do? Print a retraction? *The Denver Post would like to apologize to Julia Dorning for the comments made about her unkempt hair and dowdy looks.*"

Brown laughs, but then her face quickly takes on a serious look. "Well, at least you could say something to her."

"I don't want her to think she's affected me," I say.

"Good point," Brown says, conceding, which is a rarity for her. "Plus, all publicity is good publicity, right?"

"Well, we won't really know until tomorrow," I say into the mirror as I go back to flicking the skin on my underarms. My batwings.

Brown suddenly bursts into tears. What the —

"Brown?" I turn around and grab her by the arms. "What's wrong?"

"Tomorrow's the insemination," she says through her tears.

"Why are you crying?" I ask. "This is exciting. You could be getting pregnant tomorrow," I say, shaking her slightly as if I might force a smile out of her.

"I don't know." She pulls back from me, her finger going under her eye to wipe a tear. "I'm a freaking mess. I cry over everything. It's all these hormones they have me on."

"Of course," I say. I actually had no idea there were hormones involved.

"There's a lot riding on this, you know?" The tears start coming out faster.

"Yes," I say, placing a hand on her arm. "But this isn't your only chance. You can do this more than once, right?"

"Yeah." She sniffles.

"And then IVF if that doesn't work, right?"

Brown nods.

I know Brown, though. She has this all planned out and she wants this first time to work. It'll make up for the feeling of failing she's had since this whole fertility thing happened.

She wipes her eyes and then comes over to me and unzips my dress. I slide out of it, avoiding the mirror so I don't have to see myself in Spanx. No one wants to see that. I'm sure Brown doesn't.

"It'll be fine, Brown," I say as I literally peel myself out of the Spanx.

"Come on, let's go buy this dress," Brown says, grabbing the dress from me and hanging it on the hanger. Just like Brown. When she's done with a conversation, she moves on. I need to be more like that.

"Even with the batwings?" I ask as I start putting on my jeans.

"Even with the batwings," she says with a wink.

CHAPTER 11

"Bless your heart," Patti says to me the next morning as I enter the bakery.

"Ah," I say, nodding my head slowly. "You saw the article."

"Well, of course I did," she says, pointing a rather large spatula at me. "I mean, the way she mocked you, and that picture ... mmm," she shakes her head, lips pursed disapprovingly. "She's got your number, that one."

"Please, Patti, don't hold back," I say with unmistakable cynicism. "Anyway, she doesn't 'have my number,' I'm on to her." Well, she's pretty conniving. I definitely need to tread lightly where Lisa's concerned.

Unfortunately, or rather I guess fortunately (depending how you look at it), Lisa's column only helps the bakery. We're busy from the minute the doors open and we don't slow down until well after our normal time. We barely have time to get ready for the lunch rush.

I'm in the back trying to ice sugar cookies at lightning speed when my phone rings.

"Jules," Brown says, sounding a little frantic as I answer.

"What's up Brown, everything okay?"

"Not really," she says with a sniff.

"What's wrong?" I ask, moving away from the cookies and into my office where I can get some privacy.

"I'm at the fertility doctor," she says. "We're about to do the insemination."

"So what's the problem? Is there something wrong with … uh … the procedure?"

"No, everything's fine. It's just that Matt isn't here," she says through sniffles.

"Why isn't Matt there?" I ask, totally confused.

"I don't know. He's not answering his phone and he's a half hour late. The doctor just told me we can't wait much longer or we chance losing his … uh … swimmers that he left this morning."

"Crap, Brown. What can I do?"

"Can you meet me here? I don't want to do this on my own," she says, her voice quivering slightly.

"Of course," I say.

"I'm on Eighteenth, only three blocks from the bakery."

"I'm on my way," I say, and end the call. I grab my purse and tell Patti I'll be back as soon as I can. Only an hour until the lunch rush.

~*~

"I'm here to see Betsy Brown," I say breathlessly to a young super-model-looking woman sitting at the front desk of the fertility doctor's office. I ran the three blocks here. I've seriously got to get in shape. My heart feels like it's about to burst.

The receptionist has a nonchalance about her that instantly grates on my nerves. Doesn't she know this is an emergency? Not only is my best friend about to possibly get pregnant, but I might be having a panic attack. Seriously, my heart rate won't go back to normal.

"She's in room three. Just go in the door there," she points to a door to my left. "Take a right past the nurse's station. It's the third room on the left."

I open the door with so much gusto that it hits the doorjamb with a loud thud. I race pass the nurses station to room three and knock lightly.

"Come in," I hear Brown's muffled voice through the door.

I walk into the room and find Brown lying on the bed, her feet are up in the stirrups and a sheet covers her from the waist down. She's wearing a dressy blush colored top. It's kind of an odd sight, really.

"Thanks for coming," she says through sniffles. A tear drips down her face.

"Of course," I say grabbing her hand in mine. "I'm glad I could be here."

"I still don't know where Matt is," she says, another tear escaping. "If he's stuck in a meeting, I'm going to kill him. I mean, I know we have to do this a little backwards, but we're still trying to conceive a child here." Tears start streaming. I drop her hand and search the room for a tissue. I find a box on the counter in the small office and hand her one.

"Thanks," she says through tears.

"This is a happy day, Brown," I say, giving her a little smile. "And I know Matt would be here if he could. Something must be holding him up."

Her eyes widen. "Do you think he got in a car accident? What if he's hurt?"

I grab her hand again. "I'm sure he's fine." This is only to appease her because I'm not actually sure he's okay. My brain has suddenly run off with itself and all the possibilities. I mean, what if he's actually hurt? He could be in a ditch somewhere. He could've been in a car accident and they could be life-flighting him to the hospital as we speak. So many terrible possibilities. My heart that had just started to slow starts to pick up the pace again. Sheesh, what is wrong with me? I never used to think this way. Okay, I've always been a sort of glass-half-empty person, but I swear it's gotten worse.

"Thank you for being here, Jules," she squeezes my hand, pulling me back from my panic.

There's a knock at the door and we both look at it, hoping it's Matt. Instead, the doctor enters the room. He's not exactly what I was expecting. I was thinking an older man, maybe in his early sixties. This guy looks to be in his late forties and an awful lot like George Clooney, actually. I'm not sure I'd want someone that good looking all up in my business.

"Still no word from Matt?" the doctor asks, looking from Brown and then to me.

"No," Brown says with a sniff. "My friend Julia is here to give me moral support." We both let out little awkward laughs.

It's then that it truly sets in how awkward this situation is. I'm holding hands with my best friend while her George Clooney look-alike doctor gets ready to attempt to impregnate her. I mean, if this takes, what do you tell your kid? *I got pregnant with you by the doctor while your aunty Julia was holding my hand because your dad couldn't make it in time.* This is so not normal.

A nurse, who looks like she might be a supermodel in her off hours (what is with this office?) comes in.

"Are you two ready for this?" She motions her head toward Brown and me.

"Yes," Brown says in response, just as I was going to say that I was only a stand in for Matt. The nurse's use of the words "you two" makes me think she might have the wrong idea.

"You know, I just love being a part of something this special. A same-sex couple trying to conceive is such a beautiful thing."

Yep. Most definitely the wrong idea.

"I, uh, we ..." I start.

"It's just such a beautiful thing," the nurse repeats herself, her eyes glossing over as she looks at Brown and me.

My mouth drops open. I'm not sure what to say. Now I'm suddenly feeling like I don't want to disappoint the nurse since she's so full of emotions.

"We're so excited too," Brown says. Grabbing my hand and pulling it toward her, she gives me a quick little kiss on my fingers.

"What are you—"

Brown giggles and looks up at me. I'm so glad I can make this fun for her. And look at her, in her pretty shirt and her hair and makeup all done up. I've got a messy bun going on and I'm wearing a polo and no makeup at all. So I guess I know which role I play in the relationship. Which, you know, is offensive to all lesbians. Such stereotyping.

Dr. Clooney (I'm just going to call him that since I never got his name) must not have been listening to the conversation as he got everything ready because he turns to us as if he's just joining the discussion.

"Okay, Betsy, are you ready for this?" he asks, holding a syringe with a long thin tube thing hooked to the end.

"And you?" the nurse gestures toward me.

"Julia," Brown says, telling the nurse my name, a smile on her face as she keeps up the ruse.

"Are you ready, Julia?" Nurse Supermodel asks, her eyes bright with excitement.

"Um, sure," I say reluctantly.

"I'm ready," Brown says and then she grabs my hand tightly. I'm not sure how this works. Is there pain? Do I need to help her breathe through it? I should've asked more questions.

The nurse looks at us, tears filling her eyes again. She whispers a quiet "beautiful" as she takes in the sight. Oh geez.

"Okay," Dr. Clooney says. "That's it."

Wait, that's it? I feel like this should've been longer.

"Now you need to just lie here for about ten minutes and then you can be on your way. Make sure you and Matt have relations tonight, so that you have optimal chances."

The nurse gives us a weird look at the mention of Matt.

"He's, uh—"

"Our sperm donor," Brown interjects, still holding onto my hand.

I'm going to kill her.

The nurse looks utterly taken aback. And why wouldn't she? I mean, most lesbians probably don't have "relations" with their sperm donor.

Dr. Clooney and the confused nurse make their goodbyes and leave us.

"You idiot," I say, rolling my eyes and shaking my head at her.

She guffaws. "Well, we couldn't exactly let her down after she was so excited for us, could we honey?" Brown says, as she rubs my arm tenderly, still laughing.

"Whatever," I say, jerking my arm out of her reach.

"Hey, at least it took my mind off Matt not being here. He better have the best excuse ever." She sniffs, the emotions coming to the surface again.

"So do you think it worked?" I ask.

She shrugs. "He said we have about a twenty percent chance of it working the first time."

"So that's a one in five chance. Not too bad of odds then?"

Suddenly the door swings open and Matt runs in.

"I got stuck in traffic. There was a huge accident on I-25. And I forgot my phone," he says, his brow lightly covered with beads of sweat. He's acting like a new father already with the panic in his voice and the color drained from his face.

He crosses the room and goes to Brown, putting his hands on either side of her face, and kisses her. Then he leans his forehead against hers and whispers how sorry he is over and over again.

Brown reaches up and wraps a hand around his neck. "It's okay, baby," she says back. "It's all done."

Matt pulls away from her and looks down at the draped bottom half of her body, her feet still in stirrups. "I'm so sorry I wasn't here."

"Julia stepped in," she says. "The nurse thought we were a couple."

Matt laughs. "That's awesome."

"Okay, you two. I think my work is done. I'm heading back to the bakery."

"Jules, thanks again," Brown says sincerely.

"Yeah, Jules, thanks for being here, we really appreciate it," Matt says.

I step out of the room and leave Brown and Matt to their moment.

"Is she ready?" Nurse Supermodel asks as I pass the station on my way out of the office.

"Uh," I say awkwardly.

She gives me a confused look.

"She, um, wanted a moment with the donor," I say, keeping up the ruse for heaven knows why.

"Oh, okay," the nurse says, her voice conveying the what-the-crap feeling we are both experiencing right now.

I contemplate explaining the whole thing to her, but then decide against it. It'll be a fabulous story she can tell the other nurses.

I head back to the bakery and can't help but feel a little giddy at the thought that I just witnessed something miraculous. Brown might be pregnant right now.

Life is pretty amazing.

CHAPTER 12

Life pretty much sucks.

I mean, it doesn't always suck, but right now it sort of does. I just had a not-so-fabulous conversation with Patti and Debbie where they both told me that if I don't fix things with Kate, they're both walking. That would be my millionth lesson in why putting things off doesn't work. You'd think I'd have learned by now. Clearly, I haven't.

I don't even know what to fix with Kate. As far as I'm concerned, she's doing a great job. Sure, she might go over my head, finding different vendors for our supplies, but so far it's all been for the better. And yeah, she's kind of bossy and makes cleaning charts (I'm pretty certain her recent deep-cleaning one may have been another breaking point for Debbie and Patti) but these things need to be done. Honestly, I don't have the brain space for all of it.

I hate drama. I blame myself. Actually no, I blame *Cupcake Battles*. If it wasn't for winning, then I wouldn't have had the extra business to hire anyone else and I wouldn't be in the position I'm in now. It's all a big headache.

I'd talk to Kate today, but she has the day off for jury duty. I can't lose her either; we felt her absence today for sure. I can't lie, I'm actually secretly thrilled I don't have to say anything right now. Confrontation gives me hives. Actually, I so rarely confront people (there's usually champagne involved when I do), I don't even know if that's true. But I feel like it will.

I don't need this stress in my life right now. I don't have the constitution for all the things being thrown my way. I have wedding stress, work stress, not getting enough sleep … not to mention now I've developed some sort of weird heart palpitation. It doesn't happen all that often, but when it does it's kind of scary.

The bell on the door dings, and as if someone from above likes to kick me when I'm down, in walks Lisa.

"Hi Julia," she says, fake smile pasted on her face, her silky dark hair swinging behind her.

"Hi Lisa," I say, and my eye twitches. Dammit.

"I thought I'd stop by and see how you liked the article?" She looks around the practically empty bakery and then gives me a sad look. "I guess it didn't do as much for business as I'd hoped."

Good hell. If she'd been here only an hour ago, she would've seen the line out the door. Oh no, her stupid newspaper article only helped my already thriving business. Just what I always wanted, more business so I can hire yet another employee that everyone hates.

I need a glass of wine, and I don't even like wine.

"Sorry to disappoint you," I say, not correcting her. I know it's a mean thing to do. But I can't help myself. If I tell her business has been pretty crazy since the article hit, she'll be even smugger knowing how large her audience reaches. Plus, she'd probably take all the credit. *If it weren't for my article, poor Julia would've probably had to foreclose.* Cue sad puppy dog eyes.

She shrugs. "Well, we tried, right?"

Twitch.

Not in the mood to deal with her small talk I say, "Is there anything I can do for you, Lisa?"

"No, I was just checking in to see how things were going." She eyes the display case, which is mostly empty. That should clue her in to the fact that things are going well, but she doesn't seem to get it.

"Are you still wishing you could elope?" she asks, her voice innocent.

I hold back an eye roll. I'm not falling into that trap again. "Nope, wedding plans are coming along fabulously."

This is a lie of course. I still want to elope.

"Great," she says, her voice superficial. "If you ever need any help, just let me know."

Over my dead body, I say internally. Outwardly I simply offer a quick thanks.

"Well I better take off. I do hope business picks up for you, Julia," she says, her eyes doing that sad puppy dog thing again.

"Me too," I say, and give her my best dejected look as she leaves.

~*~

"What do you think?" Jared asks, looking around the space.

"It's, uh, big," I say, holding back a "that's what she said" comment since I'm in my thirties and all. I have to hold myself back quite often, if I'm being honest.

"That's what she said," he says.

I totally roll my eyes at him, even though I just thought the same thing in my head seconds ago. At least I showed some restraint, even if no one knows.

Jared laughs and then putting his arms around my waist, he picks me up and spins me around.

We're in Littleton looking at a location Jared found for the expansion. Yes, I've let it get this far. I haven't been able to break it to him that I'm not ready to expand. Right now seeing him giddy as a child, so proud of himself for finding this "perfect" spot ... well, I'm not sure I can bring myself to break it to him here either. I'll just go along with it for a little longer.

"Just picture it, Jules," he says, after he sets me down. "Back here can be the kitchen. Double the size of the kitchen in the downtown store. And over here will be perfect for the counter display and register." His shoes echo as he walks around the space made up of a cement floor and windows. We're talking bare bones here. "Oh, and here we can do a little stage." He points to the corner of the room left of the door.

"A stage?" I ask, confused.

"Yeah," he says, his excited eyes dancing around the room. "I thought we could do poetry slams and stuff in the evenings."

"Evenings?" I ask. "And did the words 'poetry slams' just come out of your mouth?" I feel significantly horrified.

He smiles. "I know it's a little out there. But I was thinking this location could be open later hours, like until ten. And of course we'd have to be open on the weekends as well, since this isn't a downtown location and business will probably be best on the weekends."

His excitement is contagious, I'll admit that. But later hours? Weekends? I don't think so.

"Jared," I start. I think I'm going to have to tell him now. "I don't think — "

"Jules, I know it seems like a lot, but we'll hire people to do the work. You'll still have your weekends and evenings off," he says, reading my mind. Or maybe he read the "what the hell" expression on my face.

I close my eyes. I know he thinks we can just hire people, but at least for the first year or so I'll have to put in a ton of time. There's no way we can open a brand new location and expect other people to do the work. I still have a hard time expecting the ladies to run things at the downtown location, and Patti and Debbie are perfectly capable since they'd been working at the bakery long before I bought it.

Jared walks over to me and places his hands on my shoulders. "This'll be good, Jules. I promise."

"I don't know," I say, nibbling on my bottom lip. I actually do know, but I don't know how to say it. If I took out the wedding and all the other stresses going on in my life right now, I still don't know if I'd be up for it.

I look around the space, trying to envision his ideas. I will say the thought of having two locations called *Julia's Bakery* does sound kind of thrilling. *Hi, I'm Julia. I own a baking empire.* Do I have it in me is the question … and the answer is no.

"Take time to think about it, okay?" he says, leaning in to kiss me.

"Okay," I say, conceding. I can at least think about it—maybe even entertain it—even if the answer will still be no.

"But don't take too long." He gives me a sexy half smile. "This place is a prime location, and it's not going to last long.

"How long do I have?" I ask. Feeling suddenly panicky that I'll need to give him an answer soon. Well, break the news to him soon.

"A couple of weeks, tops. I've already told the realtor that we're very interested," he says.

Good hell. He's already told the realtor that we're *very* interested? What's he going to tell me now? That he's had my brother-in-law, Jonathon, work up the paperwork?

"And I've had Jonathon take a look at the paperwork."

Crap. He's in too far. Abort! Abort! I'm not ready! How do I tell him?

Before I can even get another word out, Jared grabs me and pushes me up against the nearest wall and kisses me with so much passion my knees turn to jelly and I'm grateful for the wall behind me to hold me up. I'll have to figure this all out later since my brain is no longer functioning. Who knew empty spaces could be so hot.

CHAPTER 13

For the love of all things stupid.

I just used the talk-to-text function on my phone and sent the minister a bunch of random words, including the word budonkadonk. I mean, honestly, I've never even texted that word before in my life. Why would it ever autocorrect to that?

Autocorrect, you piece of shirt.

I meant for the text to say: "I just want to verify that we'll be meeting with you the Monday before the wedding." What I actually sent was not even coherent. I think someone needs to invent a take-back button for texting. They'd be a gajillionaire.

I should quit using my phone altogether. I've only proceeded to embarrass myself with it. I've sent texts to the wrong person, sent pictures to the wrong person (one slightly inappropriate one to my dad; I still shudder at the thought), updated my status on Facebook when I only meant to reply to someone's post ... I should not be allowed to have a phone at all. And now I've embarrassed myself once again.

There's only one thing I can do: find a new minister.

"Anna," I yell over the partial door that gives me little privacy in this dressing room. I'm in my wedding dress for my first fitting

"Yes?" She says coming toward me carrying another veil. I know this is wishful thinking, but I hope it's not for me. I'm so sick of trying on veils and they all look the same to me.

"Try this on," she hands it to me. No such luck, then. Of course, who else would it be for? Out of my entourage — which consists of me, my mom, Anna, and Bobby — I'm the only one modeling a wedding dress.

"Okay, but first I need you to find me a new minister," I say as I take the veil and set it gently on a white tufted velvet ottoman to the left of me.

"What?" She eyes me, her face scrunched in confusion.

"We're going to need a new minister," I say as I gently pull off the delicate headband veil that she had me try on last.

"No way, he's already booked and paid for," she says, with one dip of her chin indicating that there is no other choice.

"But we need to change," I plead, my face crumpling as I try to think of a way to explain what happened without actually explaining it. She and Brown would have a heyday with this one.

"Not gonna happen," she says, and then eyes me curiously. "What did you do, Julia?" Her inflection doesn't sound like she's asking a question — it's more accusatory.

"I ... oh ... nothing," I say, deciding it best to figure this one out on my own. I'm just going to text him and tell him I was letting Liam play with my phone. When in doubt, always blame the toddler. He also got the blame for the glass of wine I spilled on my parent's carpet last month. I had him in my arms so it totally could've been him, but it was definitely me. No one could truly blame the baby, so it was genius on my part.

Anna either decides she doesn't actually want to know what I've done (smart move), or she's been sidetracked by something else. She turns and walks away from the door.

I place the new veil (which looks pretty much like the last one) on my head after I shove my phone back in my purse, and then carefully walk out from the dressing room.

"Oh Julia," my mom says as I enter. She rubs her nose quickly, trying to squelch the tears that have formed in the corner of her eyes.

"What do you think?" I ask, as I stand up on the round platform in front of a three-sided mirror and examine myself.

Wow. Even I'm nearly brought to tears. It's hard to believe I'm here doing this. It almost feels like a dream. My dress is beautiful, exactly how I wanted it. It's classic, but still modern. Sleeves that go just past my elbows, a plain white fitted bodice with a bateau neckline. The skirt is long and full with a train, and my favorite part—it has pockets. I love it.

I peek a foot out from under my dress and look at the ballet flats I'm wearing. They will be comfortable and perfect—nothing like the deathtraps Anna and Brown made me wear for their weddings.

"You look beautiful," Bobby echoes from her perch on the white couch in the large dressing room that we're currently occupying.

"You know I still can't believe this is happening," my mom says, turning toward Bobby. "There was a time when Raymond and I wondered if this would ever happen for our Julia."

"Mom!" I say, my face scrunched up in disbelief. Is she really going to admit to my future mother-in-law what a loser I was in my previous life?

"Oh," she bats a hand at me, dismissing my irritation. "Bobby knows what I mean, don't you Bobby?" She gestures toward my future mother-in-law.

"Of course. I've wondered the same thing about Mark," she says with a wink in my direction.

Fantastic. I love being compared to Denver's biggest player. Actually, the comparison is better than the truth … Denver's biggest lame-o.

"Speaking of Mark," I say, as I mess with my veil. "How are things with Lisa?" I ask, forcing nonchalance in my voice.

"Still going," Bobby says, disdain spreading across her face. "Do you know he asked me what I thought of them moving in together?"

Oh dear, that probably didn't go over well.

"That's a little shocking," I say, wanting to delve deeper. "I mean, they haven't been together that long."

"I told him over my dead body," Bobby says. "My sons do not shack up."

Yes, I know all too well. If it wasn't for Bobby, I could be shacking up with Jared right now. Well, probably not. I'm not sure how my parents would feel about it either, actually. Plus, it kind of feels nice to keep everything separate until it's all official.

"Julia, I think you should try on this other veil instead," Anna says, carrying yet another veil as she comes into the room. This is the fifth one she's made me try on today.

"What's wrong with the one I'm wearing?" I ask, fussing with it in the mirror.

"It's too long in the back," she says, pointing to my backside. "The detail work on the back of the dress needs to be seen."

She has a point. It's a v-shaped back with pearl details on the zipper. It accents my backside well. My budonkadonk, if you will. Maybe I'll incorporate the word into my dialogue just to annoy Brown. She really hates made-up trendy words.

I sigh and try the veil on and thank goodness, we have a winner. That is, until we're leaving and Anna sees another one that will be "even more perfect."

Only eight more weeks. I can make it eight more weeks. I hope.

~*~

Vows. Vows. Vows.

How did I agree to this? Bobby said she thought it would be "lovely" if Jared and I wrote vows for our wedding instead of simply reciting the vows the minister gives us. And Jared thought that would be a great idea.

Does he know me at all? Since when do I enjoy speaking in front of people? The last time I spoke in front of a crowd was when I had to wing my toast to Anna and Jonathon at their reception. The toast I had completely forgotten about up until right before I had to say it. I think I sweat clean through my bridesmaids dress. It worked out okay, but that was straight-up luck.

Which reminds me … I should get Botox in my armpits just so I don't get pit stains on my wedding dress. Maybe while they're at it, they can inject that little part above the bridge of my nose. I've scowled so much lately that there are two clear and definite lines there now.

I don't want to say written vows. All I want is to say two words: "I do." That's it. Those are two big words right there. Filled with promise and commitment. What more do we need? They can even leave all that crap about honoring and cherishing each other. I mean, isn't that implied with "I do"?

I do, he does, we do. That's all that needs to be said. Then "you may kiss the bride." I've already informed Jared that if the kiss goes longer than two seconds, I'll have the annulment papers drawn up before we can even sign the marriage license. And absolutely no tongue. Because … just no. My grandparents will be there, for crap's sake.

I lean back in the black faux-leather chair, sitting in my tiny office in the bakery. I've decided that unlike everything else in my life, I won't put off these vows until the last minute. But I've been trying to write them for a month now, and I've only got this far:

Jared,

That's it. Just Jared and a comma. My ability to express myself is astounding.

I'm going to have to go for some cheesy standby like reciting a poem or song lyrics. That was a big no-no in speech class. But what do I care? It's not like I'm going to be graded on this. Just judged by half of Denver. And now Lisa. I swear her addition to my wedding is making it all even worse. In each scenario, I keep picturing her and her shiny dark locks and her smug smile. She's ruining everything.

If vows were the only thing I had to worry about, I think I'd probably be spouting words like crazy. I mean, I love Jared. There are a million reasons why I love him. I should be able to express that. But there are so many other things taking over my brain with that day. I'm worried about being in front of so many people. I'm also worried about tripping and falling as I walk down the aisle.

Dear heavens.

Vows. Think, Julia. I can do this.

I ready my hands above my laptop, ready to type.

Jared,

Nope, I've got nothing.

I'm sure Jared will have something eloquent to say to me. That's Jared, though. He'll say his vows he wrote for me only the night before the wedding, and they'll be beautiful and profound and there won't be a dry eye in the house. Then it'll be my turn and I'll fumble and stutter my way through mine, and I'll get looks of pained pity.

Eloping is sounding better and better. Too bad it's not going to happen.

CHAPTER 14

I think I'm dying.

I'm being totally serious here. My heart palpitations have been getting worse this past week, so I did the only thing I could do: I went into my office in the back of the bakery and Googled my symptoms. I mean, I guess I could've gone to the doctor, but who has time for that? Besides, up until just now I figured it was no big deal.

But there it is—clear on my laptop screen—all my symptoms point to the fact that I probably have heart disease. Heart palpitations, fatigue, shortness of breath … I've got it all. Aren't I too young for heart disease? Oh gosh, I'm probably one of those exceptions to the rule. I'll be one of those rare cases you hear about who get heart disease in their thirties and die within months of their diagnosis.

Of course the fatigue can be explained. I haven't had a good night's sleep in who knows how long. And the shortness of breath could be explained by the fact that I am completely out of shape. But the heart palpitations can't be explained. And what about the eye twitches? Of course, those only seem to happen when Lisa is around. Plus, eye twitching wasn't part of the listed symptoms. But that doesn't mean it isn't one.

Dear heavens, I don't want to die. I'm not ready to go yet. I have so much I need to do. Like marry Jared.

And ride in a hot air balloon. And climb Mt. Everest. Yeah, I'm totally kidding about that. I have no desire to climb Everest. I don't even like to climb stairs.

Not that I'm trying to be morbid here, but I wonder how many people would come to my funeral if I did die. Surely I'd be able to fill the church. I'm certain the regulars from the bakery would be there, and people from Spectraltech. My family, of course. I'm sure Anna would put herself in charge and keep changing my lipstick until she found the right color to match my pale corpse.

And what about Jared? Poor Jared. He'd be so devastated. Of course, Lisa would be right there to pounce on him as soon as the first shovel of dirt landed on my coffin. No, I can't let this happen. I can't die. I guess I'll have to go to the doctor. I'm not going down without a fight.

"You wanted to talk to me?" Kate says as she stands in the doorway of my office.

"Right. Come on in," I say.

Ah yes, the reason the palpitations started up in the first place. Chat time with Kate. Also, I've had a ridiculous amount of caffeine, so I'm sure that's not helping my heart either. But honestly, I think it mostly has to do with the confrontation I'm about to have. I've put this off long enough.

My phone pings. It's a text from Anna. Ah, and there's reason number two for my palpitations. I ignore the text.

"Have a seat," I say pointing to the chair near the door. My palms feel sweaty. Oh heavens, sweating for no reason was one of the symptoms of heart disease.

"What did you need to talk to me about?" Kate asks, obviously wanting to get right to the point. She looks kind of nervous actually. Does she think I'm going to fire her? She probably does. I need to get to the point here so she doesn't freak out. I mean, before I do, that is.

"First of all," I begin, "you're doing a great job."

I'm going with the sandwich method for confrontation or criticism that Brown taught me. You start with the top piece of bread—a compliment of sorts. Then you get to the sauerkraut and the corned beef part, where you tell them all the negative stuff. Then before you're done, you put on the bottom slice of bread where you compliment them again. Brown says it works like a charm. I have my doubts.

"Thank you," Kate says, her hands twiddling in her lap.

Oh good, the top piece of bread is in place. Now on to the corned beef and sauerkraut. Gosh, I hate this.

"You really take initiative, and I appreciate that," I say. I guess I'm still going with the top piece of bread? I have no idea what I'm doing here. I should've written down notes.

More heart palpitations. And now there's a little buzz in my ear. Where did that come from? I wonder if that's a symptom.

Focus, Julia.

"Anyway, the thing is," I say and reach up to dash off the beads of sweat that are now forming on the top of my forehead. Oh gosh, I *know* sweating was one of the symptoms. I truly might have heart disease!

"Are you okay?" Kate asks, her brows pulled together as she takes in the sight of me.

"Yes," I say, just as my breathing starts to pick up. "I'm fine."

I feel lightheaded. I might be having a heart attack right here and now. This all came on so quickly. This could be it.

"Julia, you don't look so good," Kate says, the concern on her face growing as she watches me possibly about to have a heart attack.

I take in a quick breath, but I feel like I'm not getting any air into my lungs. I try to take another breath, but my chest feels tight like I can't get anything in. Suddenly, I'm only taking quick little breaths because I can't seem to take a big breath.

This is it. This is the end!

"Patti!" Kate yells out the door of the office in a panic.

I hear Patti come running over. "What in tarnation—" she says as she looks at me and then back at Kate. "She's hyperventilating," she declares.

"Hyperventilating?" Kate questions.

"Quick like. Go grab a small paper bag from the front," she says to Kate.

I'm watching all this happen around me, and I want to tell them that that I'm not hyperventilating, I'm having a heart attack! They need to call an ambulance. But I can't get a word out since I can barely get a breath in.

Kate comes back into the office with a small white paper bag and Debbie trailing behind.

"What's going on?" Debbie asks Patti.

"Julia's hyperventilating," she says. Opening the paper bag, she gathers the top of it together.

"Oh goodness," Debbie says, her hands going to her mouth.

It's clear here that in a time of crisis, Patti is my only reliable source. Debbie and Kate are evidently not going to save me if this is truly the end. They're both just staring at me as Patti does all the work.

"Julia, darlin' I need you to breathe into this paper bag." She shows me how to do it a couple of times and then hands me the paper bag.

I start breathing into the bag. In, out. In, out. It only takes about five breaths before I can start to feel a difference. My breathing slows, not to a normal pace, but at least it's not the rapid pace it was.

"What's going on with ya, darlin'?" Patti asks with concern. She reaches up and swipes some of my hair off my forehead and tucks it behind my ear.

"I ... think... heart ... attack," I try to say through the paper bag.

"You're not having a heart attack, sweetie," Debbie says.

"No?" I ask, looking to her and then to Patti who's nodding her head in agreement.

"No, darlin', that ain't a heart attack. You just aren't breathing right." She's bent at the waist, looking at me in the eyes. "What's going on with you?"

What's going on with me? I think the better question would be what's *not* going on with me. Let's see, I'm getting married in a huge wedding when I'd rather elope. My sister is constantly up my butt with wedding requests and questions. My business is taking off so much that I'm feeling too much pressure from my employees to manage them better, and my fiancé is pressuring me to expand. Oh, and I'm also pretty sure my fiancé's ex is out to get me. Also, I haven't gotten any sleep in longer than I can remember and my health is clearly not good. To top it off, I'm probably dying.

Suddenly my eyes fill with tears.

"Oh, darlin'," Patti says, her arms wrapping around me. "You need a break. You've got too much going on."

From her mouth to God's ears. But unfortunately I have no time for a break.

"Why don't you go home and let us close up things around here," Debbie says.

That notion makes the tears grow and spill out.

"Yah, darlin', we've got this," Patti says. "You get yourself on home and get some rest. Do you want me to call Jared?"

"No," I say. "I can manage to get myself home."

"Nonsense," says Patti. "One of us will drive ya. We have a bit of time before the lunch rush."

Debbie was tasked with taking home her invalid boss. Now that my breathing is nearly back to normal and I'm ninety-nine percent sure I didn't have a heart attack, I'm starting to feel rather stupid about the whole thing. Hyperventilating? What was that all about? But still, a little time to rest is so welcome. Maybe I don't need a doctor, maybe I need a therapist.

I change into comfortable clothes and hop right into bed, dragging Charlie with me and forcing her to snuggle. I'm asleep within seconds.

CHAPTER 15

"Why haven't you seen a doctor yet?" Anna asks as we stand outside of Brown's bathroom. It's pee on a stick day — the day we find out if she's knocked up.

"Because I don't need a doctor to tell me that I need to get some rest and stop stressing," I say.

"It sounds like more than that to me," Anna says, and I find myself touched (and slightly mystified) by her concern.

"It's not," I say, not totally convinced myself. I mean, it was only a few days ago that Google had basically told me I was going into heart failure. But the truth of the matter is I'm stressed, tired, never have time for exercise, and I haven't been eating well. One good side effect of all of it is that I've lost five pounds. Not intentionally, but who cares, right?

"Any news in there?" I ask Brown through the bathroom door.

This is nerve wracking. Brown could be pregnant! And I'm really hoping she is because Anna and I got a little ahead of ourselves and brought over celebratory supplies. It's going to be very awkward if there is nothing to celebrate. And also very sad.

Brown opens the door to the bathroom.

"Well?" I ask, looking at her hands for the pregnancy test.

"I can't look," she says. "Will one of you go look and see if there are two pink lines?"

Both Anna and I get stuck in the doorway trying to make it to see the test first. When we finally push through, we find the stick sitting on the edge of the bathtub. We walk up to it slowly, almost reverently, and look down.

And there it is: two very distinct pink lines.

We both scream and start jumping around the bathroom.

"Am I … pregnant?" Brown asks from the doorway, obviously not able to comprehend it. I mean screaming and jumping around like crazy people wouldn't be considered good form if the test were negative.

"Yes!" Anna and I scream in unison.

Then Brown is the in the bathroom, and all three of us are jumping around and screaming. It's not the biggest bathroom, and I end up hitting my hip twice in the same spot on the counter. But I don't care. Brown is pregnant!

Brown Facetimes Matt who's out of town on business and shows him the positive test. They both cry, which makes Anna and me join in on the crying. Then we get out our party supplies. Champagne for Anna and me, and sparkling apple cider for the pregnant lady.

"Can you believe it?" I ask as soon as the drinks have been poured. "You're going to be a mom!"

"I can't believe it," Brown says, her face frozen in a smile.

"I hope it's a girl," Anna says.

"Anna!" I chastise her. "Who cares what sex the baby is as long as it's healthy."

"I just mean that girls are much more fun to shop for," she says. She has a point.

"So," Brown says after she takes a big gulp of her drink. "Which one of you two is going to join me?"

"Not me," I say, shaking my head. "I'm not even married yet."

"Oh come on, Jules," Brown says. "You're so old fashioned. Don't you know getting pregnant before you get married is so 21st century?"

"Yes, well even so, I think I'll wait," I say, feeling a touch of sadness that it could be a while before I am. How fun would it be to be pregnant with Brown and raise our kids together? But I think I'd like to just be married for a little while at least.

"Well, I guess since I'm married, it should be me," Anna says. "Now I just have to get Jonathon on board."

"Tell him I'm pregnant," Brown says. "Peer pressure still works."

"You know, you're probably right," Anna says cheerfully. "I'm totally going to convince him. How fun would it be to have babies that can grow up together?"

Oh gosh, what if Anna got pregnant soon and both her and Brown have babies within the same year? I'd be the odd woman out. Just imagine how many times they'd say "you'll see" once they were moms and I wasn't. My stomach sinks in the most petty of ways. I don't want Anna to get pregnant yet. Not before me. It's a terrible thing to think, and I hate myself for thinking it. But I can't help it.

That night, probably from the glass of champagne I had (I don't hold my liquor well), I dream that everyone is pregnant. Brown, Anna, my mom, Bobby … even Debbie and Patti. And I'm not. Everyone is full of advice, and they keep telling me my time will come soon, but when I look down at my stomach, there's a sign hanging from it that says "barren." Of course I wake up in a frenzy and then spend an hour reading into the dream and wonder if it's some sort of heavenly warning that I actually am barren.

I mean, there are no guarantees. What if after we're married, Jared and I find out we can't have kids? And then everyone around us starts their family, but we don't. What if? I could be happy, just Jared and me. I know that. But the thought of not being able to have children makes me feel a loss for something that's not even mine yet. It's a strange feeling.

When I finally do fall asleep again, I have my reoccurring naked dream. This time, as I'm walking completely in the nude toward Jared, everyone is pointing and laughing at me. That's a new addition to the dream. I also decide to actually look for my dress in this dream, but of course I never find it. Then I abandon all that and look for a toilet and no matter how many times I go, I still have to go. Of course I wake up from that and realize that I actually have to go in real life. Stupid champagne.

~*~

The next day at the bakery I'm exhausted, which is to be expected because of my poor night's sleep. I'm feeling fidgety and drained at the same time. It's an odd combination. It could be because of the five-hour energy I downed on the way in. It's really how I'm surviving these days.

I haven't had any more episodes of hyperventilation since that time in my office. I'm still getting the palpitations, though. I probably should listen to Anna and see a doctor. Like I have time for that. I feel like I don't even have time to make the call to set up an appointment.

Anyway, I can figure it out. I'm sure it's just lack of sleep combined with stress and an unhealthy lifestyle, which is due to the fact that I don't have any time and therefore never get enough sleep. It's a very vicious cycle.

I should try to lessen the amount of caffeine I drink, but that too has become a vicious cycle. I tried the other morning and only lasted all of three hours. I was not going to make it through the morning rush without some coffee. And of course I'm avoiding having the chat I need to have with Kate. I keep telling myself it's for my health, but let's be honest, I just don't want to do it.

Debbie and Patti aren't down my throat to say anything to her anyway. I think they're worried what might happen if I do. I know I still need to. It's so strange, I've had to confront people before, but it's like something has changed inside of me. Like all the stress and lack of sleep over the past months have caused some sort of change in my brain chemistry. I don't feel like I can handle things as well anymore, and let's be honest, I could never handle things very well to begin with. Not difficult things, at least.

"Hey Lia," I say timidly. I don't know what the heck I'm doing. I decided that I was not going to talk to Lia about my reoccurring dream, but clearly I'm not listening to myself.

She's sitting at a two-person table by the front window. She's been reading cards all morning. In fact, this is the first time I've found her without a line of people waiting. She's getting quite the name for herself in the area.

"Hello Julia," she says in her sickly sweet voice. "You're curious about something aren't you?" She asks, looking at me directly.

My eyes widen with shock. How did she know that? Man, I thought this witch thing was all hokey. But maybe there's something to it.

"Um, yes," I say guardedly. "How did you know?"

"Well, it wouldn't take any powers to see your face is pale and you keep wringing your hands together," she says as her eyes move down to my hands which are, in fact, wringing. I shake them out forcefully and do my best to keep them at my sides. Good gravy, I'm so transparent.

I clear my throat. "I was wondering if you interpret dreams?" I ask.

"Of course," she says. "Take a seat." She motions to the seat across from her.

Oh gosh, this already feels like a bad idea. Last time I sat down in front of Lia, it almost ruined my relationship with Jared. Between her cards and my crazy mind, I nearly destroyed everything. I never thought I put stock into any of this, but I guess I must, since it's got my stomach all in knots.

"Julia, I don't bite," she says to me and smiles almost wickedly. Or maybe it's a nice smile, and I'm just reading it that way. She probably does bite.

"Sorry," I say, tucking a strand of hair that's come out of my messy bun behind my ear. I take the seat across from her.

Lia's red hair is pulled away from her face by a knotted head wrap—white with little cherries on it. As usual, it doesn't go with, or even accent, the long flowing flower skirt she's wearing and the striped top. Eclectic, to say the least.

"So tell me about this dream," she says, her elbows on the table. She makes a steeple with her pointer fingers and rests it under her lips.

"Okay, so I keep having this dream that I'm walking down the aisle at my wedding, but I'm naked," I start to tell her.

"Ah, yes," she shakes her head. "That's an easy one."

"It is?"

"Sure. We all have naked dreams at one time or another in our lives."

"So what does it mean?"

"Well," she leans toward me all businesslike, "to understand dreams, we must first delve into the reality. For example, the clothes we wear in our waking life help identify us. They represent how we want to be seen by others. For example, you're always wearing jeans and a work shirt with your logo on it." She points to the shirt I'm wearing, which is a navy blue polo with a Julia's Bakery logo on the pocket. "You want others to see that you're working."

Riiiiight. I'm trying to nod my head like I'm following, but that's a big "duh" right there. Of course I want people to know I'm working. And if we're going to go there, what do Lia's clothes say about her? She wants people to know she's color blind and has no idea how to match things?

"My clothes," she continues, motioning to her radical outfit of the day, "tell people that I don't really care what they think about me. I'm my own person."

Huh, well there you go. That actually makes a lot of sense.

"Clothing also hides our imperfections, and it can represent hiding our emotional and psychological imperfections. Symbolically speaking, of course."

"Of course," I say, trying to hide my impatience. I didn't ask for an education on what clothing represents. "So what does being naked in a dream mean?"

"Well when you aren't wearing clothes in your dreams, it can mean that you feel stripped of you identity. It can also mean that you're feeling insecure or vulnerable." She nods her head once toward me, like she's basically saying that those things are true about me.

I start to take offense, but then realize she's pretty much hit the nail on the head. My wedding is definitely making me feel stripped of my identity, my sanity, and maybe even my health. Who knew dreams could be so profound? I wonder if I should ask her about the randomly reoccurring make-out dream I have about my fifth grade gym teacher, Mr. James—a fifty-year-old man who had a terrible case of halitosis. Actually, I don't want to know where that comes from.

"So, what is it about your wedding that's making you feel stripped of your identity?" Lia asks, her brow furrowed.

I'm not sure I want to get into this with Lia. I probably should seek professional help, actually. Like I'd have time for that.

"Because it's not me," I say, trying to keep it short, not wanting to go into all the details.

"Explain," she says, sitting back in her seat and resting her intertwined hands in her lap.

I exhale loudly. I guess Lia might be my best bet for therapy. Just as long as she doesn't try to throw some witchy spell on me.

"Because it's big and ridiculous and there'll be so many people there I don't know. There's a lot riding on this for it to be the perfect day, and when the pressure is on, rarely do things in my life go perfectly. Honestly I'd rather elope." I slump back in my seat.

"So what can you change to make it more you?" she asks, her head tilted to the side, a quick raise of her eyebrows.

I sigh. There isn't much I can change at this point. We're less than two months out.

"Not much." I give a quick shrug of my shoulders.

"You know, my momma used to say," she starts, and I prepare myself for the unsolicited advice—and possibly some sort of chant. I mean, her mom could also be a witch for all I know. "If you can't change the circumstances, then the only thing you can change is your attitude."

My attitude. Right. I'm pretty certain the only thing that could change that right now is some legal Colorado drugs. And I'm not sure I want to go there … yet.

"Thanks, Lia," I say ready to end this conversation. I don't want her to offer a card reading. I know what's in my future, and I'm just going to have to deal with it.

"Julia," she says, placing a hand over mine before I have the chance to stand. "I feel that I must tell you that you need to pay attention to your health."

How did she …? *What?*

"Um," I say, pulling my hand out from under hers. "Okay, uh, thanks, Lia."

"Really, Julia. I'm quite concerned." She stares at me through her glasses.

Dear heavens, has Lia had some premonition regarding the symptoms I Googled? That has to be coincidence, right?

"Thank you for your concern," I say, feeling my heart race, perspiration instantly forming on my brow.

How did she know? That can only mean one thing: she's had some premonition of my impending death. Oh my hell. I walk quickly to my office, shut the door, and take a seat in my office chair. Just in time for the hyperventilating to start again.

CHAPTER 16

Well someone woke up on the wrong side of the bed. And that someone was me. I'd like a do-over button.

First off, Jared kept bugging me last night regarding my decision about the new location for the expansion. I started to tell him how I truly felt, but then chickened out yet again. I mean, can't he tell by my body language how I'm feeling about it? Yeah, I seem to remember that men don't really do the whole mind-reading thing. They're not an intuitive species.

Then I got in a text fight with Anna over the boutonnieres. I don't know what's gotten into her. I told her I didn't care and that she could decide, and she goes off about how she's doing all of this for free (I did offer to pay, but she said that it was good practice for her future wedding planning business), and I never appreciate anything she does, and blah, blah, blah. I think we ended okay, but I can never actually tell with Anna. Honestly, it came out of left field. I think the stress is getting to her too.

My sleep was sporadic. Between being worried about my health as of late, and having another stupid naked wedding dream, I never fell into a deep sleep.

Presently I'm sitting in the office looking over the orders Kate has recently made. She's changed out the paper goods vendor, the coffee vendor, the place we get flour from, changed all produce to organic (which actually ended up being the same price in the end), and now it looks like she's done some update on my computer for my accounting software. *My computer.* Granted, she has to use the computer to place orders, but who does she think she is, messing around with stuff on my computer? All of this was done without going through me, by the way. I was okay with it at first because, heck, I need the help. But for some reason, today I just can't take it anymore.

I'm about to lose my crap.

I decide that the best thing I can do right now is to go get some coffee. And maybe a pastry. Of course our supply is very limited right now, having recently finished the morning rush.

I walk out to the front to find Kate sitting at a table talking to someone I've never seen before. He looks professional and they look like they're having a business meeting of sorts. I wonder what that's all about. Normally, I'd just grab my pastry and coffee and be on my merry way, but today I'm feeling punchy and, well, I want to punch something. Metaphorically, of course.

"Hi Kate," I say, a lot peppier than I meant to.

"Oh, uh, hey Julia," she says, looking a little sheepish.

I look from her to the gentleman sitting across the table from her. Giving her an eyebrow lift to demonstrate my desire to be introduced, or at least to know what the heck is going on here.

"Julia, this is Dan." She gestures to him with her hand.

"Hi Dan," I say, holding my hand out to shake his. "And what do you, Dan?"

"I'm, uh, from Midwest Meats," he says, obviously confused by this entire exchange.

"Are you?" I ask, a fake smile now plastered across my face. "What kind of meat do you sell, Dan?" I don't know why I keep saying his name. I sound like a car salesman.

"Uh," he looks to Kate and then back to me. I sneak a glance at Kate and she looks a little shell-shocked.

"We pride ourselves on our organic selection," Dan says, his salesman face suddenly plastered on. "And we have some great options for the bakery. I was just discussing the order with Kate."

I look again at Kate. She still looks out of sorts.

"Well, Dan, did Kate tell you that I'm the owner of the bakery?" I ask, not being able to help the smugness in my tone and probably on my face.

"She, uh, no she didn't," he gestures toward Kate. "She said she handled this side of the business."

"Well, that's funny, Dan, because I hired Kate to be a pastry chef." I turn toward Kate and fold my arms, staring her down with my most disapproving look.

"Julia," Kate finally speaks up. "I can explain—"

"Oh, I'm sure you can. Let's hear your explanation," I say. I recognize that my heart rate is picking up, and I can feel my underarms starting to sweat, but I do my best to not freak out. This would be a terrible time to lose it.

"In the kitchen. Now," I demand.

Without a glance behind me, I head to the swinging door that leads to the kitchen and open it. I take five paces forward inside the kitchen, taking care to breathe deeply. *In with the calming thoughts, out with the whackadoodle thoughts.*

I turn around and Kate is standing in the doorway, her arms folded across her chest. She looks ready to rumble.

"Julia," she starts, "it's not what it looks like. I'm just getting some pricing for organic lunch meat."

"Really," I say, feeling the temperature in my face start to rise. I'm freaking blushing right now? Seriously? "Because what it looks like is that you're going over my head. Again."

The kitchen is suddenly quiet and I look around and see that Patti and Debbie have stopped what they're doing and have full attention on me. Well, they're about to get what they wanted here, so I'm glad they're watching.

"I'm not going over your head, I'm just helping. You've had a lot on your plate these days with the wedding and I—"

"You what? You thought you could just take over?" I ask, the pitch in my voice rising. I better watch it or I'll sound like I sucked in some helium before too long.

"No," she protests. "I just—I was just trying to help."

"I think you've helped quite enough," I say, my heart rate still up, my pits still sweating, but my breathing feels under control. "I hired you to be a pastry chef, not to completely take over my business."

"Julia," Patti interjects, but I hold a hand out to stop her. This is my bakery, dammit, and it's going to stay that way.

"You're fired," I say to Kate.

"What?" Her eyes pop out of her head with surprise. "But Julia, I was only trying to help."

"And all of your 'help' has only been to undermine me and the people that were here before you. You're not the boss. You were never hired to be the boss. You were hired to bake pastries. That's it."

"Julia, I'm so sorry. Can't we just talk about this?" she asks.

"No, we can't. Please pack your things and leave," I say, sounding like the host of a reality TV show. I reach behind and scratch my neck, giving myself a second to take a quick deep breath. Although, now that I think of it, I never actually got to the hyperventilating part. Huh.

Kate doesn't say anything as she packs up her stuff and goes.

My shoulders sink and I feel the tension leave my neck when the door closes behind her.

"Julia," Patti begins.

"You got what you've been wanting," I say stopping her from going further.

"Yes, but—"

"I don't want to talk about it," I say louder than I intended.

We stand there in silence for a minute. Both Patti and Debbie have probably never seen me like this. I don't know if I've ever seen me like this.

"Sorry," I shake my head. "I just need a minute."

I walk back to my office and shut the door, falling into my chair the second I can.

What did I just do? I fired Kate! But it had to be done. It had to be.

CHAPTER 17

"What do you mean she was making the cupcakes for the gala?" I yell.

It's the end of the day and the bakery's front doors are locked, and they chose now to lay this bit of information on me. Today is Friday, which means the gala is tomorrow night. I might throw up.

"Well, I tried to tell ya, but you had those crazy eyes going like you don't got all what belongs to ya," she says, her index finger pointed at me.

"Well, I'll need your help, then," I say with a shrug.

"Can't," she says. "Debbie and I've had plans for ages now. We can't change 'em. We're goin' to a concert. Gonna see that Florida Georgia Line."

"Are you serious?" I ask, feeling my heart start to pick up speed.

"Sorry, darlin'," she says.

"Yeah, sorry Julia," Debbie says. Not even a hint of a possible change of plans in her tone.

"They're all baked and in the freezer. You just gotta frost 'em," Patti says, pointing toward the large walk-in cooler.

"I have to frost a thousand cupcakes?" I question, my eyes closing as I take in the task at hand.

"Well, you've got us for an hour or so; let's see what we can punch out," Patti says and Debbie nods her head in agreement.

At this point, I'll take what I can get. Next time I decide to go all Terminator and fire my employee, I should probably know what kind of tasks I'll be left to do in her absence. They don't teach you this in business management. Of course, that wasn't even my major so I don't know if that's true.

We get to work frosting cupcakes. Mostly in silence, but every once in a while Debbie and Patti offer up some gossip or something that's going on. I'm so drained I can barely even keep up with the conversation.

"You know, Julia," Patti says. "Deb and I were warmin' up to Kate. She really wasn't so bad."

"Now you tell me," I say, frosting what seems like my millionth cupcake, but I think I've only done fifty or so.

"No really, she wasn't so bad," Debbie says.

"You guys, it's kinda late to be telling me this now, isn't it?" I say. Seriously, isn't there a hole I could go lay in? The tile floor I'm standing on is looking comfortable at this point. I'm so freaking tired.

"Anyway, she went over my head too many times. She changed too many things."

"Yeah, I guess I'd be mad if I were you," Debbie says. She's done twice as many cupcakes as I have. Patti too.

"I don't want to talk about it. I just want to finish these cupcakes and then go home," I say.

"Oh, but you can't," Debbie says.

"Yeah, you've gotta box these and then take them over to the hotel where the gala is," Patti says, her hands wrapped around a piping bag.

"Let me guess," I say feeling completely deflated, "Kate was going to do that."

"Yep," they both say.

Good gravy. What have I done?

~*~

I managed to get the cupcakes done and delivered with literally one minute to spare. Then I went straight home to collapse on my couch, only to find Anna waiting for me on that very couch to do … wait for it … wedding stuff. I honestly can't even remember what we did. My head was in a fog the entire time. She kept saying things like "Julia, we don't have much time!" and "Julia, we're never going to get everything done if you can't focus!" Honestly, I briefly considered getting up and walking (I was too tired to consider running) out of the condo at one point, but the truth is I need her, so I better not tick her off.

I went to bed at two in the morning, only to wake up to some sort of earthquake at eight. Turns out it wasn't an earthquake, but rather a large truck. Regardless, I was awake then (mostly because my heart was racing from the scare and I couldn't calm it back down). I decided to get up and start plotting out my day since it's the day of the gala. I guess I'll be living off caffeinated beverages to keep me awake.

I have a hair and makeup appointment at noon. I totally protested it at first, but Anna felt like it would be a good chance to practice before the wedding and so therefore I was "killing two birds with one stone." Then it's dress time, and after that comes the only part

I'm looking forward to—since I'm being recognized at the gala, they're sending a limo to pick me up! I also get to walk some sort of red carpet, all Hollywood style. I keep picturing myself waving to fans and having the paparazzi snap pictures while I'm striking poses, but let's be honest—what kind of fans do I even have? Just a few regulars and a bunch of potheads who'd be too busy getting high to even show up.

Anyway, it's not like I'd want all the hoopla anyway. I'll be put on the spot enough tonight and the thought of that makes my already racing heart (seriously, I can't get it to calm down) speed up even more. What if they want me to give a speech after the award? Good gravy, I hadn't even thought of that scenario.

There's a knock at my door. Crap, I hope it's not Anna. I don't have time to do or think anything wedding today.

"Hey," my sister-in-law Jenny says brightly, as she comes in carrying Liam.

"Hey," I say, surprised to see her. I immediately reach my arms out for Liam, and he leans out for me to hold him. I'm so in love with this kid, I can't even stand it.

Lennon reaches the door a few seconds after her. "Hey, Julia," he says, sounding slightly out of breath.

"So, we should be back around two," Jenny says, putting the diaper bag down on the couch. She reaches in the bag and pulls out a piece of paper. "Here's his schedule. When to feed him, put him down. You've done all this before, but I thought I'd write it down anyway."

Lennon nods his head agreeing with Jenny. I, on the other hand, am completely dumbfounded.

"I'm sorry?" I say, looking from Jenny and then to Lennon.

"It's the sixteenth," Jenny says, looking at me like I should know what she's talking about.

"Yes," I say, agreeing. We all know it's the sixteenth. It's the day of the gala.

"You said you could watch Liam for us?" She says, the color draining quickly from her face.

"I did?" I say, my eyes widening. I literally have no recollection.

"Yeah," Lennon says. "At the Sunday dinner last month." His face scrunches as if he's questioning my sanity. I barely remember being at our monthly Sunday dinner.

"Uh," I say, trying to remember this conversation. Nothing is coming to me.

"Did you forget?" Jenny asks, panic suddenly in her voice.

"I'm so sorry," I say, bouncing Liam on my hip. "I don't even remember having the conversation. I have the gala tonight. I don't think I can do it."

Jenny's face goes into her palms and Lennon places a reassuring hand on her shoulder.

"We're totally stuck, Julia," he says. "Do you think you could still do it?" His eyes appear to be begging, which is a sight rarely seen on Lennon.

"Um, I don't think — "

"Please, Julia," Jenny pleads.

"Do you think Mom could do it?" I look to Liam and then, without warning, Jenny bursts into tears.

Was that such a horrible idea? I mean, my mom is Liam's grandma. I'm so confused right now.

"No, Mom can't do it," Lennon says, his hand still on Jenny's shoulder.

"What about Anna," I say and Jenny cries louder. Okay, so not Anna. I look around my condo in an attempt to help me think of someone more suitable to watch Liam. I'd suggest Jenny's parents, but they moved to Vegas last year.

"Isn't there anyone else?" I ask, still bouncing Liam on my hip and every once in a while I give him little kisses on his cheek. He has the softest, most adorable cheeks.

"Can I talk to you for a second?" Lennon asks, sounding urgent as he guides me and Liam into my room. He shuts the door behind us.

"What did I say?" I ask, gesturing toward the closed door where Jenny is still crying on the other side.

"Look," Lennon says quietly. "We weren't planning on telling anyone this, but..." he trails off, running a hand through his hair.

"But what?" I ask, pulling my eyebrows together. I've never seen Lennon so out of sorts.

"Jenny and I are having some problems."

"What?" I say loudly, and he shushes me with raised eyebrows. Look, if he wasn't expecting me to overreact here, then he doesn't know me at all.

"Keep it down. Jenny doesn't want our family getting involved," he says in a loud whisper.

"What's been going on?"

He exhales. "It's a lot of things." He reaches down and fumbles with the front of his untucked button-up shirt.

"We just don't seem to have time for each other anymore." He looks up at me with sad eyes. "I work too much, and she's too obsessed with the motherhood thing. Haven't you noticed that you're the only person she trusts to watch Liam?"

I'd noticed that. But honestly I thought it was because Liam is always willing to go to me, so it just made it easier on Jenny to leave him with me.

"She doesn't ever want to be away from him, Jules. She practically has a panic attack anytime I mention it. She needs a break, but she won't take one."

I feel like putting my hands over Liam's ears. He shouldn't be hearing this. Although he seems quite taken with a skin tag on my neck. I don't think he's paying attention. But don't kids get this stuff subconsciously?

"We're going to a couples counseling session today," Lennon says, sounding very glum.

"It's gotten that bad?" I ask, keeping my voice in a low whisper.

"Yes," he says, his eyes downcast. He almost looks like a little boy when he does that and I have flashbacks of Lennon and me making forts with couch cushions and digging a hole to China in our back yard together. This is before we got too cool for one another. For a while there, we were inseparable. Not seeing him like the strong, confident lawyer he's become makes my heart sink for him.

"Please Julia, can you make it work?"

I look at Liam, still pulling and tugging at the skin tag on my neck. How can I say no?

"Sure," I say. I haven't the slightest idea how I can do it, but of course I have to try. My racing heart (seriously, it hasn't slowed down since I woke up) picks up a little faster at the thought of all I have to do today. But of course I can make it work. I have to, for Lennon.

"Thanks, Julia," Lennon says, looking at me. I can see his eyes filling with — holy crap, are those tears? I don't know if I've ever seen adult Lennon cry.

"Of course," I say as reassuringly as I can. All the while, the panic in my stomach is building. How am I going to make this all work?

He opens the door to my room and walks out to the living room where Jenny looks to have pulled herself together a little. I try my best to not outwardly react to what Lennon has just told me.

"Let's go," he says to Jenny, putting an arm around her shoulders.

"Thank you so much, Julia," she says, relief in her eyes. "We'll be back by two."

"No problem," I say,

They both give me half-hearted closed-mouth smiles as Liam and I wave goodbye from the door.

"Well, it's just you and me kid," I say, and then plant another kiss on his soft baby cheek. He answers with a little baby jabber, which I'm certain means something to him, but means absolutely nothing to me.

"How do you feel about salons?"

~*~

Turns out getting your hair and makeup done with a baby is pretty much impossible. I mean, just getting him and the diaper bag to the salon was a nightmare in itself. Lennon and Jenny didn't leave a stroller so I had to carry him, which was no big deal because the kid barely weighs over twenty pounds. I carry twenty-pound bags of flour around the bakery all the time. Not for four blocks, though.

Four blocks doesn't seem like a lot, I know. But trust me when I say carrying a baby for that distance is no easy task. I even set him down and let him walk a bit, but that was like trying to get a cat to stay with me. I totally get why people put leashes on their kids now. I don't think I ever could, but now I get it.

I am out of breath and sweating by the time I make it to the salon. My poor heart is overworked, and again never settles down to a normal pace. I don't even have the time (or the constitution) to truly think about what that could mean right now (ahem, possible heart failure). I'll have to worry about it on Monday. Maybe I'll even see a doctor. Maybe.

Lucky for me, the girl at the front desk took a liking to Liam and she held him while they worked on me. Every once in a while he'd fuss for me and we'd have to take a break while I calmed him down and we found him something to shake, or tear, or throw. So far we've given him keys, magazines, sample bottles of shampoo, and combs. The glint for which only lasted mere minutes before the little stinker would get bored and move on.

I know I said I was feeling jealous of Brown, but now I'm wondering if I even have it in me to do this all the time. Good heavens, mothering is exhausting.

With my hair and makeup done, I decided the best course of action would be to call for a taxi to get back home. I know it's only four blocks, but I don't want to mess up my hair, and I mostly don't want to carry Liam back. Let's be honest here.

We make it home without too much drama. Well, there was a little when Liam tried to pull some of my pinned-up hair out. But I think I was able to stop him in time. I hope. It wasn't until I got up to my condo that I noticed Liam's face was covered in lipstick from all the kisses I gave him in the taxi ride. I quickly cleaned him up with a wipe from the diaper bag.

When my doorbell rings at two I feel as if I've run a marathon. And my heart is still beating rapidly. I don't think it's ever slowed down.

"What happened to you?" Lennon asks when I opened the door, his eyes questioning me as he takes in my hair and makeup.

"Gala, remember?" I say, feeling suddenly like we're back in our teenage years. What does he mean by what "happened" to me? Stupid younger brothers. They never change.

He gives me a little shrug. "Looks nice."

"Thanks," I say, all defensive thoughts stripped away with his comment.

"How did it go?" Jenny asks as she picks up a clapping and smiling Liam. I was only slightly jealous seeing him so excited when he looked up at her. It was too cute to truly be envious of.

"It was totally fine," I say not wanting to stress her out with how the day actually went. It wasn't so terrible. It definitely could've been worse.

"Thanks so much, Julia," Lennon says, grabbing the diaper bag from the couch. I want to ask him how the counseling went, but obviously this isn't the time to do it.

I'm not the best reader of body language, but something does seem a little different between them. Like they're more relaxed after being so tightly wound. There's definitely a difference in Jenny. I hope they can figure this all out. I mean, if Jenny and Lennon can't make it, what hope does that give me? Not that our circumstances are the same, but they've always seemed to have this marriage thing figured out.

I walk them to the door, kiss Liam goodbye (leaving more lipstick on his cheek), and watch them as the walk down the hall toward the elevators. They look like the perfect little family as they walk together. It makes me realize that I shouldn't be so quick to judge people. You have no idea what people are going through. Even your own family.

CHAPTER 18

I was barely squeezed into my dress (well, the squeezing was mostly into my Spanx) when Jared came to the door.

"Wow," he says when he sees me in my plum evening gown. "Wow," he repeats himself.

"Thanks," I say, holding back a snarky comment like "this old thing?" or "I look like an eggplant." I don't take compliments well, and honestly I did look good. Better than I normally do, that's for sure. I kind of felt like Cinderella in a purple, non-frilly dress. Cinderella with a rapid heart rate. Yep, that was still happening. I'd been so busy taking care of Liam and getting ready that I hadn't had too much time to really dwell on it. But it was still there. *Thump, thump, thump.*

I take in the sight of Jared in a tux and my racing heart gives a quick thud. He's so handsome. Like, hot-handsome. Sometimes I'm not sure how we ended up together with me and my frumpiness. I mean, I was trying for a while there, but once I got the ring on my finger I kind of let it slide a little. What can I say, there's too much going on in my life right now for me to put a lot of effort into my appearance. That may be why I got the double "wow" when he saw me.

Jared reaches for me and pulls me into him. His strong arms wrap around my waist. "Have I told you lately that I can't wait to marry you?"

"You haven't, but it was implied," I say, the side of my mouth lifting up in a half smile.

"Implied?"

"Yes, implied."

"How?"

"You haven't run from the crazy yet. So that must mean you're in it for the long haul," I say with a shrug.

His hand releases from my waist and coming up to his jaw, he rubs the base of it with his index finger and thumb. "That's true," he acts as if he's contemplating. "There has been a lot of crazy."

"I know," I say, my lips pulling into a frown. "I promise it won't be like this forever."

"Won't it?" He asks, with a slight lilt. "Because the crazy is what I fell in love with." The corners of his mouth pull up a touch.

"Oh good," I say. "It was going to be a hard life with me trying to hold all that in."

He laughs and then pulls me in for a kiss that makes my legs feel like jelly. Good thing I hadn't yet redone the lipstick that I kissed off on Liam earlier.

My phone beeps, interrupting the kiss.

"The limo's here," I say, after pulling away from him and checking my phone. I clap my hands, excited. I probably look like Liam when he claps, but who cares. I'm riding in a limo!

"Then let's go," Jared says all jovially, opening the door and ushering me out like a proper escort.

I feel like a superstar as we get into the limo. People on the street stop and gawk at the sight of us dressed up. I mean, me gussied up and Jared looking all Jared-y ... who wouldn't look at us?

I'm not going to lie, getting into the limo was a bit tough since I can barely bend at the waist. But I managed to do it without looking like a robot. Hopefully.

The limo is elegant and even has a bar inside that I'm afraid to touch because I would probably spill. Also, I planned on not eating or drinking a thing as to not cut off my circulation from the Spanx (more than is already happening now), and also because if I have to pee, I may never get myself back into the dress. So no eating or using the bathroom the entire night. Good luck to me.

I'm nervous anyway. I wasn't sure if they'd want me to give a speech or something. I jotted down a few notes and plan to wing it. I'm so not a wing-it kind of girl, but after the vow debacle (which I've still not written), I figured I'd never find it in me to write up a speech. Besides, everyone hates it when someone drones on and on. Just take the dang award and be gone with yourself.

Jared helps me get out of the limo when we arrive (it's also hard to go from sitting to standing in these Spanx). He places my hand in the crook of his elbow and we walk down the red carpet. Although there are no adoring fans screaming "we love you, Julia!" there are photographers. We even had to stop and strike a couple of poses. I'm quite sure my double chin made an appearance. At least there was no eye twitch yet.

Speaking of eye twitches, I have yet to see Lisa tonight. Maybe she got sick and couldn't make it.

"Hey you two!" An annoying voice says as soon as we enter the ballroom.

"Hi Lisa." I spoke too soon. Damn. My eye twitches, as it usually does when Lisa enters the room, and it's such a large twitch that I actually look like I've just winked at her. She winks back. How do you take back a wink? It's impossible.

"Julia, what a darling dress," she says over-cheerfully and utterly fake.

"Thanks," I say, not returning the compliment. She's wearing a tight black number with a slit up to her belly button (only a slight exaggeration). Her dark hair is down and looking glossy as ever. Her hair is the only thing I can bring myself to like about Lisa.

"It's nice to see you all dolled up," she says, hand gesturing toward my hair and makeup. "I wish I could have the guts to wear the get-out-of-bed-and-go look you do so well every day." Her eyes twinkle in the dim lighting.

Twitch.

I give her a small closed mouth smile, and then pinch Jared in the arm with my hand that's tucked into his elbow. He gives me a strange look. Such a guy — he's totally oblivious to her jabs.

"I think we should find out seats," I say to Jared and the light gleams in his eyes like he finally understands.

"I'll catch up with you later," she yells as we walk away.

Not if I can help it. This is my night, dang it. I won't let her and her ridiculously silky hair ruin it.

The ballroom is decorated in gold and black. Every table has been set to perfection, and the centerpieces look elegant with golds and creams. I only have to search for a moment before I find my cupcakes up at the front. They look gorgeous and go so well with the motif.

We find our place cards at a table at the front of the room, right by the temporary stage. My heart sinks when I see the stage. There are stairs. Stairs! I'm not exactly sure what I was envisioning, but I clearly did not picture stairs. And no rail either. I have to navigate those suckers all on my own. There's a single podium in the middle of the stage and awards lined up on a table in the back.

Jared and I take a seat at our table. We're the last people to join, apparently. I glance over at the table next to us and there sits some of my old coworkers from Spectraltech. I wave to Mr. Calhoun who looks jovial as ever, Martha sitting to his right. They are still together after they struck up a little romance at the office when I worked there. It was kind of creepy at the time, but now it seems kind of sweet. Or maybe I've just gotten used to it.

I spy a couple of people from sales and wave at them. I stretch my neck up a little, searching for Brown, but there's no sign of her. I decide to go over to the table to do a little investigating.

"Well hello there, Julia," Mr. Calhoun says as I approach. His round Santa Clause belly shakes as he talks. He stands up and gives me a quick hug. "Am I to guess that you've made the 'proverbial' cupcakes I see?" His head nods over to the cupcake display.

Oh, Mr. Calhoun and his misuse of the word proverbial. I can't believe I'm actually thinking this, but I sort of miss it. He comes to the bakery every now and then, but I'm usually too busy to have a conversation with him.

"Where's Brown?" I ask as I see the empty chairs next to Martha where a place card says "Betsy Brown" on it.

"Didn't she tell you?" Mr. Calhoun asks, his brow furrowed.

"Tell me what?" I ask, feeling instant worry settle in my gut.

"She wasn't feeling well," he says and then drops his head to my ear. "The 'proverbial' stomach bug," he says in a half whisper.

"Right," I say, feeling suddenly better. She must have morning sickness! I've heard it can be an all day thing for some people. Poor thing.

I walk back to the table I'm seated at and grab my purse to pull out my phone. No missed calls or texts from Brown, thank goodness. But I better call her just to make sure.

"I'll be right back," I say to Jared and head toward the closest exit to find a quiet place where I can give Brown a quick call and make sure everything's okay.

"Brown," I say when she picks up after the second ring.

"Hey," she says quietly and my stomach sinks when I hear her voice. She's been crying.

"What's going on?" I ask, but I feel like I already know the answer.

"I'm bleeding," she says, and her voice breaks.

"Oh Brown," I say, my fast-beating heart sinking. "Is it heavy?"

"Not yet, but my O.B. thinks I'm having a miscarriage. I'm going in tomorrow morning."

"I'm so sorry, Brown. Do you want me to come over?"

"No, Matt's here. And Anna's coming over. Plus, aren't you at the gala?" She asks through what sounds like tears.

"Yeah, but I can leave. I don't care about the gala," I say, and I truly mean it. I'm glad Anna's going over, though. I'm glad we all have each other. No pings of ridiculous best-friend-stealing jealousy this time.

"No, Jules, you have to be there. This is a big night for you. That's why I didn't call. I didn't ... I didn't want to worry you."

"Are you kidding? You should've called me. I would totally drop this night for you."

"I know, that's why I didn't call. Just ... just go to the gala, okay? I'll be fine. Matt's here, he's got my legs propped up and he's rubbing my feet as we speak," she says through sniffles.

"Okay, but text me if it gets worse, will you?" I ask, feeling tears start to form at the corners of my eyes.

"I will," she says.

We say goodbyes and then hang up. I head back into the ballroom as I hear things getting started.

"Where did you go?" Jared asks.

"Brown's bleeding," I say, feeling the tears creep in again.

"Oh no." His face goes white. "Is she okay?"

"She sounds like she's been crying a lot, but that's to be expected."

"Right." He reaches over and holds my hand in his, a very comforting gesture.

Dinner is announced and for the next while we're served a decent looking three-course meal. I wouldn't really know, though. My appetite is completely gone. I pick at a few things, but I can't stomach much. Probably not the best idea, because I downed a five-hour energy before Jared picked me up, and my stomach is feeling all kinds of strange. I could probably use some food to soak up whatever's going on in there. Although there really isn't much room with my tight undergarments.

Then it was time for the awards. There were four tables at the front of the room, all representing businesses in the Denver area that were being recognized. One by one, people from the tables were called up and presented with their award by the mayor of Denver—Mayor Hancock. As I'd expected (and feared) everyone is given a little time to give a speech.

The table I was sitting at was next in line, and when they called the first business up, my heart started beating even harder. I swear it was at a runner's pace at this point. I could feel the sweat starting to pull under my arms, like the room was suddenly a thousand degrees.

"Are you okay?" Jared asks me, searching my face.

"Uh—yeah," I shake my head like I'm trying to shake myself out of my panic. "I'm just nervous."

"You'll be fine," he gives me a reassuring smile, but I can see the worry in his eyes. I clearly don't look fine.

I start to feel my breathing pick up pace and realize that if I don't figure out a way to calm myself, I'm going to start hyperventilating right here in the ballroom, or even worse, on the stage. I start taking large breaths. Inhaling, holding it, and then exhaling out slowly. I have no idea why I'm doing this. It's not like I have any clue how to calm myself without a paper bag (which I obviously don't have in my purse — in hindsight, that might've been a good idea to bring one along), but this breathing thing just feels like what I need to do right now, and I'm desperate.

I look around the room and see Lisa. She's in her seat only a couple of tables away from Jared and me, pad of paper in hand as she jots down notes. She looks up at me and gives me a smug smile.

Twitch.

I look back at Jared and he eyes me again with concern and grabs my hand and holds it, rubbing his thumb over the back of it. I wish it was totally reassuring. I wish his hand holding would get me through this, but it's only partially helpful.

"Next we would like to recognize Julia Dorning," Mayor Hancock says.

I stand up, feeling almost like I'm having an out of body experience, and start my walk to the stairs on the side of the stage. I wonder if I went to the front and did a little roll on to the stage if anyone would think that was weird. Probably. Plus, there's no guarantee I'd be able to stand up after that, with my Spanx cutting off my circulation and all. I'd just end up lying there, like a purple beached whale.

The spotlights on the stage make it exponentially warmer up here than down at my seat where I was already sweating bullets. The warmth is definitely not helping the situation. I feel my face growing fiery hot and I know I'm probably as red as a beet. I can see the light from a camera flashing. I'm pretty sure Lisa will try to get this picture in color and on the front page if she can.

Mayor Hancock hands me my award and says a few things in the microphone. I'm not even sure what he's saying. The words are sort of a blur at this point. He stands back from the podium and motions for me to say a few words.

I stand in front of all these people and look around the room. I feel lightheaded from the heat coming from the spotlights and my queasy stomach is now making an appearance. Oh, please don't let me throw up. Not that anyone here would be too shocked by that. If they watched *Cupcake Battles* when I was on, they saw me throw up for the entire nation.

"I—" I start, but then cut off. I look down at Jared, who's looking up at me. He's trying to smile a reassuring smile, but honestly he looks a little worried.

"I—" I start again, but can't seem to find my words. It's as if my brain has gone completely blank. All I can hear is my racing heart. *Thump, thump, thump.* It feels hot and cold at the same time and my breath starts picking up again. I start to see stars, creeping in on both sides of my line of vision. Slowly moving until they're filling up my entire view, and my legs suddenly feel like they might give out.

And then, everything goes black.

CHAPTER 19

"Julia?" I hear Jared's voice. He sounds like he's in a tunnel. There's a strange ringing in my ears. "Julia?" He says again. He sounds far away, but I can tell he's panicked. I wonder what's going on?

I try to open my eyes but my lids feel like they weigh a million pounds. I can almost see when they slit open, but bright light shines through and I'm unable to open them any farther. It hurts my head. My head is throbbing and my heart is still racing and I kind of feel like throwing up.

"Jared," I try to say, but it only comes out in a whisper.

"Julia," he says. There's relief in his voice, I think. I can feel him kiss the side of my head. "You're going to be okay," he says and it almost sounds like he's trying to convince himself. Why wouldn't I be okay?

"The ambulance is on its way," I hear someone say.

An ambulance? But why? If I could just open my eyes I could see what was going on. Why won't my eyes open?

"Julia, the ambulance is coming. You're going to be okay. We'll get you to the hospital," Jared says. His voice is still far away, as if he's talking to me from across the room.

The ambulance is for me? But why? I'm so confused and so tired. So very tired. And nauseated.

Maybe I should stop fighting trying to wake up. I should just sleep. Sleep sounds good.

~*~

The sleep doesn't last long. In fact people are constantly trying to wake me up. The next while goes by in a blur. I'm being poked, prodded, and tested. I think. I'm pretty sure what's going on, but at the same time I'm not sure at all.

I know I've seen Jared, and I swear I've seen my parents too. There's a throbbing pain in my head that is so horrible, someone says they're giving me something and it feels so good all I can do is close my eyes and sleep.

When I'm finally able to open my eyes from what seems like the deepest sleep I've been in in months, it takes me a while to figure out where I am. Especially because my sight is blurry, but also because nothing seems familiar. There's constant beeping to the right of me and I can feel something like wires attached to my chest. I can only remember bits and pieces, but I'm pretty sure I'm in the hospital. Either that or I'm in Mexico and someone has stolen my kidneys. Although I have no recollection of going to Mexico, and I doubt someone stealing my kidneys would hook me up to machines.

I feel pretty dizzy. And my head feels like someone might've hit me with a sledgehammer. Maybe I finally drove Anna completely postal. I wouldn't put it past me. Or Anna.

Okay, think Julia. Think. Where was I last? I remember being at my condo, holding Liam. I remember going to the salon and getting my hair and makeup done. Now why would I do a thing like that? Oh right, the gala.

The gala! Oh gosh… it's all coming back to me. The racing heart, the heavy breathing. The sweating from the heat. It was so hot in there.

I turn my head slightly to the left. It's hard to move my head. It feels heavy and I'm so freaking dizzy.

"You're awake," Jared says in hushed tones. He's still in his tux; his tie is undone and hanging around his neck, his shirt unbuttoned at the top. He looks ridiculously sexy. Even with a pounding head and some crazy disorientation, I can still recognize a hottie when I see one.

"Your parents just went with Lennon and Anna to get coffee," he says with a nod at the doorway to the room. "And Brown sends her love, but obviously she can't be here."

Brown. I'd forgotten about that. I hope she's okay.

"What happened?" I ask, still trying to put the pieces together of what transpired tonight.

"You passed out," he says, reaching over and taking my hand in his. He rubs circles into the back of my hand with his thumb.

"I passed out?"

"Yeah, and on the way down you smacked your head on the podium."

"The podium?"

Oh dear heavens, the podium. I remember. I was getting my award and I went all crazy panicky.

"Oh gosh," I say picturing how I must've looked going down like that, like one of those fainting goats that go around the internet. And I'm sure people were recording it. Lisa will probably have it as front-page news tomorrow. Huh. I just thought of Lisa and there was no accompanying twitch. I must be totally drugged up right now.

"The doctors say you've got a concussion. They don't think it's too severe. The CT scan looked okay. And they did an EKG and everything looks fine."

"A CT scan, *and* an EKG?" I ask, my eyes going wide and I wince when I feel the pain that comes from raising my eyebrows. I close my eyes so the room doesn't spin as much. I can vaguely remember the tests, but it's almost as if it was all happening to another person and not me.

"Jules, what happened for you to pass out like that? What's going on?"

I let out a long exhale, keeping my eyes closed.

"No, wait," Jared says, "you shouldn't talk right now. Just rest, we'll talk later."

I let out another breath. "No," I say after a few seconds. "I can talk … I think." It kind of hurts my head to think, but I'm going to try. "I'm just really overwhelmed right now. With the wedding and the bakery and then there was the hyperventilating—"

"Hyperventilating?" Jared's mouth falls. "What do you mean?"

"Oh," I bat a hand at him like it was no big deal. "I had a couple of episodes where I started hyperventilating. Nothing to worry about."

"Of course it's something to worry about," he says, his eyebrows pulled together. His face is so full of worry, I want to reach out and pull him to me.

"Then there was the heart palpitations and the dizziness. Oh, and the eye twitch and the tingling —"

"Jules —"

"I was going to go to the doctor on Monday," I say cutting Jared off because I knew what he was going to say. And I actually was planning to see the doctor on Monday. Well, at least I was thinking about it. It's not like I had an appointment or anything.

"Jules, why didn't you tell me about any of this?" Jared now has my hand in both of his and he's leaning in toward me. He's so close, but not close enough.

"I … I didn't think it was that big of a deal," I say. "I mean, I just thought it was because of everything going on. There was too much happening. The bakery has been a major stress with how busy it's been and then Kate and that drama. And you were so excited about expanding."

"What?" he says, taken aback by that admission. "You're stressed because of that?"

"Well, not just that of course, but that's a part of it."

He tilts his head to the side. "Why didn't you say something?"

"You were so thrilled. I didn't want to let you down," I say, looking away from his face. The hurt expression he has right now is too much to look at.

"Then we won't do it," he says simply, and it's then that I realize the hurt on his face wasn't because I've disappointed him, it's because I didn't tell him how I was feeling. Gosh, I love this man.

"Jared, it's not that I don't want to do it," I say, wishing I could pull him closer to me. "I'm just not ready yet."

"Then we'll wait," he says.

I smile a weak smile. Inside it's a smile that reaches the sky, but if I tried to actually do that, I'd suffer the head-pounding consequences.

"What else? Is it the wedding?" He asks, his eyes searching my face.

"No. I mean, yes. Sort of."

"Do you not want to get married?" he asks quietly. His face suddenly looks boyish and utterly dejected.

"No!" I say louder than I mean to, and then wince from the pain in my head. "I don't know how you could even think that. I want to get married. And I most definitely want to marry you."

The corners of his mouth lift up ever so slightly at that.

"It's just that," I start, but then stop myself.

"It's just what?" Jared asks, searching my face again with is eyes. Gosh, I love those eyes. They're so blue, like the ocean. I want to swim in them.

"It's just that I never wanted a big wedding," I say, and instantly feel guilty for saying it.

"I know, Jules. And I know you've been doing all of this for me and for Bobby." He leans in and kisses the top of my hand very much like Mr. Darcy, and I kind of swoon a little. Or a lot. I'm not sure I could ever put into words how wonderful just a simple kiss from Jared can make me feel.

"It wasn't just for you and Bobby," I say, my eyes move to the ceiling above my hospital bed. "I did it for

Anna and my parents and our friends. But what I really want is to be married to you." I turn my head to look at him. "I wanted to marry you on a beach with only a few friends and family with us. Or in the mountains. But I don't care—I'd marry you at one of those tacky wedding chapels in Vegas, or the courthouse." I give him a little smile and he returns the gesture. "But all this hoopla—it's not me. It's not us," I say, giving his hand a little squeeze.

"I know you hate being put on the spot," Jared says, the side of his lips curled up in a half-smile that makes my heart warm.

"It's not just that. I mean, yes, I do hate being put on the spot, but it's—I don't know—everything, you know? It feels so big; so many people will be there. I feel like I have to do my best, say all the right things, be the perfect bride. We both know I'm going to totally mess this up. I mean, I keep having nightmares about it. Even my subconscious knows I'm going to mess it all up."

"Jules," he kisses the top of my hand again. "It doesn't have to be perfect. It'll be what it is. And if something happens—like you trip and fall on the way down the aisle, it will just be something we can laugh about later."

"Why would it only be me who could trip and fall? What about you? You have just as much of a chance as I do."

Jared holds in an obvious grin.

"Okay, fine. Of course it'd be me," I say, giving him my best pouty face, which only causes my head to throb at the movement.

Jared's face turns serious. "What can I do, Jules?" he asks with such sincerity I can feel stinging in the back of my eyes.

"I don't know," I say and then sigh. "I mean, it's not like we can elope now."

He lets out a quick laugh, one that ends almost as soon as it begins.

"Unless," I say, my mind starting to churn out a thought. A thought that makes me suddenly feel crazy amounts lighter than the heavy feeling I've had in my chest all this time.

"Unless what?" Jared asks, eying me suspiciously.

"Unless, we do elope," I say.

"Jules," Jared starts, and I know what he's thinking.

"Just hear me out," I say, squeezing his hands that are still holding mine. "I've been freaking out about this one day — worried that something will go wrong, but what if we got married first?" I look at his face to see what he's thinking. He looks confused. "What if," I continue, "we elope — like next weekend. We could go to the mountains or something. Just you and me."

"Jules," Jared says skeptically.

"Just listen," I say. "No one would have to know. It would be just us, only for us. And then we can come back and have our big ridiculous wedding. But the pressure would be off. There'd be no need to have the perfect day, because we would've already had one — just you and me. Together."

He looks at me, studying my face.

"Anna will kill you if she finds out," he says.

"I know, we can never tell her. Never ever."

He smiles and I smile back. He doesn't even have to say it. I know he'll do this for me. I know he'll make this happen.

He stands up, leaning over me, his nose nearly touching mine. His hand reaches up to my face and he brushes my cheek with the back of his hand and then he kisses me gently. My lips tingle in response.

"Okay," he says.

"Okay?" I ask, wanting to hear it again.

"Okay, Julia Dorning. I'll elope with you."

CHAPTER 20

I'm eloping with Jared.

I'm so giddy, I don't know if I'll be able to hold it in. It's this weekend at a beautiful resort in the mountains. Jared set it all up because he didn't want me to do anything that might cause me stress. I think I love him even more and I didn't think that was possible. He seems to be warming up to the idea more and more. Doing something secretive for just him and me. It makes it all that much more exciting.

The plan is for Jared to pick me up Saturday morning and drive to Vail. We get married and then spend the night in a beautiful condo. Then we come back on Sunday night as man and wife ... and no one gets to know except for us. Maybe someday we'll tell them. In a few decades. All the work everyone has put into everything — Anna, Bobby, my parents. I don't want to hurt any feelings. Besides, they wouldn't truly understand. Even if I tried to explain the kind of pressure it takes off me, they wouldn't get it.

Let's be honest, though, it'll be a miracle for me to keep it all in. I'm a terrible secret keeper. Especially for something exciting. Avoiding everyone I love would probably be the best route, although quite impossible. I'll just have to figure it out.

It hasn't been too much of a problem so far this week since I've been ordered by the doctor to rest. Much needed rest, actually. The only thing is that it's kind of boring. Be careful what you wish for, right? I'm all alone in my condo. Just Charlie and me, and I'm not allowed to do anything. Not even watch TV or read. The doctor has allowed me thirty minutes a day of screen time (TV, phone, iPad, anything with a screen), which is a complete joke. But that's concussion protocol for someone who's lost consciousness.

The thing is, I fainted before I hit the podium so I don't think it was the head slam that caused me to lose consciousness. Regardless, I'm trying to make it work. I've had visitors of course — my parents and Anna. Lennon too, with Jenny and Liam (they looked happier, but I couldn't ask about it with Jenny there). Jared has come over the past few nights after work. He's taking such good care of me. He's a saint, really. Like he should actually be sainted.

I've got a nice bruise on the upper part of my forehead. It was the normal purple color at first, but in the past couple of days it's taken a greenish-yellowish hue that wouldn't even be attractive on a supermodel. So you can imagine what it looks like on me. I'm not hiding it well, either. I'll have to figure out some sort of creative hairdo to cover it when Jared and I elope this weekend. The great part? If this were the big wedding day and I had to walk down the aisle with this big ole goose egg on my forehead, I'd be mortified. But because it's not and it's just Jared and me, I don't care at all. Of course I'd rather it not be there, but I can deal with it.

So the big diagnosis after the fainting/concussion incident on Saturday night was … wait for it …

anxiety with a side of panic disorder. I mean, if that's not a big duh, I don't know what is. At least it wasn't heart disease. The past months have been nothing but stress and I've never been one to handle stress well. I should've seen all this coming, but I guess I kept thinking I could make it work. Now it's become chemical. Like my brain can't even deal with it. The doctor put me on some medication that should start helping in a couple of weeks. And another med that I can take as needed when I'm feeling overwhelmed. I haven't had to take that one yet. Lying around on my couch snuggled up with Charlie doesn't make for a stressful time.

I've also been kicked off caffeine because of the heart palpitations, which is a huge bummer (honestly, how will I survive?). I keep hoping that I might be able to slowly bring it back in. Or I'll just up my chocolate intake. That has caffeine in it and he didn't say I couldn't have chocolate. Things might've gotten super ugly if he had. I mean, what else would I have to live for?

Everyone in my life seems to be on the same page right now. No one is bothering me, but at this point I'm so bored I wouldn't mind a little bothering. Even Anna has laid off on her constant wedding prep texts. I can't believe I'm thinking this, but I kind of miss them. In an odd way, it was like a constant in my crazy life.

Jared put my condo on the market. He said it will probably take until the wedding to sell it (six weeks left) and we can slowly start moving my stuff over. Plus, now that we are eloping and won't be "living in sin" we can start our life together. Of course, Bobby can't know any of this, so we'll have to keep it a secret from her. But at least I'll have the cover of my condo to go back to if needed.

The bakery is somehow surviving without me. Or Kate. Beth, the previous owner, has stepped in to help, thank goodness for her. I considered closing for a week, but Jared said that was a bad idea and even offered to work for me. The picture of him in an apron with flour all over his face made my insides mushy. He's adorable.

My phone rings and I reach over and pull it off the coffee table. I've actually been lying here counting the freckles on my arm. I'm *that* bored.

It's Brown. I've been waiting for this call.

"Hey," she says in a very even tone when I answer.

"Hey," I say back.

Silence.

"So," I say, wanting her to talk, but not wanting to be forceful.

"So," she says, not giving me an inch. Should I read into the fact that she's not crying? I mean, that's got to mean something. Of course, she could be all cried out at this point.

More silence.

"Brown, please tell me," I say. I tire easily of games, which is why I lose Gin Rummy to Jared all the time.

"I'm still pregnant," she says.

"What?" I say, sitting up too quickly and feeling suddenly dizzy.

"I'm still pregnant!" she says louder and now I can hear the happiness in her voice.

"You are?" I scream into the phone and my forehead bruise protests.

"Yep, there's still a baby in there. And get this, Jules—we got to see the heartbeat. It has a heartbeat!"

"I can't believe you led me on like that. That's information you should always start with," I say with an eye roll that she can't even see. I hope she can hear it in my inflection.

"Well, you know, I always like to be mysterious," she says.

"So what happened?" I ask.

I still hadn't gotten a good answer from her. I talked to her the day after my fainting incident and there wasn't much information to give. The doctor wasn't able to provide her a definitive answer on his ultrasound equipment. He sent her to the hospital where they could use a better machine to see what's going on, but they couldn't get in until today. Three days seems like an incredibly long time to get answers.

"They don't know for sure," she says. "The tech said that some women just bleed."

"Does that mean you're still bleeding?"

"Nope. No more blood. For now, at least. I'm on bed rest for the next week just to make certain."

"Too bad you can't come over and we can be on bed rest together. I'm so bored."

"No way, you can't even watch TV. I'm catching up on *Downton Abbey*."

A stab of jealousy goes through me. I could be catching up on *Project Runway* right now. Or even *Grey's Anatomy*. It's been so long since I've watched that. I mean, this is only precautionary right? I should just watch TV. If only I didn't promise Jared I wouldn't. And since I got him to elope with me this weekend, I guess I probably should stick with my promise.

"Oh!" I say, when I think of Jared and me getting married this weekend. Then I internally cringe. It's like the secret is so close to the tip of my tongue that I can barely hold it in. How am I ever going to keep this a secret?

"What?" Brown asks, the tone in her "what" very reminiscent of the days that we worked together at Spectraltech and spent many breaks sharing office gossip. Those breaks were the only bright spot in my days there.

"Did I tell you that the doctor told me I have anxiety?" I cringe to myself. That was a terrible attempt at recovery.

"You didn't," she says, the joy of possible gossip in her tone clearly absent. "But I probably could've diagnosed that."

"Too bad you didn't. Could've saved me an embarrassing fainting spell and subsequent concussion."

"Sorry about that. I'll be sure to let you know next time you're going crazy," she says, her voice devoid of inflection. I'm glad Brown's sense of sarcasm hasn't been snuffed by pregnancy. I've heard of people getting all sappy and sentimental from the hormones.

"Anyway, Jules, Anna and I are working on your bridal shower and bachelorette party."

"Oh gosh, don't worry about any of that."

"Yes, Anna and I knew you'd say that. Don't think you're getting out of it."

"Of course not," I say in protest. Of course that's exactly what I was thinking/hoping. "I just don't want to stress you with the pregnancy and all."

I really don't want a bridal shower and I super-duper don't want a bachelorette party. But Anna and Brown are insistent. They promise to keep it simple and "Julia-like," which I believe is code for "boring." Whatever. I do appreciate them for doing it, but honestly a big fat cancellation would've been much more appreciated.

"Don't worry. They're not for another few weeks. I should be ready to party by then," she says and my heart sinks.

"Sounds great," I say, trying to muster even just a little excitement into my voice. Then I remember that I'll actually be a married woman by then. A thrill wiggles up my throat at the thought. It actually makes the party sound even more appealing, knowing that I have a big secret that none of them will know. This eloping thing is becoming more and more the best idea ever.

Brown and I talk a bit more about the pregnancy. I can tell that Brown is holding back from allowing herself to get too excited. Even after seeing the heartbeat, it's like she can't accept that it's real. I think I'd be the same way in her shoes. Actually, I'd be a panicked mess, if how I've been acting in the past months is any indicator.

I do look forward to starting a family with Jared, but first I need to marry him. And I'm only days away. I can't wait.

CHAPTER 21

"Are you ready to marry me?" Jared asks as he comes in the door to my condo. He picks me up and spins me around.

I feel a ping of self-consciousness as he lifts me. I lost weight with the stress, but I'm pretty sure I put on a few pounds this past week when all that was left to do was eat. No TV, no reading, what else was a girl supposed to do? Plus Patti kept dropping off goodies from the bakery.

Try as I might, I can't deny the fact that there is something missing without Kate. Debbie made fruit tarts one day and while the crust was very good, it wasn't tear-inducing like Kate's. I'm starting to wonder if I was a little rash with all that. I mean, she was only trying to help make things easier for me. I could've at least sat her down and talked to her instead of losing my crap like I did. In my defense, I was going a little mental at that point.

After the quick spinning and follow-up mini make-out session, Jared grabs my overstuffed bag and we head downstairs to his Range Rover. I feel a little silly about how much I packed for an overnight excursion, but you never know what you might need when you're away from home. Even after packing the kitchen sink (only a slight exaggeration), I'm almost one hundred percent sure I've forgotten something. Something important. Not Jared's ring; I know I have that. I purchased it a while back (thanks to Anna and her over-preparedness). Whatever I've forgotten, I'm just going to let it go. Nothing I can do about it now.

We've told everyone that Jared is whisking me away for the weekend to help me recover more and so I don't have to sit around the condo all day. The only person not pleased about it was Anna. She said we had too much to do. But in the end, she agreed that I needed a little more time for my "nut-job brain" (her words, not mine).

Between makeup and my hair, I was able to cover the bruise on my head sufficiently. It looks a million times better today than a few days ago, thank goodness. I wasn't looking forward to having a big nasty bruise on my head when I married Jared. I'd do it with a bag over my head, though. Nothing is holding me back from this.

As we drive toward the mountains, we both keep looking over at each other and smiling. Sometimes I add a giggle that ends in a snort, which really takes away from the romance of it all, but hey — it's what I do.

We're holding hands and every once in a while Jared lifts my hand to his mouth and kisses the back of it. I feel so incredibly lucky to be marrying this man. My heart feels full and warm and my stomach is dancing with butterflies. The good kind.

"So our vows," he starts, after we enter the base of the mountains and begin climbing up the fairly steep I-70 drive that will take us to the resort.

Oh gosh, vows. I totally forgot.

"Should we say them today? Or save them for the big wedding?" he asks, keeping his eyes on the road, his hand in mine.

"You know, I think we should save them."

"Yeah?"

"Definitely. It'll give us something to look forward to on that day." I keep my eyes on the road, not wanting to make eye contact with him for fear that he'd see right through me. I still haven't written my vows.

"I like that idea," he finally says, giving my hand a couple of quick squeezes.

The winding mountain roads that take us to the resort are lush and green and picture-perfect today with the bright blue Colorado sky that you can't find anywhere else in the United States and the tall peaks that have year-round snow on them. I've taken these mountains for granted my entire life, I think. Maybe it's because I'm feeling a little cheesy right now, but it's almost as if I'm seeing the beauty around me with a new pair of eyes.

Jared gives my hand another little squeeze as he takes the exit off the highway to the resort. The town of Vail seems busier than I would've expected. There are bunches of people walking the streets and a ton of vendors selling their goods on the sidewalks. I look a little closer and it seems like the only thing the vendors are selling are bongs. Not so weird for Colorado these days, but a little odd for a place like Vail.

We drive under a large banner that says "Summer Fun Festival."

"Do you know what that's all about?" I ask Jared, pointing to the sign.

"Yeah, the resort mentioned it. It's some sort of arts festival, I think." Jared takes a turn and pulls into what I can only assume is the resort we're staying at tonight.

Holy crow, it's magnificent from the outside. Especially with the mountains as the backdrop. Jared drives up to the front of the resort and then parks and waits for a bellman to approach the car.

As Jared answers the questions from the bellman, I look out the window and see a group of people passing by the resort and they all kind of look like the potheads who crave the munchies at my bakery. Dreadlocks and bright colors abound. They all have about the same taste in clothes and fashion as Lia does. In fact, one of the people in the group that I'm looking at looks an awful lot like Lia. Maybe I've found her doppelganger.

After Jared gets everything squared away with the bellman, we walk into the resort hand in hand. My eyes immediately go to the vaulted ceilings. It has a French chalet look, with huge wood beams lining the a-frame ceiling. Large, comfy couches and chairs surround a huge four-sided fireplace that goes all the way to the vaulted ceiling with stacked stone detail.

We take the elevator to the top floor and walk down the hall to our room. Jared opens the door with his keycard and holds it open as I walk in. I gasp when I see the space. It has the same décor and vibe as the lobby, but on a smaller scale. An elegant sitting area and a cozy couch sits in front of a fireplace with a large ornate mantle.

"Do you like it?" Jared asks, wrapping his arms around my waist in a tender grasp.

"I love it," I say, and then reach my face up to kiss his mouth.

He pulls away not long after the kiss starts and grabs his smart phone from his back jean pocket.

"We don't have much time," he says, looking at his phone. He puts the phone back in his pocket, takes me gently by the shoulders, and plants a soft kiss on my forehead.

"So we're really going to do this?" I ask, looking up into his eyes.

He gives me a mischievous double eyebrow lift. "It looks like we are. Now hurry up and go get changed. We're meeting the officiant down in the lobby in an hour."

"An hour," my eyes widen. How will I ever get ready in an hour?

Without another word, I grab my suitcase and head to the master bedroom. The suite is so big that there are two bedrooms, a master suite and a smaller room, both with full bathrooms. Jared takes the smaller room to get ready because, clearly, he loves me.

The master bathroom doesn't disappoint. There's a glass, dual-head shower and near that, a sunken Jacuzzi tub. Placed on the large ledge of the tub is a bottle of champagne chilling in ice, a silver platter with wine flutes, and a box of chocolate-covered strawberries.

Next to those is a card with the words "Mr. and Mrs. Moody" written on the envelope. Holy crap. After today — in just a couple of hours, actually — I'll be Jared's wife. It's kind of hard to believe I've even made it here.

I take a quick shower and then start doing my hair. I keep it simple, leaving my hair down but with soft curls (I still suck at using a curling iron, but I'm sort of getting it). I was actually planning on putting it up, but I forgot bobby pins. No wonder I have packing anxiety, because I never can seem to remember everything. I wish I could say that I feel like that was the only thing I forgot, but there's a little warning in the back of my head that makes me think I've forgotten something important. I wish I could remember what it was. Clearly, it wasn't just bobby pins.

After my hair is done, I do my makeup. I keep it natural because, let's face it, that's all I know how to do.

My phone pings as I finish up my mascara. It's probably a text from Jared telling me how much he can't wait to marry me. Sigh. This whole thing is seriously so romantic.

Nope, it's Anna. So not romantic *at all*.

Thoughts on setting off fireworks at the end of the reception?

And she's back. I should've known my reprieve would only last so long. I text back a quick "no thanks," and she sends me back her obligatory "fine." She probably has it on auto response.

A feeling of guilt washes over me as I think about what I'm going to do — and Anna has no clue. She'd be hurt for a myriad of reasons if she ever found out about the eloping ... that she wasn't here and also that she's spending all of her time planning my big day, which will no longer be my "official" wedding day.

I've got to think of me, though, even though I feel oodles of selfishness when I say that. But it's true. Plus, doing all of this big wedding stuff was never for me, it was for everyone else. Maybe if I would've put my foot down, I wouldn't have ended up fainting at the gala. Of course, my brain was probably wired for anxiety. It just needed a big buildup before all the crazy came spewing out.

I look at the time on my phone and see that there's only ten minutes left. Time to get dressed. Earlier this week I was able to score a simple, white strapless cocktail number online using my half-hour of allotted screen time. I had it sent overnight because if it didn't work, I'd still have time to find something else. But it was perfect.

I was surprised that I was able to pick out something so easily, and without Anna's or Brown's approval. Not that I didn't want their approval, mind you. I had come up with a bunch of scenarios (read: lies) that I could use as an excuse for a reason to ask them what they thought, but in the end I realized it'd be too hard to keep so many secrets from them. This time it was all on me.

I spin around in front of a huge, full-length mirror just outside the master closet. I feel like I'm in a fairytale. I sort of am. If only Lisa could see me now.

I'm certainly not "dowdy" today. Although I'm sure she'd find some way to make me feel that way. *"Oh Julia! Look at that adorable white dress you're wearing. I can't believe you dare to go there when white is clearly not your color."*

Nope. I'm not letting Lisa ruin this day. Even if it's only made up in my head.

I walk out to the living area and find Jared there waiting for me. His head is down as he swipes his thumb over his smart phone. I clear my throat and he looks up.

"Hi," I say.

"Hi," he says back.

Our smiles are huge as we look at each other. Jared looks more than handsome in his black fitted suit, white shirt, and black tie. He pulls me into his arms and hugs me tight.

"Isn't it bad luck to see the bride before the wedding?" I ask after a few seconds of us hugging in silence.

"Nah," he says, his chin resting on top of my head. "I've never bought into any of that crap."

"Are you sure you want to do this?" I ask, feeling weird butterflies in my stomach. I can't believe this is all happening.

"Marry you, or elope?" He asks with a mild teasing tone.

"Uh, both," I say and he laughs.

He pulls back so he can look me in the eyes. "I don't care how it happens, Julia Dorning, I just want to be married to you."

Okay, mega swooning happening right now. I don't know how I could ever regret this whole eloping thing. It's seriously the best decision I've ever made.

CHAPTER 22

This might be the worst decision I've ever made.

Jared and I were all movie-sequence romantic. All the way down the elevator and into the lobby we kept stealing kisses, looking at each other, and smiling. It was seriously out of an incredibly dreamy film.

That was until, like a record player screech, everything came to a complete halt as we met the officiant. He was there waiting for us like he was supposed to be. But what he wasn't supposed to be was someone that looked like he'd just come from a Bob Marley concert.

I'm no expert here, but I'm pretty sure he's high. Like, just-smoked-a-fatty high. I'm not even sure what a "fatty" is. It's jargon I've overheard at the bakery by my new munchie-craving clientele. The officiant— who asked us to call him Blaze, I kid you not—is wearing a white linen button-up shirt, with what looks like a grease stain on the right pocket. He's got on khaki cargo shorts and a pair of fairly nice looking dress shoes. No socks, of course. His unkempt blonde hair is loosely pulled back into a ponytail at the nape of his neck.

Presently I'm listening to him and Jared discuss everything we need, and it appears that Blaze—even though he's clearly smoked a joint not long ago, and sounds an awful lot like Tommy Chong—is ready to officiate this wedding. He's done two other weddings already today.

Jared grabs my hand as we follow Blaze out of the resort and walk toward the chair lifts. We look a little ridiculous as we walk behind Blaze and he high-fives a bunch of people we don't know and uses the word "dude" in a variety of different ways. Proper name (Dude!), nickname (duuuuude), in the form of a question (dude?), and then there was one exchange where that was the only word spoken and it went on a heck of a lot longer than one would think it should … or could.

"Sorry," Jared whispers in my ear.

I crinkle my brow. "Why are you sorry? I'm the one who should be sorry. I made you do this," I say, feeling oodles of guilt.

"First of all, you didn't make me do anything. And secondly, I want this. I want something for just us," he says and then takes the hand that's holding mine and places a kiss on my fingers.

I smile. "You know, I don't really care who marries us, I just want to be married to you."

He lets go of my hand and puts his arm around my waist, pulling me tight to him.

So apparently we're taking the chair lifts up the side of a mountain. I really should've considered wearing hiking boots. But I had no idea what the plan was. I guess I should've asked. I think Jared wanted it all to be a surprise.

When we reach the lifts, Blaze turns to us before we're about to get on.

"So who are the witnesses?" he asks, looking behind us like maybe they'd been following us all along.

"I didn't think we had to have them," Jared says.

"It's up to the officiant, and I prefer at least one witness. Liability and all that." Blaze brings his hand up to shade his eyes as he looks out toward the resort. "No worries, man, I've got a couple of guys that can help." He points over toward the resort where a group of people are standing.

He run-walks over to the group. They're about five yards away, but we can hear the greeting as he approaches the group. Hands are slapped on backs and even a hug is exchanged with one of them.

We see Blaze gesturing over toward us and saying something that makes them all laugh. Fabulous. And then I see a person peek out from behind the group, someone who'd be easily covered because of her short height.

"Julia!" A sickly-sweet voice yells over to me.

Oh dear heavens. It's Lia.

"Julia!" She yells again as she runs (well, it's kind of a waddle) toward us.

I look to Jared and he looks back at me, his brow scrunched.

"We've been caught," I say, almost in a panic.

"Caught?"

"It's Lia, from the bakery," I say, and his brows change from the scrunched position to a much higher place on his forehead.

"Julia," Lia says as she approaches us, very much out of breath. "What are you doing here?" she asks, looking from me to Jared and then back to me again.

"Uh," I say trying to think up something, but it's kind of obvious.

"Oh my goodness, you're getting married!" she yells, bouncing around in her spot. I don't know if I've ever seen Lia this animated.

"Why are you here?" I ask her.

"I'm here for the festival," she says, her tone indicating that I should totally know that. I guess I should have known.

"Lia," I say stepping toward her, "yes, we are getting married. But you can't tell anyone."

"Oh, of course not," she says, bringing her hand up to her lips and miming them zipped.

"We're still having our big wedding," I say and look to Jared and then back to her. "We just wanted something for ourselves."

"That's so romantic," she says with a sigh. She clasps her hands together, her eyes look twinkling in the sun that's just begun setting.

Blaze walks up to us with two men that also look like they came from a Bob Marley concert. Both have long hair, one is in dreadlocks, and they too look high.

"Here we go," Blaze says, gesturing with his hand toward the two men, "your witnesses."

I gulp, rather loudly. This is so not how I pictured things going.

"Oh Julia, you need a maid of honor," she says stepping toward me.

"No," I say a little too quickly, "I mean, it's totally okay, Lia. It's really just going to be Jared and me."

"You can't get married without a maid of honor," she insists, her head nodding so quickly I wonder if she'll get a headache.

"No really, Jared doesn't even have a best man," I say pointing toward Jared.

"We can find you one, man," Blaze says.

"No!" Jared and I say at the same time.

"Please let me be your maid of honor, Julia?" Lia says, her hands clasped together and pulled up toward her chin and she looks to be actually begging.

I look at Jared and he looks back at me and shrugs.

"Okay," I say, conceding, but only half-heartedly.

She does a little cheer and then, directed by Blaze, we all walk toward the ski lifts. Jared and I in our semi-formal wedding attire surrounded by what looks like a bunch of hippies.

If my family could see me now...

CHAPTER 23

The lift takes us to the very top of the mountain and then a quick walk up a small trail finds us standing on a hillside full of wildflowers. It's breathtaking. Like, I actually forgot to breathe.

"You okay?" Jared asks, wrapping an arm around my waist to steady me.

"It's amazing," I squeak out, looking up at the pink and gold dusk sky that backdrops this magnificent location.

"I'm glad you approve," he says, pulling me into him. He places a kiss on the side of my head.

"You ready, man?" Blaze asks, and just like that I'm pulled out of my pretty mountainside-wedding cocoon. Jared's look of deer-caught-in-headlights pretty much says he's also been brought back to reality.

Besides this beautiful locale, nothing else is what I imagined today would be like. Our officiant is high, our witnesses look like they belong at a Phish concert (and they smell like it as well), and my maid of honor is a witch.

Honestly, I should've expected this. Nothing ever goes as planned in the life of Julia Warner Dorning.

"Here Julia," Lia hands me a small bouquet of wildflowers that she must've picked on the way up. "Every bride needs a bouquet," she says.

Okay, that's pretty sweet. I mean, we were in such a rush to do this I totally forgot about a bouquet. I take the small gathering of flowers from her and thank her. She reaches for me and pulls me into a tight hug. All right fine. Having Lia here isn't so bad after all. It's kind of nice to have a familiar face.

"Let's get started, man," Blaze says.

We all start moving into our places, not exactly sure where we should be going. The only person that knows anything about weddings here is Blaze. I'm not so confident in our leader, but somehow he sets us up right. At least the way he wants us to be, anyway.

He's got Jared and I facing each other with him on one side of us and the witnesses (or Dooby Brothers, essentially) on the other side, and Lia to the right of me and slightly behind.

"Let's begin," Blaze says, and Jared reaches for one of my hands, my other one holding the makeshift bouquet.

Jared looks to me and we lock eyes. And just like that we're in our own little world. This whole eloping thing may not have gone according to plan, but since nothing truly does in my life, it's kind of turning out perfect in its own way. At least it will be a great story that we won't be able to tell anyone. Maybe our children.

Blaze starts the ceremony and within a minute, my mouth has dropped open and I've noticed that Jared's has as well. Maybe it's the pot talking, but Blaze's words? Well, they're ... they're beautiful. He speaks of marriage as a promise to each other, that we should trust our love and honor each other as individuals. His words are eloquent, and deep, and poetic even.

Once the shock has worn off, I feel myself start to get all emotional. I notice that Jared's eyes are also looking a little glossy. Good heavens, who would've known that our weed-smoking officiant would bring us to tears? I'm feeling sort of bad that I ever underestimated this guy.

"The love between you now joins you as one," he says as he ends his very short ceremony. Short and, honestly, perfect.

Then Blaze has us say vows, and thank goodness they're only the repeat-after-me kind and not the spur-of-the-moment speech I half-expected him to ask us to do. Next we exchange rings.

"And now that you've exchanged vows and rings, in front of God and all who are assembled here, I pronounce you husband and wife," Blaze says and Lia squeals with delight.

A broad smile spreads across Jared's face and I join in. We're married. Jared and I are married!

"Dude, kiss your bride," Blaze says, a wry smile on his face.

Jared takes a small step forward and, putting his hands on my waist, he starts to pull me toward him. It's then that I feel something tickling my arm. I look down and there perched on my wrist is a huge brown spider. Maybe the biggest brown spider I've ever seen, and certainly the biggest one I've ever had on me.

"SPIDER!" I scream as my arms go flailing in the air, the bouquet of flowers flying all around us. I'm doing this crazy shaking-twisting-jumping thing, trying to rid myself of what I can only assume is a Brown Recluse. I mean, it's probably not, but that's all I can think of. I can't even look to see if it's gone, I just keep throwing my arms all around and basically doing a jerking and writhing dance.

Yes. The perfect ending, really.

"Jules!" Jared says, trying to calm me. He grabs my hands and holds them down to keep me from doing my spider dance. Then he inspects me hands, arms, wrists.

"Check my hair," I say, wrenching my hands from his and spinning around. I'm wiping my hands all over my body, thinking it could've crawled anywhere on me at this point.

"Julia," Lia says, in her sickly-sweet voice, "a spider is good luck!"

I want to scream "in what world?" Of course a witch would say that.

After a full inspection, Jared declares me spider free and because I know the spider exists somewhere in this now-tainted mountainside field, and that it probably has siblings, I make a beeline for the lifts, leaving everyone in my dust.

"Julia, wait up!" Jared yells from behind as I run as fast as I can in these shoes, which is actually impressively fast, if I do say so myself.

Jared catches up to me just as I'm about to get on a lift.

"Were you just going to leave me?" He says, barely out of breath, a half smile on his face.

"Sorry," I say, and then I grab his arm and pull him toward me just as the next chair lift arrives.

We hop on and as the lift makes a turn around the corner, we see the rest of the group getting on the next one.

I'm out of breath and still freaking out. I know it was only a spider, but it was a freaking huge spider and I swear it was about to dig its fangs into my flesh. It might've even wriggled its eyebrows at me in a super devious manner. I'm pretty sure this spider had eyebrows.

"You okay?" Jared asks as he tries, unsuccessfully, to stifle a giggle.

"Not yet," I say, and a large shiver runs through my body as I imagine the creepy feeling of the spider on my arm.

He scoots over, making the lift swing a little, and pulls me into him. "I had no idea you were that scared of spiders," he says, the amusement still obvious through his tone.

"I had no idea either; I've never been that close to one before." My upper body shivers once again.

"You've never had a spider on you?" Jared says, his voice full of disbelief.

"Not one that big," I say, looking to his face, which now has that familiar smirk on it. The one I used to want to slap. I kind of want to right now.

"Hey!" We both turn as we hear Blaze yell from the lift behind us. "You never kissed your bride!"

Bride. Oh my gosh, I'm a married woman. I'm officially married to Jared. Only I ruined the kiss! Is it even official unless there's a kiss?

"What do you say, Mrs. Moody?" Jared says with a little wriggle of his eyebrows.

I don't even answer because I'm swooning at being called Mrs. Moody, the entire spider incident already in the past. Not really, I'll be reliving that for a while. But at least it's put on hold.

He leans in and kisses me, gently at first, but then quite passionately. I know I said I didn't want a super long kiss at my wedding, but that was in front of a crowd. Right now, on this chair lift, just him and me and a lift full of hippies behind us, I don't care.

CHAPTER 24

A buzzing noise next to my ear wakes me up the next morning. It takes me a few seconds to realize that it's coming from my phone. I pick it up and through sleepy eyes try to see who the heck would be texting me at seven thirty in the morning on a Sunday.

Anna. Does she ever sleep?

I've missed four texts from her. All about how I need to decide how I want the napkins to be folded on the tables.

7:15 A.M.
Julia, I have an important question about napkins. Text or call me ASAP.

7:25 A.M.
Julia, where are you? Napkins! I need an answer.

7:28 A.M.
I need to tell the banquet hall today. Can you please text me back?

7: 30 A.M.
Seriously?

Why would I even care about napkins? I text her back that I want them all in the shape of a goose and then I turn off my phone. That'll annoy her for a while.

I look over and see Jared's slow, rhythmic breathing. I'm happy my crazy sister/wedding planner from hell didn't wake him up. I've got to say, waking up next to Jared as his wife might be the best feeling ever.

The sunlight filtering into the room shines off the ring on Jared's finger. It's amazing how one little band of gold can mean so much. He's mine, legally. He's now officially stuck with me. Too bad the ring can only stay on for today since we have to keep up appearances until the official wedding. It looks so pretty, though.

I'm a married woman. It's kind of hard to believe. I almost feel like an imposter in my own life. Like I don't belong here, or I'll wake up and this would all be just a dream. And it's not like this was a lifelong goal of mine or anything. In fact, for a while I went through a phase of thinking I'd probably never get married, and I was mostly okay with that. My cats and I could've been very happy together. Not as happy as I am with Jared, obviously.

Of course, now that I'm married, I have to start thinking of someone else besides myself. We're a partnership now. We have to make decisions together in all facets of our life. But even more important than that, I'm wondering how long I have to wait before I can get fat. Since he's now stuck with me. I feel a sinister laugh bubbling from within me ... and horns.

Jared stirs next to me, making a low moaning sound in his throat as we wakes.

"Good morning, Mrs. Moody," he says, his voice groggy from sleep.

"Good morning, Mr. Moody," I say and then giggle. I don't know if that will ever get old.

"You're up early. How did you sleep?" he asks. He slides an arm under me and pulls me into him and I rest my head on his chest.

"Pretty well," I say as I snuggle up to him. "You?"

"Not bad," he plants a kiss on the top of my head. I trace lazy circle patterns on his chest.

"Happy?" he asks, and by his tone, I can tell he knows the answer to that.

"So happy," I say. And I am. I don't know when I've been this happy.

The wedding was nothing if not memorable (I'll never in my life forget that spider), and last night—our wedding night—was romantic and wonderful and there wasn't a hippy or spider in sight. Which would've been awkward had there been. Especially the hippy part.

I had my doubts but I think all in all, it was the best thing to do. I can already feel the pressure of the big wedding lifted from me. I'm now ready for it. Mostly. At least I can breathe. And Jared and I will have a secret that's just ours and a day that was just for us.

"Hungry?" I ask Jared, feeling my own stomach gurgle.

"I am," he says as he rolls me onto my back and then turns himself so he's half on top of me. "But not for breakfast," he says with a quick lift of his brow.

"No?"

"Nope," he says, his mouth finding mine.

On second thought, I'm not so hungry for breakfast anymore either.

CHAPTER 25

"Wait!" Jared says as he opens the door to his condo for me. My body jerks in response.

"Oh my gosh, is there a spider on me?" I throw my purse down on the floor and immediately start to jump around. Is it the same spider? Did it lay eggs in my hair and now hundreds of baby spiders are crawling all over me?

"No," He says, placing calming hands on my shoulders. "No spiders. I need to carry you across the threshold," he smiles. "It's tradition." He picks my purse up off the floor and places it and the suitcases just inside the open door and then reaches for me.

My mind starts spitting out a zillion thoughts. Like: "He's so romantic." And, "Oh, my gosh, he'll break something ... like his back." And, "Why did I eat such a big breakfast at the hotel?" And, "If I pray hard enough, can God magically make me thinner?"

There's not enough time to totally freak out because before I can say it's not necessary, Jared has swung me into his arms like I'm as light as a feather. He's even able to shut the door and lock it once we're inside. I feel so girlie. I even giggle like a little girl as he holds me with ease.

He doesn't set me down once we get inside; he walks over to the couch in the living room and lays me down. And then, slowly and gently, he lowers himself on top of me.

THIRTY-FOUR GOING ON BRIDE

"Welcome home," he says, and then starts kissing trails down my neck to my shoulder.

And just like Little Orphan Annie, I think I'm gonna like it here.

It's about the time that my shirt is scrunched up to my neck and Jared's is unbuttoned that we hear a throat clear.

I scream and Jared falls off me like a couple of teenagers that were caught by a mom. We may not be teenagers, but we were caught by a mom. Jared's mom.

Holy crap on a stick.

"Mom," Jared says, his breath ragged as he attempts to pull my shirt down, but it's in vain. It's a tighter shirt and basically it won't budge. Please, just let me die right now. Oh please, oh please, oh please!

"Oh sorry!" Bobby says, covering her eyes. "I'll just go back to my room." She pivots and heads down the hall.

Did she say *her* room? Does she have her own room here? Why do I know nothing about this?

"Jules," Jared says, standing up from the floor. I grab his offered hand and he helps pull me to standing so I can fix my stupid shirt, which I'm burning after today.

"Oh my gosh," I cover my face with my hands. "That was so embarrassing."

"I'm so sorry," he says wearily. He puts a hand through his hair.

"Why is she here?" I ask.

"I don't know. She has a key, though."

"Well, this is awkward," I say, feeling quite sick to my stomach. Clearly I'm going to have to change the locks.

"Let me … let me just go talk to her. I'll be right back," he says.

But before he can get to the hallway, Bobby comes out with her eyes covered.

"Don't mind me, you two. I just need to grab my glasses from the kitchen," she says as she feels her way around with the hand that's not covering her eyes.

"It's okay, Mom," Jared says. "You can open your eyes."

She slowly moves her hand from her eyes as if she isn't sure she should trust us. I take a seat back on the couch, not wanting to make eye contact with her. On a scale of embarrassing, ten being the most embarrassing thing ever, this is like a billion. A hole in the floor that could suck me in right now would be incredibly welcome.

"I'm so sorry," Bobby says. "I just needed to grab my glasses. I had no idea you were here. I thought you went away for the weekend."

"We did," Jared said. "We came back today."

"Well, again, I'm so very sorry," she says.

"It's fine, Mom," Jared says, his voice softening. "What're you doing here anyway?"

"Well, I've got to stay here for a bit," she says.

"What?" Jared says, rather surly.

"That pipe that burst in my house did a lot more structural damage than they thought. I've got mold,

Jared. So I'll need to stay here until they fix it up. It should be done just in time for the wedding."

Jared looks to me, and I shake my head. I know what he's thinking. He's thinking we should tell her we eloped. But he can't do that to her. Or to me. I can't have my mother-in-law hating me. I've worked to foster a fairly good relationship with Bobby, and I'm not going to jeopardize that. We'll have to find another way.

"Can't you stay with Mark?" Jared asks. Yes, Mark. Great idea.

"No way. Did you know that Lisa moved in with him? I can't believe he'd go against everything I stand for. I don't want to be party to that. No thank you." She folds her arms. "Besides, his apartment is much too small. You have plenty of room here. I'll be quiet as a mouse; you won't even know I'm here."

Jared looks at me and I try not to display the what-the-crap look my face wants to contort into. But seriously. What. The. Crap.

My what-the-crap face also encompasses the fact that Mark and Lisa are now living together. I thought they would've broken up by now. Clearly, my prayers haven't been heard. Or perhaps those are the kind of prayers that don't get answered.

"I'll just go back to my room, you two can have the living room all to yourselves. I promise not to interrupt." She gives me a quick smile and then scoots her little petite self back to "her" room.

"Jared," I say as soon as I hear the door close. I'm using hushed tones in case she has supersonic hearing.

"I know," he says, clearly irritated. "We'll figure it out. I could put her up in a hotel or something."

"For six weeks? That'd be ridiculously expensive."

"Do you have any better ideas?" he asks earnestly.

"Not yet. But I'll think of something." I chew on my bottom lip as I contemplate our options.

"You could come stay with me," I say, but know instantly that would be a bad idea. Whether we're here or at my place, we would still be "shacking up" in Bobby's eyes. I probably shouldn't care since this is the twenty-first century and all that, but I do. I don't want to disappoint my mother-in-law. She's going to have plenty of things to hold over my head once she gets to know the real me. I don't need to start out on the wrong foot. Especially a foot she's incredibly passionate about.

"We'll think of something," Jared says as he comes over to the couch and sits next to me. He puts his arm around me and pulls me into him. He gives me a little kiss on my head, and then starts trailing kisses down to my ear and then to my neck. Like he wants to pick up where we left off.

Is he high?

"Are you high?" I pull away from him. "Your mother is in the next room."

"So?" he says, trying to pull me back to him.

"So? I don't think so," I say, lowering my eyebrows in complete resolution. Ain't nothing happening on this couch now. No way. Nuh-uh.

"Fine then, let's go to your place," he says, getting up from the couch. He reaches his hands out for mine and pulls me up to standing.

"Okay," I say, and then lean my head up to kiss him. He may have had a momentary lapse in judgment, but he's still my husband.

My husband. I'm still not truly grasping that.

"Bobby," Jared yells down the hall to his mom.

"Yes?" I hear her muffled from behind her door.

"We're going over to Julia's for a little while."

I hear the door open. "Okay," she says, sounding disappointed. Does she really want us around after she just caught us so … so … Oh gosh, I can't even say it.

"When will you be back?" Bobby asks.

"I'm not sure," Jared says. "I'll call and let you know."

Why do I feel like I've just gone through a wormhole and I'm back in high school?

This is so weird.

CHAPTER 26

Guess how long it took to sell my condo?

One week. One stinking-stupid-piece-of-crap week. Dang you Colorado pot smoking laws. If it weren't for that, I'd have sold my condo like any regular person — it would've taken months and I probably would've lost money. But no. My condo sold in a week, and I made quite the profit as well. Dash it all.

I should be thrilled, I know. But now I'm basically homeless. With Bobby over at Jared's place I can't go there. Not unless I want to be judged and end up on my mother-in-law's crap list. I could move in with Anna, but then instead of constant texts about the wedding, she'd just talk about it all day. I don't think I could deal. If I moved in with Lennon, I'd be babysitting on all my off hours. Plus, when a couple is having issues, it's not very helpful for someone to join the party. Especially family. Although they do seem like they're doing better and when asked, Lennon only gave me a quick nod. I don't think me moving in would help matters though. They need their space.

I have only one option, essentially … my parents' basement. Yes, my adult life has basically come full circle.

Right now I'm sitting in my office at the bakery figuring out another conundrum. Who the heck can I hire to replace Kate? I have to find someone and do it fast. Time is running out. I can't exactly leave for my honeymoon and let Debbie and Patti pick up the slack. They'd quit for sure. I've already asked Beth and she can help a few of the days, but not every day like I need.

I walk out to the kitchen, lean up against one of the metal tables that we do most of our work on, and let out a huge sigh.

"What's eatin' you, darlin'?" Patti asks as she rolls sugar cookie dough out.

"There are no good applicants," I say, and allow my shoulders to droop as far as they'll go.

"You know what I think," Patti says, lifting her eyebrows high in a most reproving kind of way.

"Yes, I know what you think," I say, feeling irritation pulse through me.

"Why don't you just call her? Call Kate and tell her she can have her job back," Patti says.

"Because ... because ... Oh, I don't know," I say. But I do know. It's my pride at stake here. I don't have a ton of pride, honestly. But what I do have, I guard.

"It's your fault, you know," I say, pointing an index finger in her direction. "If it weren't for you complaining about her, I wouldn't have fired her."

She puts a hand on her hip, her lips pursed together. "Darlin', all I said was you need to talk to her. I didn't think you'd go all nuttier than a squirrel turd."

"I ... uh ... wait, what?" I lower my chin, eyeing her through half closed lids.

I did go nutty on her, that's true. In truth, now that the dust has settled, I'm on medication, and Jared and I are secretly married, I can now see that Kate was quite the asset to my bakery. Sure, she changed things, but in truth she saved us tons of money by changing vendors—something I never had the time to do. Patti and Debbie may have hated her cleaning schedules, but we use them now even with her not around.

"Just call her," Patti says, going back to her sugar cookies.

"Oh, okay, fine," I say.

I head back to my office to make the dreaded call. The one where I have to eat crow.

Crow, as I've learned much too often in my life, does not taste good.

~*~

"You really should've gone on drugs earlier," Anna says as we stuff wedding invitations into envelopes.

"What do you mean?" I ask, feeling slightly offended.

"You're just so much more easy-going now," she says. "Not all nut job-y like you've been for the past few months."

"Thanks," I say without intonation. Anna truly has a way with words.

It's not only the meds that are making me feel calm, it's that all things are going fairly well in Juliaville. Well, most things are going well. I've got Kate back. She came with a price, though. I had to give her a raise and also the promise that she could manage the store at some point. I'd already thought this would be a great idea, actually, so that was an easy thing to agree to. Especially if I open a second location, which Jared hasn't brought up once since I told him we needed to put it on hold. But if we do go ahead, she'd be perfect to manage the new store.

For now I can get married — well, I can do the big wedding and then we can go on our Hawaiian honeymoon — and I won't have to worry about the bakery. It'll be in great hands.

Currently, Anna (aka the devil wedding planner) has us in an assembly line — that's how many pieces are going into this invitation. There's tissue paper, an RSVP card with matching envelope, another card with directions to the church and then to the hotel where the reception will be, and, of course, the actual invite.

She's got my mom, Bobby, me, and Brown working on it. My dad was helping, but somehow he's snuck out. I wonder how he did that. I need to know his tricks.

I get to put the actual invite in the envelope, and each time I do, stabs of guilt go through my gut. The card is beautiful with its simple white elegance and letterpress design. It's gorgeous. Of course, Anna picked it out. I mean, she made me feel like I was picking it out by giving me only a couple of choices and then dropping hints on the one she thought would work perfect until I picked it. She's pretty genius that way. An evil genius.

The guilty stabbing pain mainly comes from the wording: "Mr. and Mrs. Raymond S. Dorning, along with Barbara J. Moody and the late James N. Moody, request your presence at the marriage of Julia Warner Dorning and Jared Nathan Moody."

The marriage of ... Our marriage. But we're already married and now this whole thing is feeling like a bit of a sham. I mean, no one else will know, but still. All of the work that everyone went to. I know it was the right thing to do for Jared and me (mostly for me). I know it. But still, I can't help but feel some guilt. I clearly didn't think of all of the consequences. Not to mention it's been near impossible not to tell Anna or Brown. I keep trying to figure out a way to tell them the story without telling them we eloped, but since that's the key element there, it's just not possible.

"Julia, dear, you never told us about your weekend away," my mom says as if reading my mind. She's carefully inserting an RSVP card into an envelope.

"It was ... um ... nice?" Why do I end sentences with a question when I'm not being honest? I need to get some counseling on that. Although I doubt any counselor would help me on my lying skills.

"Well, you seem less stressed," Bobby says.

I can feel her eyes on me, but I act like I'm concentrating on a particular invite and don't look up. I don't want to give away anything with my eyes. Honestly, we should've taken into account that I'm the worst liar ever before Jared and I eloped.

"Okay ladies, we need to focus," Anna says, and I'm suddenly so grateful for her slave-mongering ways. "We have to get these done tonight so they can go out tomorrow."

Only five weeks until the big wedding. I just have to shut my trap for five weeks. It's going to be pure luck that I will, because right now I have very little faith in myself.

CHAPTER 27

"You what?" Brown yells, and I quickly shush her. We're sitting on the couch at her home and no one is around. I don't even know why I shushed her. No one can hear us.

"We eloped," I say in hushed tones. I can't seem to stop keeping up the façade.

I made it two weeks without telling anyone, but it's been building up inside me so much that I needed an ally. Someone I could rely on to keep it a secret. Someone I could talk to. So of course Brown was the perfect person. And I told Jared I was telling her and he was fine with it. Mostly.

"You freaking eloped?" Brown's eyes are wide with disbelief.

Honestly, of all people I thought Brown would be the one to take this piece of news the best, especially considering her love of gossip and the fact that she'd be the only person who would know. Ever. And also because it was romantic as heck to elope. I figured she'd see all of that.

But the look on her face isn't as excited as I thought it'd be. Maybe it's her pregnancy hormones making her act opposite of how she usually does. Maybe I need to up the ante.

"You can't tell anyone, Brown," I say, so she knows she'll be the only person who's privy to this gossip.

"Well, of course not," she says, her eyes piercing into me. "Everyone would be devastated. They've put in so much work. Why did you do it?"

Hmm, yes, a question I've asked myself one too many times these past two weeks. It's not that I regret eloping with Jared — I love being his wife. It's just that I haven't been able to *be* his wife since we can't tell anyone and I'm currently living in my parents' basement and he's living in his condo with his mom.

"Because I couldn't take the pressure of the big wedding. It was making me crazy. So I thought if we eloped then it would make it so there wasn't so much stress on our wedding day, and nothing would have to go perfectly since we were already married."

She stares down her nose at me; I can see her assessing the situation.

"Were you really that overwhelmed with the wedding?" she asks. I know she's pregnant and that was on her mind, but how did she not see all the crazy wafting from my body? I mean, I was certifiable. I still sort of am. I'm more of a recovering certifiably crazy person now.

"Yeessss," I say overdramatically. "Anna was making it so over the top and Bobby's invited half of Denver … I just kept thinking that there was so much riding on it being the most perfect day, and my nerves couldn't take it."

"So do you feel better now?" Her face morphs into something a little more understanding. I think I might be getting through to her.

"Well … " I trail off.

"Julia," she says, the understanding gone. "Explain."

"Okay, so it was super romantic and all of that—well maybe not so much the ceremony, with the officiant being high and all. Oh, and Lia making herself my maid of honor." My mouth starts spewing stuff, in random order.

"Whoa, slow down there, Bessy. Let's back it up and tell me from the beginning," Brown says, her gossip face back on.

"From the beginning. Right. Okay," I say.

So I tell her from the beginning. She knew a lot of it, but I filled in the blanks, like how I convinced Jared to elope at the hospital, to which she tells me that I should never make huge life decisions under the influence of drugs. I mean, I was on pain meds, but this had been on my mind for a while. The drugs just gave me the guts to say it out loud.

I tell her about the actual eloping and how that all went and her tone lightens up exponentially as I explain it. I feel lighter, being able to say it all out loud to someone other than Jared. First of all, Jared is a guy—and so he won't truly discuss things in detail like I want to/need to. Secondly, he was getting sick of the rehash. That's why he was "mostly" okay with me talking to Brown. He was a little against me telling anyone because he didn't want to risk it getting back to Anna or Bobby or any of our family. But especially Anna and Bobby. Brown can be a vault when you need her to, though. So I know I can count on her to keep our secret.

"So let me get this straight. Now that you're married, you're living apart. You, back in your parents' basement, and Jared with his mom in your future condo," she says, her brow creased as she retells the last part of what I just explained.

"Yep," I say flatly.

"Jules," she says, and then she looks like she's going to continue on, but instead she starts laughing. As in she can't breathe, she's laughing so hard.

I have to admit, hearing it all does point out the ridiculousness of the scenario. And it's all just so fitting. It's absolutely something that would happen to me. It's all so very ... Julia.

"Oh my gosh," she says, trying to catch her breath. "That's the best story I've heard in a long time." She wipes her eyes with a tissue that she grabbed from a box on the end table next to her.

"I'm glad I could give you something to laugh about," I say, with a quick, disdainful eye roll to the sky.

"I've been so nauseous lately, it's nice to feel something else," Brown says, leaning her head back against the couch.

"You're nauseous?" I ask, wondering why this is the first I've heard of it.

"Yeah, it just started last week," she says, rubbing her flat stomach. It's hard to believe anything is growing in there.

"That's good, right?" I ask, not actually having a clue if it is or not.

She shrugs. "I guess. It's kind of miserable, but I hate to complain about it. Especially since I should be excited about everything. But honestly, the nausea has made me pretty depressed. It's sort of sucked the fun out of it."

"Does Matt feel the same way?"

"No. He's thrilled. So I have to pretend I'm excited." She looks down at her hand on her stomach. I can see that she's having a pretty decent battle between how she should feel and how she's actually feeling. What an awful thing to go through.

"Brown," I say, putting a hand on hers, which seems to be happening more and more lately — I think we're becoming more touchy-feely friends. "I'm sure it'll go away and then you can be excited again."

"Maybe," she says.

"But even if it doesn't, don't let feeling guilty ruin this all for you. If you feel sick and not excited, then just feel sick. Don't make it worse by adding guilt into it all."

Wow, that was poignant. Especially for me. Marriage has made me wiser. Or maybe it was Oprah.

"You're right. Thanks, Jules," she says with a half-smile.

"Look at the bright side, at least you didn't have to sneak your husband in through your parents' basement window last night and then out before anyone woke up in the morning."

"You didn't!" She says, a smile back on her face.

"Oh, but I did. It felt like we were in high school, actually. It was kind of exciting."

"That actually sounds a little thrilling," she says, her mood brightening substantially at this.

"It really was," I say.

I honestly hate the running around Jared and I have to do now, but at least in the meantime we get to make some fun out of it. Like sneaking him into my parents' basement. Sure, he could just come in the front door — my parents wouldn't really care — but since we're trying to keep up the façade for Bobby, we seem to keep going with it, even for my parents. Plus, we wouldn't want it to get back to Bobby. And my mom is what I call the "innocent gossiper." Meaning, she spreads gossip like wildfire and never even realizes she's doing it.

"Well, I guess I'm happy for you, Jules," Brown says, her lips curving up for the briefest of smiles.

"Thanks," I reply.

"I guess I should start calling you Mrs. Moody now," she says, a twinkle of mischief in her eyes.

"Not so fast," I say, my index finger pointedly warning her. "No one knows I'm Mrs. Moody yet, and they can never know. This one has to go to the grave, okay Brown?"

"Your secret is safe with me." She mimes zipping her lips.

"Thanks. It feels good to tell you," I say.

"I bet it does. How do you anticipate keeping it from everyone else? You're a terrible liar," she says, her head tilting to the side as she questions me.

"I'm only a terrible liar if someone directly asks me a question. No one is going to think we'd actually elope," I say, but then feel a tiny tinge of worry travel down the length of my spine. What if someone does ask?

I only have to make it four weeks. That's it.

I can do this.
I hope.

CHAPTER 28

Mother of all things crappy, if I have to open one more piece of lingerie in front of my mom and Bobby, I might scream.

And everyone is loving it. Squealing in delight with each piece I receive. Sharing stories I never wanted to hear (oh the things that have come out of Patti's and Debbie's mouths). This is the stuff nightmares are made of.

I tried so hard to get out of this whole bridal shower thing, but Anna was not having it. And of course it's pretentious and over-the-top, just like I hate. We're sitting in my parent's living room, which has been decorated in ridiculous amounts. Anna went with a tea party theme. I don't even like tea. And now we have to sit around sipping it and I get to open gifts that are basically x-rated. In front of my mother and future (well, actually current) mother-in-law.

Bobby has been her normal refined self. Unfortunately, this whole lingerie thing has opened up a can of super disgusting worms where my mother is concerned. She's said things about her and my father that I'm pretty sure I'll never be able to scrub from my brain.

My sister-in-law Jenny is here. Poor Jenny. She's about as flabbergasted with it all as I am. I don't remember any of this at Anna's shower.

Oh gosh, please just let me die right now.

If that weren't enough, Lisa is here. My arch nemesis, Lisa. I don't know how I got suckered into inviting her, but Mark mentioned her wanting to come and caught me on a rare moment of insanity (or, not-so-rare) — so I told him to tell her she was welcome to join us. I honestly didn't think she would, but she arrived right on time, her dark silky hair in tow. If Lisa and I ever got into a throw-down (which doesn't seem that far-fetched, honestly), I'd have to do something besides pull her hair like a normal cat-fight. I couldn't bring myself to hurt those silky locks, not matter who they're attached to.

And just so she could offer yet another jab, the ever-so-sweet Lisa's gift was a certificate for a spa that does laser hair removal. She said it was for my "you know what" as she indiscreetly pointed to her upper lip indicating that hair removal was needed on me, which it's *so* not. I had that taken care of long ago. She's the epitome of loveliness. Thank goodness the meds have cured my eye twitch or I'd be twitching all over the place right now.

I, for reals, hate her.

"Open mine next," says Brown.

"I'm afraid," I say.

"You should be," she replies, her eyebrows doing a double lift.

Anna hands me a large, beautifully wrapped box. It certainly feels too heavy for lingerie. Of course with Brown, it could be whips and chains. Please don't let it be that. I look at Brown with questioning eyes and she motions with her head for me to open it.

I take my time removing the ribbon and opening the foil-striped blue paper because I don't want to rip up all of the work she put into it, and I also want to put off what I might find in here. I start pulling out the tissue paper until my hand hits something hard. Definitely not lingerie. I reach in with both hands and pull out a cutting board. A gorgeously stained wood cutting board and engraved in the center is *Mr. and Mrs. Moody*, along with the date of the wedding. It's simply stunning.

"I love it," I say as my fingers feel around the inscription. Maybe it's because of my new medication, or maybe it's because I've just opened a bunch of dirty lingerie and I've finally been given a reprieve, but my eyes well up at the thoughtfulness of this gift.

"Thank you, Brown," I say, almost in a whisper.

"You're welcome. And there's something else." She points to the box still in my lap.

I pass the cutting board to Anna and she sets it with the other gifts and then I look under another layer of tissue paper. There I find his and her matching g-string underwear that say "Mr." and "Mrs." on the front.

Brown starts laughing hysterically and everyone joins in as she pulls them out of my hand and holds them up for everyone to see. I swear I've blushed more in the past hour than I ever have in my entire life.

"Oh, Betsy, those are darling," my mom exclaims.

"Darling, mom? Really?" I say, not being able to help myself.

"They're a far cry better than your granny panties," Anna interjects.

"How dare you," I say to Anna, and then I grab the offending underwear (if you can even call it that—they don't look like they cover much) and tuck them into one of the bags I've already opened.

"You've saved the best for last," Patti says, as Anna hands me the last present—a colorful gift bag that feels rather full. I simultaneously want to be grateful that this is the last gift, and also cry because it's from Patti and there is no way she's gotten me something tasteful.

"This is from both Patti and me," Debbie chimes in and then stifles a giggle.

Oh my dear heavens, I don't even want to know.

I peek in the bag. Crap of all craps, it's basically a bag full of wedding night paraphernalia. An entire freaking bag full. Creams, his and her gels, and a blindfold and—good gracious, is that a whip?

"What's inside?" Bobby asks.

"Uh..." I sputter. "It's just, uh—"

"Oh let her see it," Patti cuts me off, pulling the bag out from me and dumping the entire contents onto the floor in front of everyone.

All I can do is cover my face with my hands as everyone in unison starts talking and laughing as they fish through the loot. Even Jenny joins in. That traitor.

I would so love for this day to be over. Like, right now.

"Oh Julia dear, look how much fun you can have," my mom says as she picks up a tube of what I can only guess is lubricant.

I hate my life.

"You know, when Raymond and I first used something like this, it changed everything for us," she says and others nod at her in agreement.

Oh no, please, no more stories. Dear Lord, if I promise to dump this entire marriage and join a convent, will you please get me out of this?

"Well if you think that's fun, you should try this," Patti says, and hands a can of something that looks like mousse to my mother.

"Oh!" she looks at the can and then giggles. "Do you really think so?"

Please. Make. It. Stop.

"Ladies!" Anna yells above the racket. "It's time for cake!"

Just like that everyone abandons my gifts from Patti and Debbie and heads over to where the cake is. Apparently the only thing that can get women to stop talking about wedding night paraphernalia is chocolate cake. I'll need to remember that for future use.

CHAPTER 29

I'm in such a good place right now.

Not emotionally or anything. I'm just currently eating chocolate.

Anna has made me limit my chocolate before the wedding and honestly, it's been tough. I mean, what is there to live for without chocolate? So when I finally do sneak a little, it's like heaven. Honestly, if heaven isn't one big chocolate fountain party, then I'm not sure I want to go.

I'm actually doing better emotionally. Even being separated from my husband and still having to pull off this massive wedding, I'm feeling so much more relaxed. Only two weeks until we can make this charade official, so that's making things easier as well.

Not only that, I've been exercising more. The doctor told me the best thing you can do for anxiety is to get exercise. I scoffed at first, of course. I may be a lot of things, but athletic isn't one of them. I have to admit getting outside does help my soul, as cheesy as that sounds.

Things at the bakery are going well. I've relinquished so many of my duties and let Kate take the reins, and Patti and Debbie don't seem to mind. I think they're just glad to have her back. Kate has stepped on my toes a couple of times, but each time I let her know (kindly, of course) and she quickly fixes it. I'm like totally using adult communication here. I'm so proud of myself.

I hear the jingle of the bells from the door to the bakery opening. I have my back to the entrance while I wolf down this triple chocolate brownie of which dreams are made from.

"Hello Julia," Bobby says to my back and I nearly choke on the last bite of brownie. I was not expecting her.

I quickly wipe my mouth with the back of my hand and then turn around. "Hi Bobby," I say, trying not to open my mouth too wide for fear there is chocolate all over my teeth.

"Can I have a quick word?" She asks, and then her mouth goes into a thin straight line.

Dear mother of all things crappy, what have I done now? Please don't let her have found out about Jared and I eloping.

"Sure," I say.

She takes a seat at a table and places her purse in her lap. So I guess we have to sit down for this discussion. Even lovelier. I open the door to the kitchen and ask Debbie if she can man the front for a minute and then walk over to the table to take a seat across from Bobby. The chocolate brownie is suddenly feeling like a huge rock in my stomach as my belly swirls with nerves.

"What can I do for you?" I ask Bobby, hopeful that this isn't the same scenario as the last time she visited me at the bakery.

"Did you tell Lisa that you hated roses?" she says, getting right to her point.

Oh em gee, that's it. I'm actually going to have to kill Lisa. Or have Lia put a spell on her. I mean how much havoc can one person wreak on my life? I do enough damage to myself; I don't need the help.

"No," I say emphatically. "I never said that."

Bobby looks down at her purse in her lap and I'm having serious bouts of déjà vu. Although it's not déjà vu at all. I've literally been in this exact same situation not all that long ago.

"Well she told me that you said that you hated roses and that you didn't know why I was making you have them at the wedding."

I wrack my brain trying to think of what I actually said because obviously words were twisted here. I can't even recall the conversation. It probably wasn't even with Lisa. She probably just overheard me talking, that little snitch. I guess I'll have to do the only thing I can do here: be honest.

"I don't hate roses," I tell Bobby. "They're just not my favorite."

"Well why didn't you say something, then?" she asks, her brow furrowed.

"Because I don't really care that much," I say.

"So you don't care about your wedding," she says, oozing aggravation.

"No! I mean," I pause trying to think of what I mean. "I just mean that I don't mind the flowers we have. Besides, it's all set. We only have two weeks until the wedding, so it doesn't matter. We can't change anything."

Gah! I'm terrible at wording things.

"You know, if you'd just say something, you wouldn't have to settle for something you don't like," she says, not quite as huffy as before.

"I don't say anything because, well, I feel like this is your wedding too," I say.

"What do you mean?"

"You only have sons, so you'll never get the chance to plan a wedding. I want this wedding to be about you, too."

She sits for a moment and I wonder what she's thinking about.

"That's really sweet," she says, her eyes looking a little watery.

"Anyway, I thought you weren't going to listen to Lisa anymore," I say, wishing once again that Mark would just break up with her already.

"Oh," she purses her lips together briefly. "I don't know why I let that girl get under my skin."

"You're not alone," I say, rolling my eyes and shaking my head.

We sit in not-so-comfortable silence for a moment.

"What happened to make you dislike her so much? I mean, besides the obvious reasons," I ask, feeling like this is the perfect time for her to finally tell me.

She sighs. "I caught her cheating on Jared," she says.

I'm not sure what I was expecting, but I wasn't expecting that.

"You caught her cheating? How?" I ask. I mean, that's really random. Your boyfriend's mom catches you cheating on said boyfriend?

She sighs again. "It was just one of those wrong place, wrong time moments for Lisa. And right place, right time for me."

I nod my head, trying to get her to give me a little more information than that.

"I was out to dinner with a friend, and we just happened to try a new restaurant we'd never been to before. It was across town. I don't think I'd ever been in that area of town before, actually. Anyway, the restaurant had tall, secluded booths curtained off throughout, and my friend and I thought it'd be kind of fun. We could gossip and no one would hear us."

She looks up at me and I nod for her to continue.

"Anyway, so we're enjoying our dinner and enjoying the seclusion of it all, but we could hear some … uh … things going on in the booth next to us."

"Oh, gosh," I say, trying not to conjure up all the "things" she could've been hearing.

"I felt like I should complain to the manager or something. But as I got up to do so, the person in the booth next to me was exiting her booth as well. So imagine my surprise when I come face to face with Lisa."

My eyes bug out of my head, even though I was pretty sure who that person would be.

"I, of course, assume she's with Jared and being completely disappointed in him, I tear open the curtains, only to find someone else. Lisa begged me not to tell him and that it was a huge mistake and gave me all of those excuses everyone seems to use when they get caught cheating."

"Wow," is all I can say.

"So then I tell her that she'd better break up with Jared or I was going to tell him myself. And so she did. She broke off that ridiculous engagement, but she used some excuse like they'd grown apart or something. I never told Jared that I caught her cheating."

"Why didn't you tell him?" I'd think that if it were my son, I would want him to know.

"I didn't want to break his heart. I didn't see the point of it. Lisa was out of our lives, and from the looks of it, Jared seemed kind of relieved that it was over. So I never said anything. But then she waltzes in with Mark, and I keep hoping he'll move on from her like he does all the rest, but he seems completely taken with her. And her with him."

"Aren't you worried she'll cheat on Mark?" I ask.

She shrugs, "It would probably serve him right if she did. But no. She looks at Mark in a completely different way than she ever did with Jared. I hate to say it, but I think they might actually work out."

So Lisa was a cheater ... on my poor Jared. I mean, I'm truly grateful she did or I probably wouldn't be sitting here with Bobby. But still, how terrible. I wish I could say it was totally shocking, but after all the crap she's put me through, it's not.

It looks like I need to give up on my prayers that they'll break up before the wedding. Bummer.

CHAPTER 30

I can't think of a time that I've laughed this hard.

Honestly, my stomach actually hurts from laughing. And there's not an ounce of alcohol involved either. I'm in a hotel room playing "Would You Rather" with Anna and Brown. Brown has just announced that she would choose eating Brussels sprouts for the rest of her life rather than having everyone one else in the world laugh like Fran Drescher. I think I'd choose the same. But then that got us on a tangent of trying to do that terrible nasally laugh that Fran Drescher does, and it's hilarious. It also might be one of those things where we're laughing so much and it's getting late, so everything sounds funny. If anyone else were to walk in right now, I doubt they'd find it as hilarious as we do.

Anna and Brown respected my wishes and planned my bachelorette party just the way I wanted it. Only the three of us, eating a bunch of junk food and hanging out in a posh hotel. We're in a junior suite at the Hotel Monaco and it's stunning with its bright colors and modern furniture. This was one of the venues that Anna had taken me to for the reception and now I'm wondering why I didn't pick it. It's gorgeous.

It's been the bachelorette party of my dreams, really. We made a pact not to talk too much about the wedding and simply have fun. The only thing I did do was read my vows to them. Yes, I was finally able to write them. Anna said they "didn't totally suck" (I'm pretty sure she was kidding—I hope), and Brown—being Brown—had me reword a few things that didn't make much difference in the end. All I care about is that they're done and passable.

"I'm exhausted," Brown announces while eating out of a carton of Ben and Jerry's. I think this baby only craves sugar because that's all she seems to be eating. I've seen Brown eat more sugar in the past five weeks than I have in all the years I've known her.

"Me too," I agree, yawning.

"You two are so old," Anna says, looking at the clock in the room. It's only eleven thirty.

"Yes, well, I'm trying to grow kidneys right now," Brown says, patting her belly. That's her excuse for everything these days. She must read online about every milestone her baby is making because she always knows what's happening with its growth. "I'm growing a spine." "I'm growing a liver." "I'm growing fingers." Sometimes it's like she's the only pregnant person that ever existed.

It's not getting on my nerves—I love it. It's definitely getting on Anna's, but I think that's more because she's jealous. I don't have any desire to be pregnant right now. I can barely handle my life as it is.

"I can't believe it's only a week until the wedding," Anna says, laying her head back on the bed we've been sitting on. "Can you believe you'll be a married woman in a week, Julia?"

Brown gives me a raised eyebrow that only I catch. I do feel terribly guilty not telling Anna. Her and Brown are my best friends, and it feels like a betrayal on so many levels.

But what's done is done. And frankly, I'm a little proud of myself for not spilling the beans. Every week that passes seems to get easier and easier. Plus there's the fact that even though Jared and I are married, we haven't been able to be a married couple at all. His mom's house is nearly ready and it looks like she'll be staying with Jared right up until the wedding. And I'm still in my parents' basement.

"I don't know if I've said it enough, but thank you for all of your work on the wedding, Anna," I say, feeling suddenly sentimental. I mean, this wedding would've been a total disaster without her, and I can say this with complete confidence.

"Yes, well you've been terrible to work with," she says with a smirk. But then the smirk turns into a tiny smile. She's teasing me, but she's only half joking. I totally understand. I probably have been terrible to work with. Not that she's been a walk in the park, either. I'm not going to go there right now, though.

"I know," I say with a sigh. "I'm trying to be better."

"I've noticed that in the past few weeks you've seemed to calm down," she says.

"Must be the drugs," I say. I'm not discounting the anxiety medication I'm on; I'm sure that's helping. I know it is, actually. But I do think eloping with Jared has given the big wedding less importance and now I don't feel so scared of it.

"Well I haven't done much for this wedding, but I'm going to take credit for getting you and Jared together in the first place," Brown says, and then spoons some more ice cream into her mouth.

"Uh, I think I can take some credit there, too," Anna says, looking almost defensive.

"I'm pretty sure you both can take credit there," I say. It's true, if it weren't for Anna and Brown, I'm quite confident my neurosis would've either ruined things before they started, or killed it soon after. I'm a victim of my own brain sometimes. Okay, a lot of the time. But I'm learning to handle it.

I guess I have Jared to thank for bringing me closer to both Anna and Brown. Until he came into my life, Brown and I were only work friends taking smoke breaks (well, Brown was doing the smoking) and going to the odd lunch now and then. Now she's an essential part of my life. A true best friend.

Anna and I were barely sisters up until Jared came into the picture. If it weren't for all the shopping and makeover things we did together, I don't know if Anna and I would be as close as we are today. She's now my sister and my confidant. We may show it differently than other siblings, but we love each other. More now than ever.

Without even knowing it, Jared gave me my life back. I'd hope that I would've eventually found it myself somehow. But who knows. Things worked out how they were supposed to. I'm totally confident of that.

CHAPTER 31

Well we made it. It's finally time for the big wedding. Everything appears to be going well. No one is running around frantic. Even Anna seems calm. It's like now that the pressure of the perfect day is no longer an issue for me, it's affecting everyone. The flowers showed up on time, the minister is here and ready to go (and not high). A clear traffic pattern has everyone arriving on time. We could possibly start the ceremony when we're supposed to, which is unheard of.

There's just one itty-bitty problem. I've been throwing up all morning. I'm no doctor or anything, but I'm fairly confident I have the stomach flu.

That was not a twist I was expecting, nor had I factored this one in. You got me again, karma.

Presently, I'm leaning over a toilet, after Anna made me try some soda crackers and Sprite to help calm my stomach. It worked for about ten minutes before it all came up.

Honestly, I'd lie on this bathroom floor all day if I could. I'm in a robe and my hair is up with a scarf wrapped carefully around it, as to not mess it up. See? There's a silver lining: my hair's up so at least no one has to hold it back while I spew. That's essentially the teeniest, tiniest silver lining ever.

"I take it that didn't work," Anna says from the other side of the door. Clearly she heard the up-chucking.

"No," I say, my throat feeling tight. I kind of want to cry, and I totally would if it weren't for the fact that it'd ruin my makeup and Anna would most likely kill me. Although, at this point, death isn't sounding so terrible …

"Come on out, Brown's here," she says.

I decide that lying down on the bathroom floor isn't my best move at this point, so I acquiesce and leave the bathroom.

"Hey Brown," I say, wrapping my arms around my midsection. "Got any miracle cures for the stomach flu?"

"You look pale," Brown says as soon as she gets a glimpse of me.

"Yes, thank you," I say sarcastically. I've been puking my guts up all morning, of course I look pale.

"Too much to drink last night?" she asks, her eyebrows lifting high.

"Um, no. It was the rehearsal dinner and you were there. Since I have a terrible track record of drinking at rehearsal dinners and messing things up, I decided to refrain," I say, remembering last year when I nearly ruined Anna's wedding at her rehearsal dinner. Fun times.

Come to think of it, I was feeling a touch sick last night. I thought it might be nerves or something, which is silly because I wasn't really feeling nervous.

The rehearsal dinner was at the Paramount Café, which has a lot of meaning for Jared and me. It was where we officially started our relationship.

"That's true," Brown says looking over at Anna and winking. "Nope, definitely not a hangover, then. That, I can fix. But the flu? Not so much."

"Thanks for trying," I say, and then lie down on the chaise lounge that I'm so grateful they have in this dressing room.

The room is actually rather quaint. I was picturing a ruddy old church classroom, but they must do a lot of weddings here, because this room is definitely fit for a bride. Beautiful drapery hangs around the windows and a lovely vanity is set up in the corner that we can use to do makeup and hair. Although we had the hair stylist and makeup artist meet us at the hotel this morning, so there's not much use for it today. Thank goodness Anna is here for touch-ups before I walk down the aisle. That's *if* I'm able to walk down the aisle.

I don't feel the normal achiness that I usually get when I have the flu, thank goodness, so hopefully I can just sit here for a few minutes and miraculously feel better. I do believe in miracles, and we're at a church, after all.

"What can we do for you Jules?" Brown asks.

"There's really nothing," I say closing my eyes as I lean back on the chaise. "Anna's already tried. I think I just need to rest."

"Well, you can't rest too long," Anna says. "We still need to get you into your dress and touchup your makeup. You're set to walk down the aisle in an hour."

I don't have the heart or the energy to tell her she might have to wheelbarrow me down at this point.

"How are you feeling, Brown?" I ask wearily, still keeping my eyes closed, trying not to think of the situation I'm in right now.

"Pretty good, actually," she says brightly. "I mean, I still have a little morning sickness, but it hasn't been that bad."

I could tell she felt better last week at the bachelorette party. The nausea was no longer overshadowing the pregnancy. And I know she's not that far along, but she's already glowing, I swear.

"Are you pregnant yet, Anna?" she asks. I briefly open my eyes to see that Brown has taken a seat on the couch and is watching Anna as she steams a part of my dress, which is hanging up on the door.

"No, and it's likely not happening soon," Anna says.

"I thought you were going to accidentally forget to take the pill," Brown says. I can hear the humor in her voice. I sincerely hope she's kidding.

"That was a thought," Anna says, no humor in her voice. Dear heavens, will this kid ever learn?

"I mean, it happens all the time. I had a friend who took her pill just six hours late and she got pregnant," Brown says.

My eyes pop open. "That's ridiculous. That's not how the pill works," I say to her.

"Uh, earth to Julia, that's totally how it works. You have to take the pill at the same time every day."

"I know that, but missing six hours won't get you pregnant," I say, shaking my head.

"Tell that to my friend. She swears that's how she got pregnant," Brown says.

"Anyway," she says, directing her attention back to Anna, "what if you accidentally missed a day or something?"

Anna, bats away the idea with her hand. "I think I'd rather Jonathon and I be on the same page instead of tricking him into it."

Well, I jumped to conclusions. Maybe Anna is growing up after all.

We sit in silence for a bit, and something starts to nibble at the back of my mind. It's one of those nettling thoughts that I'm not even sure what it is exactly, but there's like a tiny voice wanting to be heard in the deepest part of my brain and I can't seem to grasp a hold of it.

It must be about the pill. That was the thing I'd forgotten on my trip with Jared when we eloped. I didn't take it for two days. It was near the beginning of the pack, so I wasn't too concerned. I mean, there was no way I was ovulating. I remembered when I got back from the trip and started right back up. It was then that I realized that according to my pill I'd have my time of the month during our honeymoon, so I called my doctor and we did one of those tricks where you skip your period with another packet of pills, so I've yet to start my period.

Hold on a second …

I didn't take the pill for two entire days. What if Brown's friend was telling the truth? If taking it later in the day would cause her to get pregnant, what about two whole days? And what do I know about when I ovulate? It's not like I've ever had a reason to track it.

I wait a bit of time until Anna and Brown have moved onto a completely different topic and then say, "Hey Brown, how many weeks after you found out you were pregnant did the morning sickness kick in?"

She gives me an odd look.

"Just curious," I say, and pick a piece of fluff off my robe to prove my nonchalance about the whole subject. I will not freak out. Not yet, at least.

"Um …," she starts counting something on her fingers. "About six weeks, I think."

Sweet mother of all that's holy.

I stay perfectly still, assessing the situation. I need to get a test. I'm sure I'm not pregnant, but I need to find out just in case. And I need to do it now. I can't wait until after the wedding. It'll bother me the entire time.

I once again wait until Anna and Brown change the subject so the whole pregnancy talk is over, and I can do this without either of them catching on.

I'm actually a little shocked Brown hasn't put two and two together. She's usually ridiculously good at figuring things out. Maybe she has pregnancy brain already. I've heard you forget things when you're knocked up.

Once they're discussing when they should get into their bridesmaids dresses, I carefully stand up from my chaise and grab my purse and walk to the door.

"Where do you think you're going?" Anna asks as I open the door.

"Um," I say, trying to think of an excuse. "I'm just going to run to the drug store. I'm going to grab some antacid and see if that will help."

Wow, that was a quick lie for me. I usually stumble and stutter them out.

"There's one a block down the street. I'll go get it for you," Anna says. She moves to go find her purse.

"No!" I say louder than I intended. "I mean, I think some fresh air will help this stomach bug."

"Julia," Anna says, looking me up and down, "You can't go outside like that."

I catch a glimpse of myself in the mirror. I'm wearing a white robe, slippers, and my hair up in a scarf that makes me look rather crazy-old-lady-ish. But I don't care.

"I'll be discreet, I can just pop out the back," I say, one foot out the door.

"You can't!" Anna says frantically. "What if someone sees you? What if Jared sees you? That's bad luck!"

"Seriously Jules," Brown says. "I can go grab it."

"No!" I say. Good gracious, I'm a freaking adult. I can go where I want.

"I'm a freaking adult, and I can go where I want," I say out loud, and they both look at me like I've lost it.

Anna rolls her eyes. "You don't have much time Julia," she looks at her watch.

"Just let her go," Brown says to Anna. "She's clearly having some wedding jitters. Heaven knows I had them." She really did, and I had to talk her down on her wedding day. She winks at me because she knows it's not that. I'm not sure what she thinks it is, but I'm eternally grateful that she always has my back.

I don't even wait for Anna's reply. I step out the door and then carefully work my way out the back of the church. I'm heading in the direction of the drug store (which thankfully doesn't have me going through the parking lot of the church), as quickly as my slipper-clad feet can carry me.

I have to navigate around some potholes on the way (I took a shortcut through another parking lot and a very shady alleyway) but within a few short minutes I'm inside the drugstore and making a beeline to the pregnancy tests.

I've never bought a pregnancy test before; I don't even have a clue where to find them. I look in the section where the tampons are located and I find kits for other stuff, but no pregnancy tests.

Crap. I'm going to have to ask someone. Of course I do. In fact, I'm pretty sure the pregnancy tests were right here before I walked up to the aisle, but karma knew I was coming and had them moved just so I could add to my humiliation.

I walk over to the pharmacy counter—me, looking like I do, and feeling nausea sweep over me in full force—and ask the attendant where I can find a pregnancy test.

"Oh, we keep them back here," says a young man, who, according to his tag, goes by Barry. "They get stolen a lot."

Wow, that's pretty sad, if you think about it. Of course at this point, I'm so desperate to have one, I could see myself grabbing it and running, totally forgetting to pay. So maybe more times than not people are just so frantic at the possibility of bringing another person into this world that they temporarily lose their mind. I can definitely relate.

"Okay, so can I get one?" I ask, furrowing my brow. I mean, I would've assumed my asking where they were would have been enough information for him to grab me one. It's not like I'm doing research for further use.

"Sure," Barry says, making a one-eighty degree pivot and going to a back counter where there are boxes and bottles stacked.

"Do you want digital or regular?" he asks rather loudly.

Digital or regular? Isn't it supposed to be two lines or something like that? Is one better than the other? It really should be much easier than this.

"Uh, I'm not sure," I say, trying to keep my voice low and hope that he'll follow suit.

"One's considered more accurate than the other," Barry yells, obviously not catching the clue. "With digital, there's no question. It simply says 'pregnant' or 'not pregnant.'"

Oh, yippee. People are lining up behind me. This is becoming super fun by the minute.

"I'll take digital then," I say, feeling slightly frantic and oh-so-very nauseated.

"Digital it is," he says in a loud, peppy tone. "Oh wait, do you want one test or two?"

"Just one," I say, a little more snap to my voice than I intended. Why would I want more than one? To confirm?

"So you want just one of the digital?" He asks, his voice growing ever louder.

"Yes," I almost hiss.

He brings the box up to the counter and sets it down in front of me.

"I can check you out here, if you like," he says.

"Great," I say, pulling my wallet out.

Barry scans the barcode on the box and then types some stuff into the register.

"Huh, that's weird," he says, picking up the box and looking at it. "I think this is on sale, but it's not giving me the sale price." He meanders back to the shelf where he grabbed the box and looks around. Meanwhile the line behind me is growing longer by the minute.

"It's fine," I squeak out, "I'll pay whatever price. I'm kind of in a hurry here."

This gives the pharmacist pause as he turns to look me up and down.

"I'm getting married, and my wedding is in—" I look up at the clock on the wall and then back down at him, "forty minutes."

Barry looks at the pregnancy test in his hand and then at me and a smile spreads across his face. "I think you bought the cart before the horse," he says.

Well, that's some nerve …

"Listen," I say, my hands going to my hips, "not that it's any of your business, but I'm already married. We eloped six weeks ago. And anyway it doesn't matter. Getting pregnant before you're married is totally twenty-first century. Everyone knows that."

A loud gasp escapes from someone behind me. Seriously? Are people really that judge-y? I turn around to see who it was that made the noise and — holy crap in a jar — it's Lisa. Her eyes are wide, and her hand is covering her mouth like she's just heard the pope died.

I close my eyes. Not only have I just revealed to my arch nemesis that Jared and I eloped, but she now knows I might be pregnant.

For the love of all things sucky.

I make my purchase, slip the test into my purse, and then walk over to Lisa.

"So," I say, and then begin to nibble on my bottom lip.

"So," she says, a small smile appearing on her face.

We stand there in silence. Me in my headscarf, white robe, and slippers. Lisa in a form-fitting deep-red cocktail dress, her dark hair shiny as ever.

"How do you get your hair so shiny?" I ask out of the blue.

"What?" she asks, totally confused.

I shake my head. Clearly, a diversion isn't going to work here. I'm a terrible diverter, and Lisa isn't a toddler.

"Look," I say, and then exhale. "Obviously, I would appreciate you not repeating anything you just heard."

She just looks at me.

"Lisa, I don't have to explain my choices to you, but I'd be grateful if you'd keep this to yourself until Jared and I have said something. There are a lot of feelings that will get hurt if this comes out from the wrong person." Or at all, really. But I'm not going to tell her that. I see now that we'll probably have to tell. Maybe we can wait a month or two after the wedding.

She contemplates that for a moment. Almost as if she's assessing whether to use this bit of info against me or not. Is she truly that evil?

"Look, I know you don't like me, Lisa—that's pretty obvious. I'm not even sure why. It's not like I've ever done anything to you." Whoa, where is this coming from? "And I don't know where this thing is going between you and Mark, but if it keeps going," I pause to take a large breath, "we're going to have to figure out how to get along."

"What do you even mean?" she asks, her eyebrows pulled together so close they almost form a V.

I eye her, my forehead scrunched. So I'm going to need to spell this out for her?

"Let's see," I start counting off with my fingers, "you've insulted me, my bakery, wrote an underhandedly mean newspaper article about me, in fact, *all* of your comments toward me are underhandedly rude. And you've managed to get my mother-in-law angry with me, not once, but twice, with your big mouth."

"I…" she starts but then stops herself. She does this twice more.

Aha! I've stumped her. She has no words. This must be new for her.

"I'm sorry," she says, almost inaudibly.

Wait ... what? She's sorry? Did she really apologize just like that? No excuses, no underhanded jabs?

"You're sorry?"

"Yes, Julia," she rolls her eyes. "I'm sorry. I didn't mean to make you feel bad. I had no idea I was so underhandedly rude."

I say nothing. Can someone really be that obliviously rude? I don't think it's possible.

She sighs. "I guess, I'm ... oh, I don't know. I mean, I ruined what I had with Jared and now it's like I have this chance with Mark, but I feel like the whole thing's tainted with Bobby now. Because of my previous actions." She looks away from me and down to the floor. I know what those "previous actions" are, but I'm not going to tell her that. "And I'm not the same person. I really like Mark and I want things to work out for us."

Well, that makes one of us.

"Anyway," she continues, "then I find out Mark is Jared's brother and all I want is for Bobby to like me and then I see you and you're just all..." she trails off, motioning at my outfit with her hand.

I roll my eyes. "A disaster?" I interject.

"No!" She says, emphatically. "You're just so ... so ... cute. You get away with your natural look that took you probably minutes to do, while I struggle for hours for this." She gestures to herself with her hands. "Do you know how much time I spend in the gym, at the spa, and at the dermatologist to do all of this?"

I'm dumbstruck.

"Not to mention the expense of it all," she keeps going. "Do you know how much Botox costs? It's not cheap."

"Well ... I .... Er..." I try to speak.

"Anyway, you just do you," she says, gesturing once again to me. "And I guess I'm a little jealous. Or a lot."

I look down at my robe. "You're jealous of me?"

"Don't rub it in, Julia."

"I'm not. I'm confused. I mean, look at me," I point to myself, "And look at you," I point to her. She's a flawless goddess in a skin-tight cocktail dress, and I'm all homeless junkie in a robe and headscarf.

"Yeah well, things aren't always what they seem on the surface, are they," she says.

I ponder her words for a moment. I don't know if anyone has ever been jealous of me, or at least admitted to it. It's usually me that's the jealous one.

"Don't you have a wedding to go to?" She asks, looking up at the clock that's on the wall behind me.

I turn around and look at it too. Only thirty minutes left.

"Crap, yes I do."

"I'm glad we talked," she says, a half smile on her face.

"Me too," I say, returning the smile.

"I'll see you in thirty minutes, then," she says.

"Yep," I say, nodding my head. I turn and start walking toward the door.

"Julia," Lisa says from behind me.

"Yes?" I turn back and look at her.

"Your secret is safe. I promise. Or I guess I should say 'secrets,'" her eyes move to my purse where she and I both know the pregnancy test awaits.

"Thank you," I say, and then give her a small closed-mouth smile.

"Oh, and Julia?" she calls me back just as I start walking away again.

"Yeah?"

"Moroccan Oil," she says, running a hand through her silky locks.

"Huh?" I scrunch my eyes at her.

"It's the secret to shiny hair."

"Oh, right. Good to know," I say.

"Now you know one of my secrets," she says, a twinkle in her eye.

I just smile. I'm pretty sure my secrets outweigh hers by a freaking ton, but whatever, I'll take it.

CHAPTER 32

Pregnant.

Holy crap of all craps. I'm pregnant. Me. Julia Dorning Moody is knocked up.

I so totally can't even right now.

I'm sitting on the floor in the bathroom because I was finding it hard to stand. Also, I barfed right after I saw the results and it was just easier to stay down.

I'm not sure what I should do. Obviously I need to tell Jared, but I'm thinking it's pretty safe to assume that with Bobby's traditional ways, I'm quite certain a baby before marriage would not go over well with her. And six weeks into it, it's going to be easy to do the math. Only, the reality is the pregnancy didn't happen before the marriage; we were already married. So what do we do? Tell our families—who've put their time and energy into this wedding to make it the best day ever for us—that we ran away and eloped? Or do we say we had a major oops before the wedding? It doesn't seem like either option will go over very well.

One thing's for sure: I need to talk to Jared. My stomach drops at the thought. I don't know how he's going to take it because we were planning on waiting at least a little while. Plus we don't live in a family-friendly condominium. We'll have to move. We're totally going to have to uproot everything because I forgot my pill. How will he take it? I guess there's only one way to find out.

"Anna," I yell from my spot on the floor.

"Yes?" she says through the door.

"I need to talk to Jared. Can you get him for me?"

"Can't it wait? We need to get you dressed and your hair done," she says.

"No, it can't wait. I need to talk to him now."

"Okay, but only through the door," she says. "And make it fast."

"Anna, I don't care about stupid traditions. Would you just get him for me?"

Seriously, our lives are about to change completely, and Anna's worried about some stupid superstition about how Jared and I can't see each other before the wedding? Plus, we're already married. So there's that.

A few minutes later there's a soft knock at the door. "Jules?" I hear Jared's voice and I swear just hearing it makes everything feel better.

Even if he's not thrilled with the idea, he'll learn to be. We both will. Although I can't lie, part of me is feeling something verging on thrilled. It's just being slightly overshadowed by the fact that we may have to come clean about eloping, and also the morning sickness. I could do without that.

I stand up slowly and go over to the door, opening it.

"No!" Anna screams when she sees me open the door.

"Get over it Anna," I yell back and open the door wide enough for Jared to come in, then shutting the door behind him.

He looks very double-oh-seven in his tuxedo. I kind of want to attack him right here in the bathroom, if it weren't for Anna screaming outside the door to "make it quick." And the looming feeling of wanting to barf. How will I endure nine months of this? How will everyone endure my whining for nine months?

"How're you feeling?" he asks, pulling me into his arms. Tears immediately form in the corners of my eyes. Just being in his arms makes me feel so safe. I can handle anything with Jared's arms around me.

"I," I cut off with a sniffle. The tears have now accumulated and are moving down my face.

"Are you crying?" He pulls back to see my face. "Jules, what's wrong?" The concern on his face makes the tears come faster.

"Um, well," I don't know how to say this. So I pull out of his arms and take him by the hand over to the test that's sitting on the top of the toilet. I nod my head toward it.

"Is that—" he cuts off as his eyes widen when he sees the pregnancy test. "Is that what I think it is?"

I nod my head yes hesitantly. I'm looking at his face, but I'm still not sure how he's feeling by his facial expressions. He looks confused. Or maybe scared. Or both. He's probably not quite sure how he feels. I know I'm not.

He looks at the test and then looks back at me, and then looks at the test again. He reaches out and lifts it up, as if he can't believe it's real.

"But … how?" he asks, looking at me.

"Um," I wring my hands together. How will he take this? "I sort of forgot to take my pill for a couple of days."

I search his face. But his expression is still more contemplative as he takes in this information. Oh gosh, please don't be mad at me. It was a simple mistake that has now changed our lives forever. So yeah, kind of a big mistake.

"You forgot your pill," he repeats in a monotone voice looking down at the test again.

"Jared, I—" I start to apologize, but the hand that's not holding the test comes up to his face and covers it. And his shoulders begin to shake.

Oh, pile of crap, I think he's crying. My stomach sinks. I've ruined things.

"Jared?" I ask softly, putting a hand on his shoulder.

He takes his hand away from his eyes, and I can see them—actual tears streaming down his face. My heart beats faster and my mind goes numb trying to come up with something to say. Some way to save this.

But before I can, he puts the test down on the counter and then he does something I wasn't expecting—he puts his arms around me and buries his face into my neck.

He whispers something into my neck so quiet I can't even catch what he's saying.

"What?" I ask softly.

He pulls his head back so he's now looking in my eyes. "Thank you," his voice breaks a little when he repeats what he had said.

"Thank you?" I question, my eyes searching his for answers. Thank you for what? For giving him a reason to jump ship? For making our already complicated lives that much crazier?

"Thank you for this," he says, picking up the pregnancy test again and looking at it.

"Oh my gosh, you're happy?" I say, seeing the biggest smile spread across his face when he looks again at the test with that definitive "pregnant" on the tiny screen.

"Of course I'm happy," he says, his smile growing even wider. "Aren't you?"

"I don't know. I mean, yes—I think I am—but I'm also freaked out. Jared, this changes everything. And it wasn't planned, and it was stupid of me to forget to take my pills … I just didn't know how you'd take it."

"Jules," he takes my hand in his, "when you said you'd marry me, I didn't think I could be any happier. But this?" He holds the test stick out in front of us. "Marrying you and having a family with you, well," he stops, because his voice breaks again and tears form in his eyes.

Then tears form in my eyes. Well, actually tears start to fall like waterfalls from my eyes. I think I'd been try to keep them at bay for too long. I make a snorting noise because, well, that's what I do in perfect moments like this. Jared takes me in his arms and we cry together. And it's all just so beautifully cheesy.

"We're having a baby," he says, his arms still around me.

"We are," I say, feeling emotions pour through me that I've never felt before. Feelings of excitement, elation, and a tad bit of what-the-crap. I'm pretty sure these are normal feelings. I hope.

But then again, what do I know? I have no idea what "normal" is in this situation. All I know is that I was a terrible babysitter when I was younger. I spent most of the time talking to my friends on the phone and eating their food and completely ignoring the kids I was hired to watch. I've never been much of a baby person, or a child person for that matter. I mean I love my nephew, Liam, but I'm not going to lie, when he has a dirty diaper or is unusually whiney, I immediately hand him back to his parents. This kid's going to be with me all the time. All the diapers. All the whining. I have to deal with all of it. What if I suck at it?

And what about my own life? I'm a bit of a disaster at this point. I mean, yes, I've sort of got a handle on the anxiety thing — well, I'm properly medicated (which coincidentally can be taken while pregnant according to the doctor, I had no idea why he would say that at the time, maybe I looked bloated) — but this is all new for me. I'm still a mess. My life is still chaotic. A baby certainly won't make that better. From what I've seen, it'll only make things harder.

"What's wrong, Jules?" Jared asks after he's pulled his head back and sees the look on my face.

"I'm going to totally mess this kid up," I say, suddenly feeling the weight of all this land on me. And it feels like the heaviness of an elephant.

"Jules," he says, a half smile on his face. "You'll be great. And besides, you aren't doing it alone, remember? I'll be there to help mess him up too."

I punch him lightly on the arm. "Don't joke. And wait, did you say 'him'?"

He just smiles.

I touch my stomach. "It could be a girl, you know."

"Yes, and I'll love Julianna just as much as I'd love Jared Junior." He smirks.

I punch him again.

"We have a problem," I say, not wishing to ruin this moment further, but it needs to be said.

"What problem?"

"What do we say to our families?" I felt suddenly nauseated at the thought. Or maybe it's the pregnancy nausea. It's hard to tell anymore.

"What do you mean?" he asks, confused.

"I mean, we're having a baby. It won't be hard for them to do the math when I have this baby seven and a half months from now."

"Oh, so what. We're married, so Bobby can't be mad," he says, batting my worry away with a flick of his wrist.

"Yes, but Bobby doesn't know that," I reply. "So do we admit to our families that we eloped? Or do we let them think we had a little oops?" I ask, my hand going down to my stomach again. Hard to think of this baby growing inside of me as an "oops." That seems kind of harsh. See there? I'm already defending the little tyke. Maybe I won't be so bad after all.

"Hmm." Jared considers that for a moment. "I guess we better tell them we eloped."

"But they'll hate us!" I exclaim. "They went to all this work for this big wedding, and you know your mom will blame me." My shoulders fall. All of my work to keep on the good side of my mother-in-law will be ruined.

"Julia," Jared hooks a finger under my chin and lifts my face up to his, "don't you think she'll be so thrilled that you're giving her a grandchild that none of this will matter?"

"I never thought of that."

"So we'll tell them. But after the wedding," he says with a single nod of his head.

"Okay," I say.

He seems so at peace with it all. I wish I could feel the same. Anticipation bubbles in my stomach as I think about telling everyone. I wish I could just send them an e-mail while we're on our honeymoon. Or a text. That'd be super tacky, but maybe it would be something we could all laugh about later. *Remember that time Julia sent us a text to tell us she was preggers and that they had eloped so it wasn't one of those twenty-first century out-of-wedlock babies? That was hilarious!*

"JULIA!" Anna pounds on the door. "In case you forgot, you're getting married in fifteen minutes!"

I tuck the pregnancy test in my toiletry bag and Jared gives me one last hug and then opens the door.

"Don't worry, I'll keep everyone entertained until she's ready," he says to Anna with a smirk.

"That's not comforting at all," Anna says, oozing sarcasm, and then her eyes widen when she sees me. "Holy crap, what happened to your face?"

I turn and look in the mirror, and although the waterproof mascara has stayed intact, there are trail marks of tears through the rest of my makeup, and my eyeliner has smudged so that I'm looking rather goth. The red eyes aren't helping matters either.

"Jared," Anna says, trying to steady her breath, "what did you say to her?"

"Nothing," I interject quickly. "We were just discussing … uh … stuff."

"Well, now I have to fix this," she motions at my person with her hands moving wildly around, "and get you ready in fifteen minutes. Why do you insist on ruining your own wedding? A crazy trip to the drugstore, crying your makeup off in the bathroom. Seeing your fiancé before the wedding?"

"I better leave, I think she's about to blow," Jared says to me in a stage whisper loud enough for Anna to hear.

"Get out of here!" She yells at him and he practically runs out of the room.

"Brown," Anna yells. "You better get over here. We have massive work to do."

CHAPTER 33

Lucky for me, I don't throw up again. I'm finally able to keep some soda crackers down and my stomach feels like it settled. Or maybe all of the nerves I'm feeling before my dad walks me down the aisle cover up the nausea. Like two negatives that cancel each other out.

The church is filled to the brim with people. Many people that I know, and so many that I don't. But it's no matter, this day is about all of them and no longer about Jared and me. We had our day. A hippy and spider filled day, but it was ours.

My dad tucks my hand in the nook of his arm and we start walking down the aisle to a violin quartet playing *The Wedding March*. On the way down, I see some of my old coworkers from Spectraltech. I also see Debbie and George, Patti and her husband, Randall, Kate and someone I don't recognize; all are smiles as I pass them. Lia, in her normal mismatched attire (although a slightly dressed-up version) beams at me as I walk past her. She gives me a little wink, and I know what she's referring to. Our little secret. I do feel a little bond with her, knowing that she's been at both of my weddings.

Up at the front of the church sits our families. Bobby, Mark, and Lisa on one side, my mom, grandparents, Lennon, Jenny, and Jonathon on the other. Liam, dressed in a tiny tuxedo, bounces around on Lennon's leg.

As we approach the end of the aisle, I see Brown and Anna standing up at the front smiling at me. They look gorgeous in their bridesmaid's dresses. It's hard to believe all of this hoopla is for me. It's quite overwhelming.

"I love you, Julie-Bear," my dad whispers to me as we get to the end of the aisle, right before he's supposed to hand me off to Jared.

And there go the waterworks.

"I love you too, Dad," I whisper back, tears brimming in my eyes.

He hands me to Jared and tells him to take care of me and then Jared starts to tear up as well. Honestly, we're already married, but all of this hoopla is seriously hard on the emotions. Also, there was a massive lack of sleep last night. Oh, and I'm full of pregnancy hormones.

The minister goes into his spiel and Jared and I wipe tears away from our eyes as we promise to love, honor, and cherish one another.

"The bride and groom would now like to say their own vows."

The minister turns to me to go first and I let out a slow exhale. I was not looking forward to this part, and even with the eloping thing, it's still feeling like a lot of pressure to get it right.

"Jared," I start. "I'm not sure what I did right, but I must have done something to deserve a man like you. A man with so much integrity and such a big heart, I feel like I've been blessed beyond belief." I basically mumble over the last part. Dear heavens, why would I put four B-words in a row? I should've paid someone to write this.

I clear my throat and Jared gives me a little smirk. "I promise to take care of you to the best of my ability," I continue, "even if it means I have to relinquish some of the control, or at least make you feel like I did." This gets me a chuckle from the audience.

"My only hope is that I can make you as happy as you've made me."

There's an audible "ah" from the crowd and Jared swipes a tear from his cheek. The two of us are quite the blubbering pair.

"Jared," the minister motions to him.

"Julia, I think I fell in love with you the moment I found you hiding under that conference room table," Jared says, and everyone laughs, even though they are probably totally confused by the visual. I kind of want to pinch the hand of Jared's that I'm holding for even bringing it up, but I hold back. From the back, a boisterous laugh echoes through the church. Mr. Calhoun, I presume. He was the only other person there on that fateful day. And that's what it was: fate.

"And every day since has felt like an adventure," Jared continues. "You make me laugh. You make me feel like I can do anything. I have no idea what the future will bring for us, but I do know that I'll work to make you feel my love every day of our lives."

Another "ah" runs through the crowd as I swoon over this man that I love so much.

The minister starts speaking again, and has us exchange rings. This time when I put the ring on Jared's finger, it's there for good.

"Ladies and gentlemen, I present to you Mr. and Mrs. Jared Moody," the minister announces once we both have our rings. "You may now kiss your bride," he directs to Jared.

Jared pulls me in, wraps his arms around me, and gives me a sweet, tender kiss that lasts slightly longer than I'd told him I would allow, but I honestly don't care.

Everyone cheers as we walk back down the aisle and exit the church.

I must admit marrying Jared for the second time was just as fantastic as the first. And this time, there was no spider.

CHAPTER 34

The start of the reception is a blur of hugs and congratulations. I've been hugged by so many strangers today, it's a darn good thing I'm not a germaphobe.

I know I said I didn't want over-the-top for my reception, but Anna has gone above and beyond. The ballroom looks fantastic with twinkling lights and stunning flower and candle centerpieces for the tables. The chairs are covered with gold lamé wraparounds that accent the cream colored tablecloths (about the only décor I picked out for this reception), and the formal place settings sparkle under the dim overhead lighting. Gorgeous flower arrangements adorn nearly every flat surface. Over in the far right corner I can see Patti, Debbie, and Kate taking pictures by the cake that they made. The cake is exactly what I wanted … because I told them exactly what I wanted and I'm their boss.

In the other corner of the ballroom sits the candy bar. I think it might be my favorite thing here. It has soft, muted colors, but still looks fanciful, like something you might see in an old-fashioned sixties diner. The champagne fountain is nowhere to be seen, thank you very much.

The only thing I don't love is the huge dance floor in the center. But that's not Anna's fault. I hate dancing. I'm all Elaine Benes from *Seinfeld* on the dance floor. Only liquor can make me daring enough. Since I can't drink anything now, I'm just going to have to avoid it.

I take mental pictures of everything, even though the flash from the photographer's camera can be seen twinkling around the room every few seconds, so I'll have actual pictures of it all. But I want to remember everything how I see it. Because I'll one day be telling this baby growing in my belly all about this day. I'll probably save the hippy elopement until he or she is older, for obvious reasons.

"Hello there, Mrs. Moody," Jared says in my ear as he wraps his arms around me from the back. I tilt my head back and lean against his shoulder.

"Hello there," I say. I've been Mrs. Moody for a while now, but I'm definitely not used to it.

His hand reaches down and caresses my stomach. I quickly push his hand away in case anyone caught sight of us.

"That's a dead giveaway," I say, half laughing. The fact that Jared is so thrilled about this baby makes me excited too. I'm not even worried about how much I'm going to mess this kid up. At least for now.

The DJ — who's definitely trying too hard with his quick talking 1960's radio nasal voice — announces that it's time for our first dance.

"Ugh," I say quietly to Jared.

"Is it that terrible to dance with your husband?" Jared asks, the left side of his lips pulled up in a mocking smile.

"Well, actually..."

"Come on," he says, grabbing my hand and taking me to the center of the dance floor.

All eyes are on us, and the room is quiet as Bono starts crooning "All I Want Is You" from large speakers. There'd be no Etta James for us. Even though the words to "At Last" fit pretty well for this moment. The U2 song was playing on our drive back from eloping, and it was a pretty amazing moment when we both looked at each other and had the same thought that this should be what we dance our first dance to.

Both Jared and I share tears on the dance floor. Funny that everyone around us thinks we're just happy to be married. In reality, we're mostly caught up in the fact that we'll be parents in the near future. It makes this moment even more beautiful having something that just him and I know. And Lisa too, I guess. Although I never confirmed with her. She only saw the pregnancy test.

After the song ends, the DJ brings everyone to the dance floor and I'm stuck out there having to dance. Jared does silly moves that somehow totally work and everyone keeps their eyes on him rather than the foot-shuffle-snapping thing I'm doing.

Just about when I've had enough with the dancing, the DJ announces that it's time for toasts and the service staff starts handing out flutes of champagne. I grab one because we decided that I'll pretend to drink it so I don't bring attention to myself if I ask for something else.

Mark is up first. I feel a slight bit of nausea while his shoes make tapping noises as he goes over to the

DJ to grab the microphone. Not nausea because of the pregnancy (although it's definitely looming), but worry about what will come out of Mark's mouth. He can be a bit of a loose cannon. Actually "bit" is putting it lightly.

"Hey everyone," Mark says too loudly and feedback rings throughout the ballroom. Grumbling noises run through the crowd and I see my grandpa cover his ears with his hands. He takes a step forward, away from the speakers and then tries again. "Hello everyone," he taps the microphone. "Is this thing on?" He taps it again and looks around the room. Seriously, did he not just deafen us all with the feedback? The microphone is *on*.

"Okay, so I'm the Best Man. So I guess I have the duty of giving a toast. I'm Mark, by the way." A chuckle moves around the room. "Jared is my brother, and Julia is now my sister," he says, very doofus like. I love Mark, but honestly, I would've rather had Mr. Calhoun give the speech and use his favorite word "proverbial" inaccurately over and over again. At least it would've been safe. With Mark you just never know.

"So, I was told by the maid of honor to keep this short," he tips his head over to Anna, who's glowering at him, "so let me just say that Jared has always been a great brother, even when he used to beat me up." A few people giggle, probably more for support because it wasn't that funny. "And," Mark looks nervously down at the floor, "when our dad died, he really stepped up and helped our mom with me, and I've always looked up to him because of that." Okay, well maybe Mark wasn't a bad choice after all. I sniffle back some tears. "He deserves nothing but the best, and Julia," he turns to me, "I think he's found that in you." He raises his glass to Jared and me. Jared, whose arm is around my waist, pulls me in tight to him and kisses the top of my head.

Wow, Mark actually came through.

"So here's to Jared and Julia," he goes to lift his glass. "Oh, wait, one more thing. Congrats on the baby, you two," he nods over at us with a big smile. Then he lifts his glass again and takes a big gulp.

I can feel my heart beating in my throat. It's gone completely and utterly quiet in the ballroom as everyone looks at Jared and me. I catch a glimpse of Bobby, who's sitting at a table to my right. She looks stricken, and rather pale. My parent's jaws are both nearly on the ground. Anna and Brown, who are standing across from me, are like wide-eyed twins.

"Jared," I say in a whisper, because that's all that would come out.

"Wait, didn't everyone know?" Mark says into the microphone as he looks around the room at blank stares.

My stomach swirls and I suddenly feel overwhelming nausea come over me. "Jared, I think I'm going to be sick," I say, putting a hand on my stomach.

"What?" he asks, searching my face like he might find a way to fix the nausea.

"I'm going to be sick," I say again, and before I can upchuck in front of all of these witnesses, verifying the news that Mark just laid on everyone, I hitch up the bottom of my dress and hightail it out of the ballroom. I make it to the bathroom before the entire contents of dinner come back up.

What in the actual hell? Why would Mark say that? Did Jared tell him? I don't think Jared would've told him. How'd he know, then?

Oh my gosh, Lisa. Lisa told him. Even after she promised not to tell anyone. Why would she do that? I guess I now get to tell everyone her hair secret. Like that's really a fair trade. What are we going to do? All of our family and friends and complete strangers now know that I'm knocked up.

"Julia?" I hear someone say my name as they enter the large, multi-stall bathroom. "Julia?" she repeats.

I open the door and peek out. It's Lisa.

Feeling sick from just throwing up and all of the drama that I'm sure is ensuing inside that ballroom, I let into her.

"How could you?" I ask, my voice is full of malice as I march over, pointing my index finger at her as I do. I want to be showing her another finger at this moment.

"I'm so sorry, Julia," she says, and her face actually looks sincere. Fake sincerity. I don't think there's a sincere bone in this girl's body. "I didn't mean to say anything to him, it just slipped out. And I told him not to say anything, but you know Mark. He probably didn't even hear me."

I close my eyes as more nausea rolls through my stomach. I might be making a second round.

"Get out," I say, pointing toward the door.

"Julia, I promise, I didn't think he'd announce it to the whole room." She looks stricken and sick to her stomach herself.

"Julia?" Jared asks, as he peeks his head into the woman's bathroom. "Is there anyone else in here?"

"No," I say, motioning with my hand for him to come in. "Lisa was just leaving."

"I sent her in here to find you," he says as he walks in the bathroom, putting his arms around me and pulling me into him. I lean my head against his strong chest and breathe in the scent of him. I refrain from punching him for sending Lisa in here, of all people.

"I'm so sorry, you guys," Lisa says, her eyes actually look like there might be tears there. "I had no idea Mark would say anything—"

"How did you even know?" Jared interrupts.

"She saw me buying the pregnancy test at the drug store," I say.

"I told Mark that it might not even be happening, but I guess he wasn't listening. I'm going to kill him," she says, tossing her glossy dark hair back with her hand.

"Not if I kill him first," I say with a huff.

"No one's killing anyone," Jared says, still holding me tight. "It was a simple mistake."

"A simple mistake," I repeat, pulling my head back from his chest so I can look him in the eyes. "Now everyone we know and love, and a bunch of people we don't know, know that I'm pregnant."

"And they don't know you eloped," Lisa says, realizing how much worse the situation is, especially with Bobby.

"Wait, how did you know that?" Jared asks, confused.

I let out a harrumph. "She overheard me telling the pharmacy tech at the drug store."

"Why were you telling him?" Jared scrunches his face.

"Because he was judging me for being pregnant on my wedding day. I could see it in his eyes," I say.

Jared shakes his head, but the corners of his lips turn up slightly. "Jules, we have to tell them."

I let out a resounding sigh, accepting what I already knew we'd have to do.

"Come on," he says, releasing his hold around me and taking me by the hand. "Anna is getting our families together so we can explain."

Oh gosh, Anna is going to be so mad at me. "Can't I just stay in the bathroom and you tell everyone?" I plead.

"We're doing this together, Jules," he says. "Besides, the eloping was your idea so you should be the one to tell." Aha! He's nervous too.

"Some knight in shining armor you are," I say, disgruntled.

We walk hand in hand out of the bathroom with Lisa right behind us. Our family is all gathered together right outside the bathroom. Plus Brown, Debbie, and Patti.

I hear Patti say "bless her heart," and I hold back and eye roll.

I swallow big as I look to Anna, who appears to be seething. This isn't going to be pretty.

"We have something to tell you," Jared starts, and my mom mouths "oh my gosh!" and covers her smiling mouth. At least she's excited. I need at least one cheerleader.

"It's true, Julia's pregnant," Jared says, and Brown screeches with excitement. There are varied expressions going around. Some look happy, some look confused, some look like they might choke me or Jared (mainly Bobby).

"But," I say looking at Bobby, "it's not what you think." I look to Jared who gives me a confirming dip of his chin. "Remember all the anxiety I was dealing with?" I get some nods from a few people. "Well, a lot of it had to do with today. I felt like there was too much riding on this one day. Everything had to be perfect and everything had to go right." I don't mention that one of the bigger issues was all the people who were invited—no need to tick off Bobby more than I already had.

"So after I ended up in the hospital, I convinced Jared to elope with me. That way it'd take the pressure off. Today wouldn't have to be perfect, because we would already be married. I'm sure a lot of you won't understand why we did this, but it really did help me. Today was even more wonderful because it didn't carry the weight that I'd been giving it." I throw the last part in hoping that they all will see how much we still appreciated this day and all of the work that was put into it. Because it's the truth.

"So when did ya elope?" Patti asks.

"When Jared took me away for the weekend. About six weeks ago," I say.

"And how far along are you?" Brown asks, a big smile on her face.

"My guess is six weeks," I say with a shrug of my shoulders.

"Well, then I'd say congratulations are in order," my dad says, raising his champagne flute that he's still carrying.

I look to Bobby to see if I can read what she's thinking, by the look on her face. She looks as if she's trying to piece things together in her head.

"So," she says, after a few seconds of quiet, "I guess that explains why you were so upset about me living with you, Jared," she says. A small smile appears on her face and then she breaks out laughing.

I look to Jared. He looks confused as well.

"Mom?" he questions.

"It's just too funny," she says, wiping under her eyes. "You elope and come home expecting to start your lives together, and instead you have to live apart because your old-fashioned mother-in-law is living in your house." She starts laughing again.

My parents join in with the laughter, and I can feel Jared's shoulders shaking lightly next to me. I look up to see him chuckling along with them.

Well, I guess she's taking this well.

"Mom," he says, when she finally stops laughing, "you're going to be a grandma."

When Jared says this, it's almost as if this is news to her. Like she can finally wrap her brain around the situation. She beams up at him.

"I'd say that's cause for celebration," she says. "Someone get us more champagne. Not you, Julia, you need to take care of my grandbaby in there." She walks over to me and pulls me into a hug. "Congratulations, my dear," she says softly in my ear.

When she pulls away, I scan around for Anna, and see her and Brown talking. While Bobby is hugging Jared, I walk over to her.

"So," I say, and then nibble on my bottom lip.

"So," Anna repeats.

"Do you hate me?" I smile sheepishly.

"A little," she says, but then she smiles. "But I'm mostly happy for you." And then she pulls me into a hug. She must be drunk. This is not typical Anna. She's rarely happy for me and she never hugs me. I'll take it, though. She can sober up and be mad at me later. Right now I just want to enjoy this moment.

"Now it's your turn to get knocked up," Brown says to Anna.

"Actually, after seeing Julia throw up her guts today, I think I'll wait a little longer," Anna says, her nose scrunching up with mock disgust.

Brown starts talking about how we get to do this all together and go on family vacations together and have barbecues … and maybe our kids will marry each other and we can then be in-laws. She's totally getting ahead of herself and I love it.

Anna seems genuinely happy for the both of us. Not an ounce of envy — or at least not any that we can see. I'm still willing to bet she's drunk a little too much. I guess we'll just have to see.

All around us our family and friends are bustling with talk of babies and grand-parenting, and they all seem elated. Lennon has baby Liam give me a fist-bump (his newest trick) and then gives me a congratulatory hug. The thrill in the air is palpable as they all drink a toast to Jared, me, and this baby growing in my belly.

And just like that, everything feels right in my little world.

"Julia, I'm so sorry," Mark says, walking up to me after the toast, Lisa in tow. "I had no idea that it was a secret. I promise it wasn't Lisa's fault. Don't blame her for my big mouth."

At least he can admit that he has a big mouth. Lisa looks so pitiful standing next to him, I almost think he might be telling the truth.

"No worries," I say and I can see the relief in Lisa's face. I don't think she did it on purpose, and even if she did, I don't truly care. Everything turned out just fine. And maybe even how it was supposed to.

The rest of the night goes off without a hitch, all things considered. We don't get on the microphone and explain things to everyone. It's none of their business, anyway. The people that mean the most to me know, and that's all I care about. Anyway, I'm sure word got around, probably singlehandedly by Bobby.

There's more dancing, the bouquet and garter toss (Lisa fought someone for the bouquet—guess she's dying to be next), and I don't have to threaten annulment after the cake cutting because Jared feeds me a bite of the lemon pound cake with lemon curd and raspberry filling like a gentleman. I, on the other hand, am not so kind. I smash the cake all over his mouth. And then, in front of my friends, family, and half of Denver that I don't even know, I lick some of it off. What can I say? I was feeling a little giddy at this point.

By the end we're all exhausted, our feet are hurting, and I'm pretty sure my cheeks are bruised from all the smiling, but this has been the best second wedding ever. Even with Mark announcing my pregnancy to everyone. That might've been the icing on the cake. It makes me wonder if I actually could've survived if we'd skipped the whole eloping thing. But we'll never know now, and honestly, if I had to do it all over again, I'd have done it the exact same way.

Jared and I run through bubbles as we leave to get in the car and head out to our hotel. Everyone whoops and hollers as we go, and Jared's car is quite the mess with versions of "just married" written all over the windows. I only get a quick look, but I believe there are a string of condoms tied to the back. What a waste that was since that ship has sailed.

As we drive away with everyone cheering behind us, Jared grabs my hand and lifts it to his mouth. He places a soft kiss on my fingers and then gives me one of his best sexy smiles. I think about how much has happened since he first found me hiding under that conference room table, and I'm grateful for all of it. And there is still a lifetime together to look forward to.

EPILOGUE

Seven and a half months later …

The sound of a baby crying makes both Jared and me burst into tears. It's loud and shrill and probably the most beautiful sound I've ever heard.

"Here's your baby girl," the doctor says as he lays a tiny bundle of beauty on my chest. She's covered in red gunk and some white powdery looking stuff. I know I told the doctor before she was born that if he laid that grossness on my chest I would not pay him (I saw the doctor do that with Brown and her baby boy and there was no way I was going to allow that). But that was before. I couldn't care less right now. She's beautiful and perfect and she's all mine. I mean, mine and Jared's. But I did all the growing and two hours of pushing while he did basically nothing, so I think she's a little more mine than his.

"Hello, Julianna," Jared coos as she fusses, making jerky movements as she tries to make sense of this world she's been thrust into.

"Jared," I chide.

"Well she needs a name, so I'm giving her a temporary one," he says as he carefully touches her little hand.

Jared and I could never agree on a name. We went around and around trying to come up with the perfect name. I said we should combine our mother's names, just like in the *Twilight* series, and call her Bobkat. Jared did not appreciate it because he's never read the books nor has he seen the movies, but I laughed enough for the both of us.

"I know it might be a little unorthodox, but I was thinking about the name James," I say.

James is the name of Jared's dad. Jared's head drops and his shoulders begin to shake.

After a moment he lifts his head up and with tears streaming down his face, he says, "It's perfect."

"James Katherine Moody," I say, peering down at this wonder that I'm holding in my arms. Katherine, after my mom of course, so now our daughter has a shout-out from both sides of the family.

Our daughter. I still can't believe it. I'm a mom.

As Jared wraps his arms around our baby girl and me, I snap a mental picture. I never want to forget this moment.

There have been so many life experiences in the past few years that I've tried to take a mental picture of because each has been one of the best moments of my life. The day I moved out of my parents' basement and into my own condo. The moment Jared kissed me for the first time. The first time I walked into the bakery and knew I had to work there. The moment I signed the papers that made the bakery mine. The time I won *Cupcake Battles*. The night Jared asked me to marry him. The day we got married on the side of a mountain with a bunch of hippies. The moment when I found out I was pregnant. And now this.

I have no idea what the future holds, but I can't wait to find out.

The End

Visit Becky's website and sign up for fun
giveaways and e-newletters

www.beckymonson.com

Join Becky on Facebook:
https://www.facebook.com/AuthorBeck
yMonson

Twitter: @bmonsonauthor

Instagram: bmonsonauthor

ACKNOWLEDGMENTS

It takes a village to write a book.

I could not have finished this book without help from the following people: Kathryn Biel, Jennifer Peel, Karen Browning, Lori Schleiffarth, Robin Huling, Julie Dirks ... and so many more. It's nearly three in the morning, so I'm having trouble remembering everyone. But just know that I appreciate you all.

I also need to give a shout-out to Dr. Pepper and chocolate, for you were both major players in the finishing of this book. My creativity (and love handles) have flourished thanks to you.

Thanks to my editors, Kaylynn Flanders, and Heather Godfrey. You save me! Thanks for making me sound somewhat smart.

Thank you to my cover artist, Angela Talley Smith for your incredible talent and ability to make the ideas in my head happen.

To my family and friends and everyone else who has had to listen to me bounce story ideas off you and deal with my whining ... you are very patient people. I adore you all.

And to my loves – Rob, Audrey, Max, and Violet. Everything I do is for you. You are my sunshine.